DULL BOY

DULL

BOY

SARAH CROSS

• Dutton Books •

DUTTON BOOKS

A member of Penguin Group (USA) Inc.

Published by the Penguin Group

Penguin Group (USA) Inc., 375 Hudson Street, New York, New York 10014, U.S.A.
• Penguin Group (Canada), 90 Eglinton Avenue East, Suite 700, Toronto, Ontario
M4P 2Y3, Canada (a division of Pearson Penguin Canada Inc.) • Penguin Books Ltd,
80 Strand, London WC2R 0RL, England • Penguin Ireland, 25 St Stephen's Green,
Dublin 2, Ireland (a division of Penguin Books Ltd) • Penguin Group (Australia),
250 Camberwell Road, Camberwell, Victoria 3124, Australia (a division of Pearson
Australia Group Pty Ltd) • Penguin Books India Pvt Ltd, 11 Community Centre,
Panchsheel Park, New Delhi – 110 017, India • Penguin Group (NZ), 67 Apollo Drive,
Rosedale, North Shore 0632, New Zealand (a division of Pearson New Zealand Ltd.)
• Penguin Books (South Africa) (Pty) Ltd, 24 Sturdee Avenue, Rosebank, Johannes-
burg 2196, South Africa • Penguin Books Ltd, Registered Offices: 80 Strand, London
WC2R 0RL, England

CIP Data is available

Published in the United States by Dutton Books, a member of Penguin Group (USA)
Inc. • 345 Hudson Street, New York, New York 10014
www.penguin.com/youngreaders

Designed by Jason Henry

Printed in USA • First Edition
ISBN: 978-0-525-42133-7

1   3   5   7   9   10   2   6   4   2

FOR PETER,
WHO ALWAYS SAVES THE DAY
—S.C.

DULL BOY

Maybe I Need a Costume.

Trust me—I don't want to wear a costume. Skintight spandex isn't really my thing, the ski-mask-plus-bathing-suit combo didn't exactly inspire confidence when I tried it on (please forget I even mentioned that), and where am I supposed to find a leather jumpsuit? But at this point I have to consider all my options.

And before you start thinking I'm a complete freak, I should probably admit something:

I have superpowers.

When other guys my age stay up too late on a school night, they're probably on Xbox Live or finishing some last-minute homework. Right? I'm in the garage with all the lights off, dead-lifting my mom's car because I don't have a three-thousand-pound weight set, and hoping she doesn't notice. Or I'm soaring through the sky, flying under cover of darkness because night is the one time I can risk it. The only time I can really be myself.

Sometimes I wish I didn't care what would happen if anyone knew the truth about me. But I do care. I have to keep this a secret. No one can know—not my parents, not my friends . . .

It's just that it's getting harder to hide it.

Now that I have these powers, I feel like I can't shirk the responsibility that comes with them. If I can maybe make a difference, shouldn't I be out there, giving it my all? I've been patrolling my town for weeks, looking for some way to be useful—and I'm getting antsy, more ambitious. Rescuing cats from trees is fine, but what about real emergencies, like flash floods and fires and people being held hostage? There's only so much I can do while pretending to be normal.

IT'S FRIDAY—ANOTHER AFTERNOON spent pounding the pavement in search of crimes to stop and people to help. And, as usual, I'm coming up mostly empty.

School let out hours ago and it's already getting dark. I cruise by the elementary school, scoping the playground for would-be vandals and thinking about everything I still need to do tonight. The place is empty, except for one little kid playing basketball by himself.

I stop to watch him.

The kid dribbles the ball against the pavement twice, then hurls it at the hoop, throwing his whole body forward. The ball sails wide. He chases after it, sniffles thanks to a monster runny nose, and wipes his face on his sleeve.

He's totally oblivious, lost in what he's doing. *Pound-pound. Huhn!* The ball hurtles toward the net, drops off before it even comes close. *Sniff!* He scrunches his face. Tries again.

I should get going—the closest I've come to doing anything useful was picking up and returning a dollar someone dropped, and I still have to buy something for Henry.

But giving this kid a few pointers won't take long. I'm no basketball star, but—

"Air ball!" A pack of rowdy fifth and sixth graders bound across the playground, laughing at triple volume like they've got someone to impress.

The kid tenses up, stops his basketball mid-bounce. Almost in sync, I rise from my stakeout spot. These guys are tiny to me, but they're giants to the kid—I can tell by the way he shrinks back as they approach. I drift closer, hackles up like an angry guard dog.

Before I get there, my cell starts ringing, cranking out a tinny version of Black Sabbath's "Iron Man."

Not now!

wat u doin? It's a text from Nate, my sort-of friend, the guy who weaseled his way into our group after he took my spot on the wrestling team—a spot he'd *never* have if I hadn't voluntarily stepped down.

@libry talk ltr, I tap back.

He *knows* I'm supposedly at the library, thoroughly engrossed in my extra-credit science project. What's up with bothering me? Henry's surprise party isn't till eight.

I bump the volume down on my phone—no more interruptions!—and glance up just in time to see the kid's knees hit the pavement. When he tries to get up, the older guys shove him down again.

I cross the remaining distance in like three strides, jaw tight with my best vigilante scowl. I'm wearing all black; I have a ski cap pulled down over my eyebrows. I'm channeling Batman, protector of the playground instead of Gotham.

One of the bullies is kicking the little dude's basketball around like it's a soccer ball. It rolls over to me and I stop it with my foot.

"Hey! Why don't you pick on someone your own size?"

I'm nowhere close to being their size, but whatever—it's a classic line.

"Oooh, like you? I'm so scared." The alpha bully rolls his eyes. He and his friends start snorting and flopping around, bumping into each other—I guess to, uh, insinuate that I'm retarded? They're throwing out lines like, "You want me to leave him alone; come make me," and "What are you, his girlfriend?"

Hilarious stuff.

"It's cool," I say, strolling closer. I toss the basketball into the air a few times—casually, like I'm messing around. But when it's on its way down for the last time, I bring my hands together and pop it like a balloon.

Their tough, no-fear expressions crumble. "Oh, snap!"

All five take off across the playground. The alpha bully trips on his shoelaces and one of the other kids charges right over him; a third kid screams that his older brother's gonna kick my ass—but he waits until he's at least a hundred feet away from me to do it.

"You all right?" I say to the little kid. His head's down,

but he nods, sniffles; he's busy examining the hole in his jeans. There's blood on the frayed denim.

"You broke my basketball." *Sniff!*

Oh. Crap. Yeah, I did, didn't I?

"Sorry about that. I'll buy you a new one, okay?" I crouch down next to him, dig out my wallet, and offer him twenty bucks—more than half of my buy-Henry-a-last-minute-birthday-gift budget.

Sniff! He smears his tears with the back of his hand. "I don't want to play anymore. I'm too small."

"Pff! Too small? You're just getting started!" I ruffle his hair and he laughs, even though I'm pretty sure that's an annoying gesture. "You might be eight feet tall one day!" He squints at me skeptically, and I grin. "Stranger things have happened."

I extend a hand to help him up, and a sudden chill races down my spine, makes my body convulse.

It's hitting me again.

I hunch my shoulders, tug my hat low so it covers my ears. The weather's been almost "balmy" lately, according to my mom. But my body's shaking like I got caught in a blizzard. My skin's slicked with cold sweat.

I try to tell myself it's because I need to eat, or I'm getting sick, but I know it's not that simple. Something's wrong with me.

"C'mon," I say. "I'll walk you home. And if any of those kids are waiting for you, they'll have to deal with me."

"Okay." He takes my hand with his tiny, tear-covered one. "Thanks."

Aww. See how nice that is?

For a second I forget that I'm a first-class deceiver, a destroyer of property and all-around screwup.

It doesn't take long to be reminded.

When I pull out my phone again, it's full of texts from Nate and Milo, and a voice mail from my mom.

Mom: *"Don't be out too late! I want you up early tomorrow mowing the lawn. And I swear to God if you break the mower, Avery . . . (sigh) I've got a whole list of chores for you to do. Don't think you're not going to do EVERYTHING you can around here to pay back—"*

I delete it; I already have that lecture memorized: she's going to give me more hell about destroying Henry's dad's car, blah blah, hell, blah. *Not* that it was destroyed. I just . . . broke the door and shattered some windows when I slammed the door too hard. It was an *accident*. And it was totally his choice to buy a new one.

Nate: *dude y r ur grdes so bad if ur alwys at libry?*
dont 4gt ur settng up 4 h's bday. u got party stuff from lacey rt?
h will luv bday banner n plates! so old school lol
hllo were r u Av?

Milo: *get ther erly it gets crwded*
u ther yet? wat u buy hm?
BURP!

By the time I get the kid home, it's almost seven; I'm

supposed to be at Roast by seven-thirty so I can hang Henry's "Happy Birthday" banner and set out all the party favors and "Happy Birthday from Pikachu!" plates and napkins and stuff. It's kind of lame, but . . . I guess it's supposed to be funny. I dunno; it was Nate's idea.

I also have to buy Henry a present. *This* is important. Because even though Henry's my best friend, I've blown him off a lot lately. Like, he'll want to hang out and play Xbox, or practice moonsaults on his trampoline, but when he calls I'm halfway across town waiting for some crisis to occur, so I end up resorting to my I'm-studying-at-the-library lie.

But what's the alternative? Tell him the truth?

Tell him that I quit wrestling after I broke Mike G.'s arm not because Coach made me, but because my strength was out of control and I was afraid I might hurt someone again?

And that, um, not only do I have *powers,* but that I feel like I need to do something good with them so I'm more than just a destructive force?

He'd think I was totally delusional. Or he'd make me show him, and *then* he'd believe me—but that would be worse. Because he'd brag to Milo and Nate. And then the news would be everywhere.

I can't come clean and fix everything, but I don't want Henry to think I've forgotten about him. We used to do a lot of cool stuff together. Like in seventh grade, when we plotted out this whole wrestling rivalry, and we put on WWE-style shows between classes. He'd hit me with a folding chair that we stole from the orchestra room, and I'd elbow drop him in the hallway. We spent a lot of time washing chalkboards that year, but it was worth it.

Those are some of my best memories. I've just been busy lately, and "all heroism, no play" means that the only "super" I've been to my friends lately is super lame. I need to make it up to them, to prove I'm not a deadbeat friend. I'm hoping a kick-ass birthday party will help.

Unfortunately, since I *made* that kid take the twenty bucks, most of my money's gone and I have to go the cheap route and get Henry a bargain-bin Incredible Hulk T-shirt—and hope he just thinks it's ironic. Then I zip home and climb in through my open window, grab some wrapping paper and the decorations, slap on some cologne— because hey, there will be girls there—and fly to Roast under cover of darkness, cutting through the woods or empty parking lots whenever possible.

I really shouldn't be flying, but if I get there any later, Henry's surprise will be ruined—and then I'll really be screwed. My friends barely trust me to pull this off as it is. I just hope they appreciate it, because if anyone saw me flying, I would be dead. DEAD. Scientists would have me in a government lab in about five seconds, checking to see if my pee could cure cancer.

Vivisection leaves a bad taste in my mouth.

Roast is crowded when I get there, just like Milo said it would be. Basically, every kid who doesn't feel like going to Denny's is here—late-night hangout options are slim. Tack on adults who don't like sports bars, a scattering of poets, and you've got table availability that's almost nil.

But I won't be deterred. It's Henry's birthday; I'm on a mission.

I stake out a spot by the massive coffee roaster (it looks like a furnace, but smells better), and wait for a four-person table to open up—then, when it does, I pounce, throwing all my stuff down to claim it.

Paper Pikachu hats tumble out of the bag. A few sophisticated hipsters gape at me, appalled.

"Birthday party," I explain. And then I ignore them.

I go to town decorating, setting out the matching paper plates, napkins, noisemakers—every ridiculous item you can imagine. Nate's friend Lacey even stuffed a few balloons in the bag, so after I order something (a cupcake and a smoothie, so the manager doesn't kick me out), I sit down and start blowing them up, tying them off, and then taping them to the table.

Awesome. Henry's gonna pee his pants laughing.

I need permission to hang the birthday banner, so I pop one of the paper hats on my head and beeline to the nearest employee: a girl around my age who's dressed all in black. She's busy pushing a broom around, messy brown hair hanging in her face. I figure she won't mind being interrupted.

"Hey, do you mind if I—"

"The sign-up list is over there," she says, jerking her head toward the counter. In a . . . not-very-friendly way.

"What? Aren't you here for open-mike night?" Then she squints at my head. "What the hell are you wearing?"

"Uh . . ." My hands go to the Pikachu "I Choose *You,* Birthday Boy!" hat; suddenly it seems like a bad idea. "Nothing." I slip it off my head. God, this is gonna seem even stupider. "Do you think I could, uh, hang this banner? For my friend's birthday?"

She blows a piece of hair out of her face, scowls. "I don't care if you hang your*self.*"

"Uh . . . okay, thanks." I slink away from her, cringe all the way back to my table. Yikes. What's her problem?

The banner is rainbow-colored. It's shiny and metallic, and crinkled tinsel dangles from the edges, like fringe on a scarf. It's the most obnoxious thing I've ever seen.

I'm just about done hanging it when the applause starts. Followed by microphone feedback, and the obligatory "Welcome to Roast's open-mike night! Thank you all for coming!"

Ugh. No offense to poets, but I hate poetry. The only thing worse than people expressing their innermost feelings is when they have to make them rhyme.

I settle into my seat and take a big slurp of my smoothie; lean my head against the wall, anticipating agony. There's a girl sitting at the table across from mine who looks like she's getting ready to read—she's in the middle of some weird transformation: from geek to goth?

She's busy wriggling into a black t-shirt with a metallic silver coffin on it, tugging it on over a tee that says:

I ❤ ROBOTS. She takes off her glasses and blinks a few times before one of her friends—this cute blonde: wavy hair, pink hoodie, tiny-hearts-and-cupcakes charm bracelet on her wrist—starts lining the girl's eyes with black eyeliner.

"Stop blinking, pleeease," the blond girl singsongs.

"Sophie, you're poking me in the eye. It's an unavoidable reaction. I'm—*ow!*—protecting my cornea."

"Tell your cornea to take one for the team. Otherwise you're gonna look like a raccoon."

There's one more person at her table: a guy, my age but, uh, sensitive-looking? He's the only person here who's more overdressed than I am. He keeps adjusting his trench coat, like he's trying to pull it closed more, twisting the collar and tightening it around his throat. I hope he's not the blond girl's boyfriend. Probably not, since geek-to-goth girl is sitting between them.

Trench-coat boy is shuffling through some papers, glancing around with pale blue wide-open eyes, this overly serious nervous expression on his face.

"Are you sure you want to read this?"

"Of course I'm going to read it," geek-to-goth girl says, standing up and pinning anarchy-symbol buttons all over her pants. Then she rolls her pants up to her knees to reveal pink-and-black striped tights. "That's why we came here. There's an eighty-seven percent chance that she'll respond favorably this time."

Anyway: so the open-mike thing starts, and the first

person to bound up there is the geek-goth-punk-circus girl. Seriously, I don't know what she's supposed to be. Tack on a pirate patch and it might start to make sense.

No, it wouldn't.

"Hi. I'm Darla Carmine," she says, leaning into the mike, "and the poem I'm going to read is called, 'More Than Meets the Eye.'"

Hmm. Maybe I judged this girl too harshly. I cross my arms over my chest, nod my tentative approval. This might be awesome. I hope it's about Optimus Prime.

She reads, complete with dramatic pauses and Shakespearean gestures:

There is more to me than meets the eye.
More than the girl you see when you walk by.
What is happening to me?
Are there others like me?
I am powerful, but I am afraid.
Will I be used? Abused?
I'm so confused.
Tonight I look around, and see that I am not alone.

WTF kind of poem was that? That was horrible! It's worse than the limericks I wrote for our poetry unit in seventh grade. Plus, the whole time she was reading it, she kept looking at the angry floor-sweeping girl with these "meaningful" glances.

Wait—was that a lesbian-crush poem?

Hmm.

Then she says, "Thank you," and takes her seat to the sound of polite applause.

The angry floor-sweeping girl snorts—she's like right next to me, sweeping up stray pieces of tinsel. "That poem sucked," she says.

To me? Uh . . . I look around. Either that or to the voices in her head.

"Word," I say, giving her a we-agreed-on-something, that's-a-basis-for-a-civil-friendship nod.

"Yours will probably be worse."

Or not. "How many times do I have to tell you? I'm not here to read a poem—it's my friend's birthday."

"Uhhh . . . your invisible friend?" She does this blink-blink, you're-a-moron thing, then points at my mostly empty table.

"They're coming," I say. "They're just late." Like . . . twenty minutes late. People are hovering around my table; they keep asking if they can take the chairs and I have to shoo them away. Finally I whip out my cell and call Nate, because this is getting ridiculous.

"Dude, where are you?" I say when he picks up.

There's music in the background, a girl's laugh. A tinkly voice saying, "Is that him?"

"Av?" Nate laughs his life-of-the-party laugh. "We're at Henry's house. Where're you?"

My mouth opens but no sound comes out.

EVERYTHING IN MY BODY gets hot.

No.

Not here. Please.

I try to breathe—not to look embarrassed, or off my game. To stay *cool*. Especially now that I have an audience. I've been using my extra-loud cell-phone voice, mostly for angry girl's benefit, so she knows I'm not some loser.

But I *am* a loser. My friends—at least two of them, since I know Milo was in on this—lied to me. Tricked me. Because I'm that gullible. That stupid. That unimportant.

My hand trembles until it's in a tight fist against my head. Nate's voice is gone, the music is gone, replaced by the sound of plastic cracking, all the guts in my phone compacting, tiny pieces raining down on the table. Like insect parts.

I crushed my phone.

I take a deep breath. And then another one.

Lower my hand to the table, knock the pieces to the floor.

You don't know what it's like. You don't *want* to know what it's like.

I feel like I need to break something, and then another something, and then more somethings—and then myself. Like this feeling *isn't* going to go away. Ever.

It isn't hormones, it isn't adrenaline—something's wrong with me. I've got all this power, all this strength, all this aggression in this *normal-looking* body, and I feel like I can't contain it, like I'm going to explode. And working out doesn't help. Running doesn't help. Flying *sort of* helps, because the push and pull to stay in the air is so intense—but that comes with its own dangers. Being caught. Apprehended. Poked, prodded, tested.

Exterminated.

I need to call Henry. He must think I'm the shadiest friend ever—and maybe that's not far from the truth.

"Your battery died, right?"

My head snaps up.

It's the blond girl from before—Sophie? She's leaning her hip against my table, her smile brighter than the sparkly rhinestone charms dangling from her pink cell phone. "I hate when that happens. Do you need to borrow mine?"

"Yeah, I kind of . . . Thanks."

"Just try to be careful," she says—and winks. "This brand is really fragile."

"Heh . . . um . . . I will." I dial like the thing's made of crystal, hold it like it's a precious artifact. I think the whole place can hear me when I swallow, it's so freaking loud in my ears.

At the table across from mine, Darla—the "poet"—is

staring at me so hard that it looks like her eyes are going to pop out. There's a big coffee puddle on the table in front of her; her lips and chin are wet with coffee dribbles—like her coffee just exploded out of her mouth like a geyser.

I'm hoping that's a coincidence.

Henry answers on the fourth ring.

"It's me," I say. "My phone died."

"You're not pissed, are you?" He sounds uncomfortable. Behind him Nate calls out, *Get over it!*

"Pissed at *him*," I say warily. Because—

There's party giggling in the background.

Lots of:

Oh my God!

So he really believed . . .

That's so mean!

Translation: *That's hilarious! I'm glad it wasn't me!*

"It was a joke, Av. No big deal, okay? We still want you here." Fidgeting. "We just figured, uh . . . I mean, you're always blowing us off anyway and it gets kind of tired. So . . . it was like payback."

"You knew?" Something stabs me behind my eyes, and I squeeze them shut, thinking:

Lie to me, okay? I lie to you guys all the time; it's not that hard. Freaking lie to me. I don't want to know the truth.

"We still want you to come over. Just call your mom and get her to drive you." And then Henry's voice changes like everything's forgiven, like we're all friends again. 'Cause being sorry on your birthday? Yeah, I'm sure that sucks.

"It's awesome, Av. Lacey's cousins from Immaculate came and they are *smoking* hot—"

I hang up.

"You know . . . it's your party, and you can cry if you want to." The angry floor-sweeping girl plops down in the chair next to mine, stretches out her nicotine-fiend-skinny legs, and grabs my cupcake, biting into it before I have a chance to snap at her that I'm *not* crying.

And I'm not. I'm just allergic to some perfume that someone's wearing; it's burning my eyes and they're watering. Crap like that happens, okay?

"Uh, that was mine," I say. "It's not like it just magically sprouted there so you could eat it."

"I'm doing you a favor." She shrugs. "I ate, like, four of them out of the case before. The frosting tastes like paste." Her hair falls into her face, and she sweeps it out of the way with her fingertips.

When she pulls her hand back, her forehead is marred by four thin red scratches.

"People suck," she says. "It's a fact of life. And if they screw you over . . ." She narrows her eyes, more thoughtful than aggressive. "You're probably bigger than they are, right?"

"Uh, mostly. Milo's a heavyweight, but he doesn't really—"

"Good. So you kick their asses. It's like a public service. It teaches them that screwing people over is bad."

"Right," I say, trying not to stare at the tiny beads of blood that are now dotting her scratches. I almost ask her why she's being not-hostile ("nice" might be pushing it), but figure I'll ruin it if I do.

Her nose twitches; she plucks a piece of cat hair off her sleeve. "Anyway, I can't sit here and console you all night—I'll get fired. I have to stop that girl before she spews another gallon of coffee on the floor."

"Wait!" I fumble for the wrapped present, dig it out from under my chair. "Do you like the Incredible Hulk? Because I don't really need this anymore."

"What?"

"It's a shirt. Probably too big, but . . ."

"I'll find a home for it."

Her fingers dig into the package, nails raking up thin slivers of the wrapping paper. It swings loosely at her side as she heads over to harass Darla and her friends.

The blue-eyed guy, skin almost translucent, like a ghost's, apologizes; he's already sopping up the damage with a napkin. Darla manages a smile (hard to do in the presence of sweeping girl's scowl) and says, "Hi! Catherine, right? What did you think of my—"

"Stop spitting your coffee out. This isn't a zoo." And then she walks away from them, disappears into a storage closet; comes back with a mop.

Sophie scoots out of her chair and squeezes past Catherine (is it Catherine?) and the other patrons carefully, like she doesn't want to touch anyone. There's glitter on her cheeks, and when the light hits her face a certain way, she sparkles.

"Everything okay?" she says.

....

"Could be better," I say, handing her phone back. "My friend's mom's car broke down, so this party"—I gesture to the decorations—"is officially over."

My breath catches; her skin is touching my skin, our hands united at the sides, two sets of fingers still closed around her phone. And, yeah, I'm touching a cute girl, so maybe it's natural to feel out of sorts—but for a few brief moments I could swear there's something holding us together. There's this tugging sensation—like a Band-Aid pulling on my skin—and then the pressure eases off like it was never there, and she's putting her phone away, smiling awkwardly, fumbling with the clasp on her purse.

"That's too bad," she says, words tumbling out in a rush. "Well, maybe next time, right?"

And then she spins away from me, her skirt flaring out; she hurries into the bathroom and slams the door.

Did I do something? I mean, I kind of got the impression that she didn't want to be touched, but it's not like I did it on purpose . . .

Trench-coat boy is burning a hole through me with his blue eyes. That "sensitive side" I saw before? Looks like it's on hiatus.

I need to get out of here.

I gather up the party supplies and dump them in the trash, sling my coat over my shoulders, and exit the coffee shop, to the sudden sound of applause. I know it's got nothing to do with me—it's a poetry thing—but in a way, I feel like they're applauding my decision to leave. Just call me hypersensitive. Or self-absorbed.

Outside, it's mostly dark. Streetlamps light up this part of Main Street, but farther down, they're either broken or nonexistent. Most of the shops down there are closed.

So of course that's where I go.

I need to walk; I can't stand still. The heat I felt earlier dissipated along with my anger. I'm cold again, almost shivering—but no matter how high I zip my coat up, how far I pull my hat down, I can't warm up.

And I wonder if this is the trade-off. If my body might be devoting so much energy to making me tougher, more powerful, that it's sapping strength from somewhere else. Maybe my brain, my heart—*something*—isn't getting what it needs. Maybe it's killing me from the inside out.

Morbid much? I try to think about something else—*not* myself—when it hits me: I need to apologize. Whatever I did that made Sophie freak out like that . . . she needs to know it wasn't intentional. If that makes any difference at all.

I hike back up Main Street toward Roast, but stop before I get within full view of the streetlights. I hang back, sticking to the shadows, because Sophie and Darla and the trench-coat guy are outside. I feel weird approaching them all together; that guy seemed pretty pissed at me.

Sophie's hopping from one foot to the other, her hands pulled into the sleeves of her sweatshirt. Darla's pants are rolled back down, so she doesn't look like a goth pirate anymore. And the guy? He's still scanning the area with his psychotic blue eyes, chin tucked to his chest.

"I think you need makeup remover," Sophie says. "That bathroom soap—"

"It's all smeared," Darla says. "And now my eyes are red. Crap. This is not going to go over well . . ."

"Just tell your dad it was a makeover gone wrong. Blame it on Nicholas."

"Very funny," the guy says. "And then he'll ask my dad why I'm wearing eyeliner. No thanks."

Darla sighs. "She wasn't receptive *at all.* I got the feeling we were more, like, annoying her."

"Speak for yourself," Sophie says. "I had nothing to do with that poem."

"Just because I'm the only one *bold* enough to take on the challenge—"

Sophie giggles. "Whooooa, simmer down there, Mr. Wayne."

Even broody Nicholas manages a smile.

Darla sticks her tongue out. "Make fun of me all you want—but this is serious stuff. People like the Ice Queen—"

The *what*? I edge closer.

"God, do you *have* to call her that?" Sophie rolls her head back, like she's looking up at the stars. "She has a name."

Darla sniffs. "Bottom line, she's a manipulator and a predator and she can't be trusted. If *she* makes contact before we do—"

Then Nicholas speaks up: "That was him, wasn't it? The guy you told us about."

Huh?

Darla nods. "Shocked the hell out of me."

"Yeah, but . . . it was kind of cool, right?" Sophie holds on to the lamppost with one hand, swings around it. Grins a big, beautiful grin. "I wish he would've done more."

"No, you don't," Nicholas says firmly—like this is the last word on the matter. Whatever the matter is.

An SUV pulls up. Headlights shine on their squinting faces, illuminate the sidewalk in front of me. I press my back against the darkened building, hope those lights didn't just give me away.

Darla hitches her backpack onto one shoulder. "You sure you don't want a ride? It's pretty late, Soph."

"I'm fine, you guys. My mom's just doing her running-late, workaholic thing. She's not going to abandon me." Sophie unzips her purse, pulls out a beat-up paperback, and shoos them toward the car with it. "She'll be here in like, ten minutes or less. I promise."

"Ohhh-kay," Darla says, frowning a little as she climbs into the SUV, Nicholas right behind her. The driver beeps and Sophie waves good-bye.

And then they drive off, and she's standing there alone, reading with one foot propped on the lamppost, a manga cracked open in her hands.

Every once in a while the door to Roast opens and a few people spill out—but mostly she's alone, quietly flipping pages, paying next to no attention to what's going on around her.

I keep taking a few steps closer and then wussing out,

second-guessing myself. This bothers me, because I didn't used to be so insecure. After last summer, when I lifted Mrs. Pearson's car like it was nothing, saved her kid's life, and became a local hero (and passed it all off as "adrenaline"), I was riding a wave of confidence I thought would last forever.

But that wave broke when I busted Mike Graves's arm in a wrestling match.

It wasn't the first strength malfunction I'd had, but it was the worst. It ended my time on the wrestling team and severed a tie between my friends and me. And I hurt someone. I heard—I felt—a bone crack.

It changed everything. Before, being "destructive" meant breaking our washer and dryer (oops) or kicking a hole in the garage wall after I accidentally dropped the car on my foot. I figured I'd get my strength under control eventually, and in the meantime the only pain I was causing was to my parents' bank account. One day I'd be rich or famous and pay them back. Until then, it was their own fault for passing on their faulty genetic material, or letting me chew on uranium as a baby, or rescuing me from that spaceship in the backyard or whatever the hell happened.

'Cause if you're wondering? Yeah, I know we haven't been over that yet: I have NO idea why I'm like this.

Anyway.

As soon as I hurt Mike, it was like I constantly had to be careful, to keep my distance, to make sure it didn't happen again. I was boring—no fun to hang out with because suddenly my friends were breakable. That meant no more play-fighting with Henry, or putting Milo in a headlock when he tried to fart on his cat—because what if I snapped his neck? What would I do then—kill myself, because I was such a menace to society? Because I'd paralyzed one of my friends? I don't want to be that person.

Sophie pulls out her cell phone, thumbs a message to someone, bites her bottom lip. I want to go over to her. I have a *perfectly valid* excuse: I need to apologize, even if I still don't know what I did. Maybe she's really religious? Maybe that's why the touching thing . . .

You know, just talking to her would be good, too—a happy ending to a so-far crappy night. Okay, I'm walking toward her, going over the options in my head. Trying to be cool, like my heart's not beating a mile a minute, like I'm not going to slam my head directly into a brick wall if she shrieks and runs away from me.

Before I have a chance to say something, another car pulls up: a silver Jaguar XF, all shiny and perfect like it just drove off the lot.

Sophie perks up when she sees it—maybe she's a car fan? Or it's her parents' car? I can say . . . I can go up to her and say, "Sweet car," and she'll be like, "I know, right?" and from there . . .

The driver's-side door opens while the car's still idling; the driver gets out and it's not who I'm expecting. It's a young guy, maybe seventeen, dressed like he stepped out of a magazine: dark-wash designer jeans, white button-up shirt with diamond cuff links (what is he, a gigolo?), and pointy leather shoes. He flips his platinum-blond hair out of his face and Sophie's lips break into a big smile.

She shoves her manga into her bag and hugs him—in a friendly way, but with her cheek pressed to his chest. If he's not her brother, I already hate him.

"Thanks," she says. "I hope it's not—"

"Never any trouble," he says, opening the door for her like he's some kind of Prince Charming. Agh! And he has an accent! Freaking lothario! He's definitely not her brother. He sounds French almost, but mixed with something weirder, more *interesting*.

Sophie giggles as he kisses her forehead; ducks under his arm and darts into the car.

There's something seriously weird about this. I want to jump out of the shadows (yeah, very normal) and yell, "Don't go with him!"

But who am I to say that? I mean, she *wants* to be with this guy. Sure, she lied to her friends—but if your friend dressed up like a goth pirate, you'd probably lie to her, too. It isn't my business. I don't know her. We're not together. And *I'm* the freak. What would we have to talk about, anyway? My exciting days of fake-studying at the library? The awesome group of friends I *don't* have?

So I force myself to walk away, back down the dark part of Main Street, where I almost hope something happens that *is* my business—a mugging, someone starting a fight—so I can make a difference. Bust in and be someone. Get my blood flowing. Because I'm freezing; my body's shaking; my breath—I blow it out, *fwoosh*—is like smoke in the air. I'm storming downhill, hands stuffed in my pockets and balled into fists. When I slip.

On ice. A patch of ice about as big around as a car, stretching from one side of the sidewalk to the other.

I fall and land smack on my ass. Spit out my mom's favorite four-letter word and . . .

Stop.

Listen.

Was that a whimper? A . . .

An old woman's voice, pleading: "Please don't hurt me."

3

*P*LEASE *DON'T HURT ME.*

I take a deep breath, rise unsteadily to my feet. There's not much light here—just a dim glow from the lamps farther up the street—but I can see it now, through the window of the store in front of me: ornate furniture, jewelry dangling from a statue's long fingers. Walls lined with framed mirrors, with shelves of antiques, porcelain tea sets, vases, glass decanters.

And in the middle of it all, two masked men with guns. An old woman cowers before them, her arms drawn to her body like she's trying to make herself smaller.

My heart skips. I'm pretty sure I'm not bulletproof.

But neither is she.

I crack the door open before I have a chance to reconsider. Maybe I can defuse this. I just have to be calm and keep *them* calm and—

One of the thugs turns his gun on me. Pivots and it's in my face—and as much as I want to fix this, I can't breathe. I'm staring down the barrel, trying to force my lungs to open up, my throat to open up.

"Easy," I finally manage. "I know you don't want to

hurt anybody. You can take all the antiques you want, just don't—"

"I'm not interested in a bunch of old furniture, kid!" The bottom part of his ski mask is cut off. Spittle glistens on his lips. "We're here for the money!"

"Okay . . . you'll get it." I hold my hands up in that classic thug-placating way: *I am no threat to you.* "I work here with Grandma sometimes. I know the combination to the safe."

The gun barrel flicks upward. "Open it."

I make my way slowly past him, my back to the wall, heart beating so hard it feels like it's gonna punch a hole in my chest.

If I do this right—*please, please let me get us both out of this*—I can save her. I won't be defined by the bad stuff, the accidents, the debt that's gonna give my dad a heart attack, the lies I've told Henry and everyone else. I'll be a hero again.

A good person.

My breath shudders through my lips, visible in the air in front of me, as I fumble around at the back of the store. I have no idea if there even *is* a safe.

"Please let my grandmother go," I say. "She has a heart condition."

"Get me my damn money and shut up."

"I will," I say. "Sorry . . ."

My foot catches on a rolled-up Persian rug and I trip; my hands flail out and make contact with a solid chunk of darkness in the moonlit store: a steel box, about the size of a minifridge. Is it . . . ? My hand finds the dial and then I'm sure.

"Hurry up." The gunman's footsteps—short, frantic—make the floor creak.

"Please, please don't hurt me . . ."

I swallow hard. *Don't mess this up.*

I crouch down like I'm working the combination, spin the dial with one hand while I test the safe's weight with the other. It's bolted to the floor.

Easy enough.

I wrap my arms around it, legs bent to either side, and pull—back arched for leverage. The bolts rip free with a grating, metallic shriek.

"What the—"

Before he gets the word out, I'm up. The safe probably weighs around two hundred pounds, but to me it's like a paperweight. I toss it at the thug who's been tailing me, yell, "Catch!"

His reaction is automatic. He drops his gun, flings his arms forward in an attempt to protect himself—but it's not enough. The safe's momentum knocks him back and off his feet, sends him crashing into shelves full of precious heirlooms, antiques that shatter in an explosion of sound.

The gunman and the safe fall together, half buried by an avalanche of glass and porcelain. A mirror slips free of its frame and breaks over his head. He's stunned—we're all stunned: his partner and the old woman are looking on in disbelief. But I can't count on that to last.

....

I only have a few seconds before the second gunman regains his composure. I have to make them count.

Blood pounding in my ears, I snap toward thug number two, already imagining the scene if I'm too late: a bullet tearing through my chest, my heart exploding in a bloody mess, splattering against the wall. I see it again and again: the shot and then nothing but red.

I wrap my hands around his fist. I'm breathing hard, desperate to keep him from pulling that trigger.

He screams—

And I feel the structure of his hand crumbling, his fist folding in my grasp, until I'm holding something lifeless and broken.

He doesn't stop screaming.

My stomach twists. Bile rises into my throat.

Shaking, I let go of his hand. The gun drops to the floor.

It doesn't go off. It sounds hollow.

Everything I hear right now sounds like that:

The first gunman struggling to push the safe aside; the thud and tinkling crash as it turns over, pulverizes the shards of shattered glass. Heavy footsteps as he limps over to his partner, who's cradling his hand, mouth open and crying out silently like he can't even express the pain anymore, it's so intense.

The old woman slinking back into the shadows, quickly, fluidly, debris crunching under her heels.

The thugs as they stumble out, shouting, "This wasn't what I signed up for, you crazy bitch!"

....

"This kid's some kind of monster-freak!"

The door as it slams behind them. More thuds as they slip on the ice outside. And then the shivering starts up again. My body temperature plunges as the room transforms.

If I thought I was cold before, I didn't know what cold was. Living ice crawls across the floor like a slow-motion flood. Shattered glass mixes with ice crystals, turns into subzero flora, diamond-white spikes. I'm paralyzed as I watch, stunned into silence as a porcelain-pale woman enters the room.

She has platinum-blond hair and wears a white fur coat, spiked white stripper heels—like a Playboy Playmate crossed with Cruella De Vil. Some kind of sexy, domina-trix nightmare.

Maybe this is my brain freezing over—along with my heart—because I'm obviously not human, not even *close* to human. Humans don't cripple people, don't destroy limbs and extremities as easily as they'd open a door. Isn't that what makes us different from—I don't know—sharks?

"Don't be afraid," she says, pink-white lips parting in a smile. "You are among friends." Her words are tinged by a strange accent. Familiar, but . . .

"I'm dreaming," I say. "I hit my head." My lips feel numb, fat and swollen as they try to form words to make sense of this. "Someone shot me."

"No," she says, "you are unhurt. Leilani, come here, won't you?"

The old woman glides toward us, spine straightening,

features blurring as she gets closer: wrinkled skin becomes smoother, warmer; thin white hair uncoils, spills long and dark down her back. Her eyes grow fierce and more exotic; her lips fill out, too, till she looks like a teenage Victoria's Secret model. *With powers.*

"Hello," she says.

I scramble back, slipping and nearly impaling myself on an ice spear. "What's going on?"

The blond woman sighs, draws a pale hand out of her glove. "Avery, please don't feign ignorance. It will make this very tiresome."

"I'm not feigning anything!" How does she know me? Has she been watching me?

"Surely you suspected you weren't the only *extraordinary* person in the world."

"I don't know what you're talking about," I say. *Okay: calm down. Give your story. And most importantly, LIE.* "I came in to help that old woman. I felt bad. That's not extraordinary." My heart's racing; my tongue tumbles over the words. And I can't stop shivering.

How much did she see? How much does she know?

"Of course not." The blond woman smiles. She looks mature somehow, in control—but her skin is as smooth and perfect as plastic. "You're nothing special at all. Just a dull boy—is that it?"

"Yeah," I say. *Dull boy.* Totally normal. "Exactly. And I have a curfew, so, uh, if you don't mind—"

The woman shakes her head, like: *Nice try.*

She raises two fingers to her lips and blows, exhaling

frost like fairy dust. The snow-white cloud swirls wildly and gradually takes shape, revealing a brittle ice butterfly perched on her fingertips. The butterfly's wings creak back and forth mechanically—an eerily empty imitation of life.

"My name is Cherchette Morozov . . . And we share a very special bond."

What was it? Was it lifting the car? Did she see me fly? For months I had worried that I'd screw up, let something slip. That I'd be found out. And if it ever happened, I had a plan. One simple, poorly thought-out plan: deny everything.

"No idea what you're talking about," I say.

Playing dumb. Yes. I am sooooo good at that.

"I know what you are going through," Cherchette says. "You are hiding, you are afraid. But this does not have to be the case. You do not have to spend your life in fear that you will be hurt, or will hurt someone else."

She bends her fingers and the ice butterfly skitters down, spreads its fragile wings as it rests in her palm. "That boy at your wrestling match—you broke his arm. Very brutal."

Cold sweat trickles down my sides, my back. "That was an accident."

"Was it? Ah well, accidents happens." She smiles. "That's what they say, isn't it? But if they continue to happen, opinions will change. People will say you are a monster. You will be punished."

I shake my head, start to protest: "No, there—" *There won't be another accident like that.*

But when I curl my fingers into fists, I can feel the gunman's broken hand against my palm, like a mangled phantom limb. My stomach clenches up all over again.

. . . some kind of monster-freak . . .

"You don't know the full extent of your powers, Avery. You can't possibly. They will grow and change as you do, increasing in intensity and in their unpredictability, if you are not taught to properly control them."

I want to say: *I don't have powers!* But looking in her eyes . . . it's clear. She knows.

I hang my head, concentrate on breathing through my nose, inhaling icy air. It scrapes my lungs, steals my breath. When I exhale, I feel empty inside. Like I've lost something.

"I'm not here to frighten you, Avery. I've come to offer you a different life. I offer you sanctuary, guidance, a community—a *family*, if you will—of like-powered individuals. You'll have a fresh start. All you have to do is come away with me."

"Come away with you?" I blink at her, genuinely confused. "Why would I—"

"Do you love your parents, Avery?"

Her words cut me like ice. Tears sting my eyes, steam in the cold air.

I whisper it. "Of course I love them."

"Then don't you want them to lead the lives they were

meant to live? They will never be able to help you, or teach you about your powers. They will be left frustrated, wondering what they've done wrong, and why you continue to cause trouble for everyone around you. They will never understand what you are going through, why you insist on bringing them so much heartbreak.

"And if you tell them the truth, they will try to help you, but they will be clueless as to what you need. They will take you to doctors, scientists, psychologists. You will be no more than a test subject. You will lose your freedom, your humanity. You're anything but a dull, simple boy, Avery—but they will destroy you, crush everything that is special about you. I want to save you from that fate. Won't you let me?" She flutters her eyelashes, blue and flecked with ice crystals. Coyly. Menacingly.

I crouch down, hold my head. Press my palms to my eyes to keep the tears in.

"I am not exaggerating, Avery. The world will hurt you. And it will not look back. That is why I offer you my protection. A new home, where you can learn about your powers and live without fear, no longer forced to hide your gifts from everyone around you. It's the only way you will truly be safe."

"She's right," Leilani says.

"Shh, let him be," Cherchette murmurs. "He will come around."

"I, if I—" My voice comes out in a croak. "*If* I said yes. If I wanted to go with you, what would I—what would happen?"

"You need only to contact me," Cherchette says. I hear her heels as she crosses the room: stiletto spikes cracking the ice. She kneels down and slips a card into my jacket, tilts my chin up with her hands.

"I know you are overwhelmed right now, and will need time to make your decision. I will check on you again very soon." She smiles almost warmly, her perfect skin refusing to crease. Her eyes glint a dark, arctic blue.

And then she's closer to me, closer, and her lips brush my cheek, searing my skin with a white-hot frozen heat. "Be good now," she whispers.

My cheek burns where she kissed me. I sit there in a daze as the ice around me melts, and I don't snap out of it until blue and red lights flash through the window, until I hear the police officers get out of their cars, until I'm sitting in a puddle and the wreckage around me is dripping, disintegrating, and I realize I have no excuse, no explanation—that "I don't know" or "it was an accident" isn't going to cut it this time.

I stand up with my hands up before someone can yell at me to put them there.

4

*L*AST SUMMER, I BECAME A HERO. *Totally by acci-dent.*

I was riding my bike around my neighborhood on a boring Wednesday afternoon, sweating my ass off and daydreaming about having parents who would let me run the air conditioner while they were at work, when I heard a scream. A freaking-out, oh-my-God-I-just-backed-over-my-kid-with-the-car scream.

I slammed my feet down to stop, dumped my bike, and ran over.

Mrs. Pearson, the kid's mom, was in shock, eyes locked on her little guy: a toddler with his leg trapped under the wheel. She was not doing that calm, together act you need in a crisis.

"We can lift it," I told her. "Come on, help me!" But she didn't take a step; her hands fluttered around her mouth, she was totally hysterical. So I grabbed the back bumper, stood near the middle, and tried to brace with my legs. I was used to working out for wrestling, but you wouldn't look at me and think, Whoa, amazing strong guy is here! *And I sure as hell didn't think that about myself.*

I had an adrenaline rush like you wouldn't believe. I felt like I was going to choke on my own racing heart. Or be sick.

I lifted that car off the ground like it was a box of old clothes—like it was my bike instead of a car. And—

I was so stunned by how easy it was that it scared me.

Mrs. Pearson scrambled to get her son, and then backed away, clutching him to her chest. Still, I couldn't let go. I was stuck with the license plate almost staring me in the face, muscles tensed and full of blood, thinking, over and over again: These are not my arms. Who is this person?

Finally, I calmed down. I lowered the car to the driveway.

Sweat was pouring down my neck, my back; I sat down in the grass and kept pushing my hands through my hair. Even when the ambulance pulled up, and the paramedics packed the kid onto a stretcher and brought him in, I was still sitting there, hands rubbing up and down my arms, wondering if I was at risk of breaking myself, or if I'd imagined the whole thing.

I must have looked shell-shocked. The paramedics asked me if I felt like I'd pulled a muscle, hurt myself. And then somebody contacted the news stations, and that was that. Reporters beat my mom to the scene and took about a million pictures, interviewed me while I was still in a daze.

How did you do it? How did it feel?

I told them I wanted the kid to be safe. And that adrenaline is an amazing thing. And that I was proud to be an

American—because how can you dissect someone who says that?

As stunned as I was, I knew something was wrong with me. That I'd stopped being normal the second I lifted that car.

When my mom arrived, she wrapped me up in a huge hug and kept telling me how proud she was. I asked if we could turn on the air conditioning at home, and she laughed, and managed to get me through the crowd and into the car, and we went home, and you better believe she turned on the air for me. She even stopped yelling at me about my messy room and about leaving my socks everywhere—for a few weeks, anyway.

We fielded interview requests; I got one of the keys to our city; we even appeared on some nationwide morning shows via satellite: me, my mom, my dad, the supergrateful Pearson parents and their happy, healthy toddler.

It was amazing, it was the best feeling I'd felt in my whole life.

It was too good to last.

A re you crazy? Are you CRAZY?! Why do I even ask these questions?"

It's 11 P.M. We just got back from the police station. My mom's pacing like a caged tiger, practically tearing her hair out.

I'm sitting on the countertop, drinking some tomato soup that I microwaved. I have a blanket around my shoulders, like I'm the victim instead of the screwup—like somebody pulled my half-drowned body out of a lake.

If only.

"*Why* would you try to thwart a robbery, Avery? Were the nine and the one buttons on your cell not working? *Why wouldn't you just call the police?!*"

"I don't *know*," I say. "My cell died; I couldn't call. I felt like I should do something."

I wish I could tell them I saw a woman in danger, and that's why I risked it—but none of the info is fit to confess. The old woman I tried to save was a *shape-shifter*, for crying out loud. The whole thing was a setup.

What was I supposed to tell the police? I'm not hurt, other than the frostburn on my cheek. Nothing was stolen. The safe was ripped out of the ground—which is the one thing that points to a robbery and saves my ass, since no one thinks I was responsible for that.

"It wasn't smart, Avery." My dad kneads his forehead—I think he aged twenty years tonight. "We know that you were trying to be helpful, but you could've been hurt."

"If he wants to be 'helpful,' he could load the dishwasher like he's supposed to," my mom says. "Breaking into antique stores and racking up thousands of dollars' worth of damages while almost getting himself killed is not 'helpful.'"

"I didn't break in," I mumble. "The door was already open."

My mom shakes her head, pours herself another cup of coffee.

Dad sighs. He's got his checkbook out. Heart-attack time.

"Look: aside from the financial burden, things are going to be fine. The owner's agreed not to press charges. We're going to get through this and learn from it. Your mother and I are just grateful that nothing worse happened."

"But there are going to be some changes around here. Take a look at these." My mom fans out some brochures on the counter next to me. The covers show clean-cut teens frolicking on a grassy lawn, smiling and holding hands like they're at Girl Scout camp. On one, a cartoon bird tows a banner that reads: CLEAN AND SOBER JUST IN TIME FOR COLLEGE! On another: FROM DELINQUENT TO DELIGHTFUL!

I spit my soup back into the mug. "You're not serious."

"It's an alternative school," my dad says. "One of the officers recommended it. They've had a lot of success with the troubled youths they've placed there: kids who need more supervision, but who don't really belong in the system."

"I don't need to go to a school like that! I'm not 'troubled'!"

"Avery . . ." My dad flips through his checkbook. "The numbers don't lie."

I flop over on my bed, restless, staring into the dark. My parents are still up and talking downstairs. Occasionally my mom's voice gets strained. Right now she's complaining that she's "tried everything," that maybe there's nothing left to do but ship me off somewhere else.

Maybe there isn't.

I feel like I'm in a vise, being squeezed from two directions, and if I don't do something about it, I'll be crushed by the pressure. I slip the card Cherchette gave me out of my pocket.

There's a phone number printed in silvery ink. All I have to do is call.

I keep taking these big breaths, breathing in and not letting go until it feels like my lungs are going to burst. But it doesn't help. I'm going crazy in here; I have to get out.

Normally I would wait for my parents to go to bed before I leave, but there's nothing "normal" about tonight. I met a woman who makes ice move like it's *alive,* and who confirmed that there are other people with powers in the world. Now that I know that, lying in bed and flipping through the same *Sports Illustrated* swimsuit issue while I wait for my parents to nod off seems more insane than flying. So screw it, I'm going now.

I throw on a black hooded sweatshirt and shove open my window, then slip my legs out and drop down, landing on—and crushing—the same pathetic bush I always crush. I'm lucky my parents aren't more attentive gardeners, because I've been doing this routine since October. As far as I know, they've never noticed.

I trek through the yard until I get to the woods behind my house—then go deeper, just to be safe. It's damp tonight. My cheek feels raw where Cherchette kissed me, like I did a face plant onto concrete. The moisture in the air cuts through to my bones.

When I get to the clearing I use as my taking-off point, I take a long look at the sky. The one place where I can leave all this other crap behind, where no one can touch me, scream at me, blame me, laugh.

I own the sky.

I can barely remember *not* owning it. It's like my memories of flying are so intense, they block out huge chunks of time when I was normal, plodding along on the ground like everyone else, getting pumped about running a race or something—like *that* was freedom. Wow.

The wind in my face. Nothing solid holding me down.

Learning about flying wasn't like learning about my strength—it's not like I jumped off the top of my house and didn't hit the ground one day. I do a lot of idiotic things (uh, juggling the washer and dryer? Bad idea.), but that definitely wasn't one of them.

Flight was more of a gradual discovery. A restlessness that wouldn't go away, a sense of untapped potential that gnawed at me until I pushed myself off the ground.

I never had one of those wake-up-in-the-middle-of-the-night, oh-snap-I'm-floating-above-my-bed moments. Flying is something I *do*, not something that just happens. I don't feel like a balloon; it's not like I'm floating, aloft but stripped of my sense of gravity, or power.

When I fly, I focus. I'm aware of every muscle, every turn of my torso; the way I shift my shoulders, the way I adapt to the air. It's like I move through it because the air knows to resist me, and I know to resist it back. Like we have an understanding, and I'm on a different plane of existence—swimming through the air.

I soar, with my head thrust back and my arms stretched out at my sides. I spin sometimes—I show off—even though there's no one to impress. I deafen myself in the wind, fly until my skin is cold and my heart is beating harder than ever. I suck in the deepest breaths I've ever breathed.

There's nothing more thrilling, more invigorating, than the challenge of keeping your body aloft, with the possibility that, at any second, you'll lose control and crash to the earth. That freedom and then that finality—they're linked. And not to be morbid, but it's like how youth is so treasured because it only lasts so long, or flowers are beautiful because they bloom and then they wilt. It's like I want it even more because I know it shouldn't be happening—because I feel like it could be taken away. I mean, even pro athletes only have so many good years—and there's no precedent for superpowers. What if there's an expiration date?

I can't bear the thought of losing this. My flight is the one thing I have that's totally my own—no one's ever witnessed it; it's never hurt anyone and it never will. Without it, I don't know if I'd be fully myself. I'd be dead, lifeless, dull. When I'm flying, I'm more than normal, more than most people will ever know—but it's undeniably who I am. And there's peace in that—in being here, now, *myself.*

Tonight, when I launch myself into the damp, cool air, up past the treetops, into that massive, starlit sky . . . everything's left below me. Any anxiety, any confusion, remains on the ground where it belongs.

I'll get through this—I have to.

Because somewhere—maybe worked up by the same feelings, facing the same dangers—there are other kids like me.

And I'm going to find them.

UN-FREAKING-BELIEVABLE.

Sitting across from me, in the guidance office of my new high school for troubled losers, is the worst excuse for a jaded misanthrope badass I have ever seen.

And the worst part is I think I sort of know her.

"So what are you in for?"

The anarchy buttons, the black eyeliner, the coffin T-shirt, and the weird striped tights are gone. She's completely transformed since I last saw her.

"What am I 'in for'?" I blink at her, trying to mask my confusion but probably failing. "Nothing. My parents enrolled me. Why are *you* here?"

She's still wearing glasses, but now they're paired with glittery eye shadow and big gold hoop earrings. Her jeans are like ten sizes too big and belted around her hips so that her boxers puff out like a deflated hot-air balloon.

"My probation officer recommended it," she says, propping her pink Timberlands on a table that's covered with the school's glossy brochures. "No one wanted to mess with me in juvie 'cause I was psycho."

I'm sure.

Darla unzips her giant parka and blows a bubble-gum bubble, then pops it. Underneath her jacket she's wearing one of those R.I.P. T-shirts, the kind that are supposed to commemorate the glorious life of your dead homie. Only it looks like she made it herself, with the help of Photoshop and some iron-on transfers, since I doubt there are a lot of gangsters mourning Marie Curie.

This girl is so damaged.

"You know you're totally giving yourself away, right?"

"Are you hollering at me, dog?" She slouches even lower in her chair, like that'll be the magic trick that negates her posing.

I don't even know how to respond to that. "Um . . . okay. You know dead scientists aren't really 'gangsta,' right?"

She flushes. "You know Marie Curie?"

"Not by sight, but her name's right there on your shirt, and I'm not a moron. I don't belong in this school. And I'm not staying here . . . if I can help it."

"Oh. You're not? Huh." Now when she sinks in her seat she looks like she's hiding, face ducked behind the huge collar of her parka. "Crap," she mumbles.

"Something wrong?" Man, this girl is weird. I still can't figure out what she could have done to get sent here, unless she shoplifted those huge pants and then wrote the judge one of her crappy poems.

I haven't forgotten that whole coffee-spewing incident either, and the fact that she's starting at this school on the very same day *I'm* starting . . . well, it's suspicious. But I mean, it's possible this is a coincidence—she might just be deranged.

"Kind of. I, um . . . at the risk of sounding completely insane—"

The secretary interrupts before Darla can finish, hands us our schedules, and tells us to hurry on to class, assuring us that we *don't* want to get detention here. I check my schedule: "Remedial English—sounds promising. You going there, too?"

"No, I have . . ." Darla scans her printout. "Intro to Rehab." Her eyes grow wide, like a person on a sinking ship who just saw the last lifeboat leave without her. "All right, well—we need to talk later! Okay? At lunch?"

"Sure," I say. I need someone to sit with anyway, assuming no one will have stabbed me by then. "See you later. Hope your first class is, uh, helpful."

"Um, yeah. Thanks!" She sways back and forth, and her eyes start to roll back in her head.

"Whoa!" I catch her before she clonks her head on the table. "Are you all right?"

"F-fine," she says. "I just need a little . . . reassurance."

Darla's breathing really hard, almost hyperventilating. She starts digging around in her huge parka, and I steady her until she finds her purple inhaler.

"Asthma?" I say. "That must be rough."

"I'm fine now. You can go. *Really.*" She waves me away and I leave her to take care of her medical business in private. But I'm not a hundred percent convinced that she's okay, so I stop at the doorway, peek back to make sure she's breathing properly.

She doesn't have her inhaler anywhere near her mouth. She's holding it away from her body, about as far away as you would hold a leash if you were walking your dog.

Darla presses a button on the inhaler, and blue electricity crackles between two outstretched metal nodes. Then she sighs and starts to calm down, like she can breathe again.

I haul A to my first class.

By third period I have exactly one friend (Darla Carmine), 280 potential enemies, and a boot print on my pants from getting kicked in the ass on my way down the hall. (And no, I didn't retaliate—I just gritted my teeth and kept walking.) Thank you, anonymous donor.

It turns out that Darla and I have science together third period, and when we arrive the teacher is all smiles. "Aren't you lucky—we're doing a dissection lab today!" She assigns us seats at different tables, then reminds us that "the scalpels are not to be used as weapons."

Great. As if cutting up a cow eyeball isn't bad enough— it also means arming the resident psychopaths. That'll do wonders for my concentration.

Darla and I exchange looks. Her telltale geek pallor goes a shade or two lighter.

"Scalpels?"

I shrug and try to look reassuring. "Maybe everyone'll be too grossed out to get violent."

The classroom fills up with every variety of thug and delinquent imaginable. It's not as big of a shock as it was at first, when I walked into Remedial English and saw two thugs stabbing each other's hands with pencils until they bled, while a huge guy with a ten-o'clock shadow squished a smaller kid's head into his armpit, and the teacher calmly diagrammed sentences with her back to the class—but I wouldn't say I'm used to it.

Overall you've got: the Thugs 4 Life, busy giving each other ink-pen tattoos (Gothic letters and knives stabbing into skulls), who've been in and out of juvenile detention centers since they were eight; the low-maintenance Burnouts, who break into the janitor's closet at least once a day and huff cleaning fluid and bug spray; the *high*-maintenance Burnouts, who chug Robitussin and snort Ritalin on their way to a full-out coke habit; the Bonecrushers, who beat people up and send them to the hospital, but whose parents have enough money to keep them out of juvie; and the Mary Janes, who dress like they're in preschool but threaten to "cut you" if you look at them the wrong way.

And then Darla, the gangsta-impaired electroshocker, who seems to be even more out of place here than I am.

While the teacher's explaining the lesson, Darla whips out the most complicated cell phone I've ever seen (it's purple, and looks like the illegitimate techno child of a satellite and a Swiss Army knife) and starts texting up a fury. I start doing this subtle-yet-crazed put-it-away gesture that gets increasingly frantic as every crook in the room turns to watch her. Like moths to a flame.

The thing is, half these kids could afford to buy the hottest cell on the market. But beating someone down and stealing their property must be more satisfying—judging by the gleam in every fiendish eye.

This could get ugly.

Just as I'm making a mental note to cut my next few classes so I can tail this girl all over school and make sure nothing bad happens to her, there's a knock at the door. Darla finally notices me waving at her. She stashes her cell phone and we all turn our attention to the door.

"Just a moment," the teacher says, setting a tray of rancid worm corpses on her desk. A uniformed police officer escorts a slouching, black-clad girl into the room.

I almost choke on my next breath. It's Catherine—the floor-sweeping girl from Roast.

Is this like a twisted reunion or something? What's going on?

She looks really irritated, halfway to snarling, and she's clutching a package of Wonder Bread by the plastic tuft at one end. There's something pathetic about the clash of the bright red, yellow, and blue packaging against her black clothes. Her hair hangs in flat, soggy tendrils, like she just took a shower or got caught in the rain. She scowls and shakes it out of her face.

"Found another truant," the officer says, patting his belt.

I know he thinks he's doing something good, but that smug expression rubs me the wrong way. I've had enough authority figures look at me like that to know there's *always* more to the story. I mean, it's not like he brought her in carrying a crack pipe—she's holding a loaf of white bread. Get off your frigging high horse.

"Catherine," the teacher says. "So glad you could *finally* join us. What's your story this week? The flu? An exotic vacation?"

"I'm not truant—I had to stop at the store," Catherine snaps.

"Take your seat." The teacher gets all no-nonsense and points to the back of the room—to the table where *I'm* sitting. Catherine swings her Wonder Bread and grumbles all the way back. She raises her eyebrows when she sees me.

"What are *you* doing here?" she says under her breath. "Did Pikachu tell you to kill someone?"

The teacher slams a tray with a dead worm pinned to it onto our table.

Harsh. She treats everyone else's worms with more respect, setting the trays down like they're harboring a formaldehyde-infused scientific treasure.

"Shut up or I'll make you a sandwich out of that," I murmur back.

I think I see the corner of Catherine's mouth turn up in a smirk. "Yeah, right."

Darla's voice carries over to our side of the room, high-pitched and quavering: "I work best alone, actually." I glance to see who her partner is.

....

It's one of the Burnouts. Not too dangerous, but skeezy enough to have Darla freaked out. He's leaning close to her, leering, his greasy hair hanging in his face.

Uh, did he just stroke her shoulder? That's a mistake.

"This is a team effort," the teacher says. "Working together is part of functioning properly in society."

"Five bucks says he eats it to get high off the formaldehyde," Catherine says quietly.

"That's so sick. No way he does that. You're on."

"Remember to use the tools," the teacher says. "There will be no pinching, biting, or squeezing the worms. You are to find and identify every item on the work sheet . . ."

Ugh. This is so disgusting. I try to remind myself that, technically, this is more educational than the rest of the crap I've done today—but I can't bring myself to cut into the worm. I don't even want to *look* at it, let alone identify its anus and genital pores.

There's another knock at the door and the teacher excuses herself. "Keep working!" she says. As soon as the door slams shut, this massive dude sitting diagonally in front of us swivels around in his seat. He's wearing a blue football jersey that says *Big Dawg* across the back, and his legs are packed into cargo shorts like two pasty sausages. He looks like he's been mainlining bovine growth hormone since he was born.

"Hey, Catherine." He grins. "What happened? Your drunk dad forget to drive you to school again?"

"Shut up, dumb-ass."

It takes a second before I realize that's *my* voice.

Every head turns to look at me—this is way more exciting than worm theater. The Burnouts' eyes are wide and wobbly. Even the Thugs think I'm insane.

"Kill him, Big Dawg!"

"Rip his head off!"

Big Dawg's nostrils flare. He stands up slowly, like a stout Godzilla savoring the moment before he crushes Tokyo.

I start to shove my chair back, but Catherine puts her hand on my arm to stop me.

Big Dawg cracks his knuckles. *Krrrk. Crunch.* "What's your name, new kid?"

So I tell him.

"Pirzwick, you're the dumbest new kid I've ever met. I'm gonna break your bones in so many places, you'll be begging to be put on house arrest so I don't paralyze you."

Nice. I have to bite my tongue (literally) to keep from telling him where he can stick *that* threat. Followed by: *My bones don't break that easily. I could hurl your ass to the next county if I wanted to.*

But of course I can't say that.

I grit my teeth and prepare to get punched in the face.

Catherine tilts her chin up to lock eyes with Big Dawg. "You know why I got kicked out of my old school? Some bigmouthed jock pissed me off—so I cut his eye out."

She draws her fingernail down the length of our worm, slits it fully open so that the guts are revealed.

"And you know what's sooo funny?" She grins at him.

"He was making fun of my family, too. That'll be such a coincidence."

"Whatever, bitch," Big Dawg snorts. "You're crazy."

"No shit," she says. "Glad you figured that out."

Big Dawg scratches his crotch and retreats, grumbling about how Catherine's a "crazy bitch" all the way back to his seat.

One of the Mary Janes flings a worm at her patent-leather-shoe-wearing rival, then starts screaming that she's a boyfriend-stealing skank. Hair pulling and jumper tearing ensue, and the focus shifts away from us.

Catherine jabs a few pins into the worm to hold the flaps of its flesh open. She scans the work sheet, looking angry all of a sudden, not cool and collected like she was a moment ago.

"So we're back to this, I guess."

"I guess," she snaps.

I wait a few seconds before I ask her what I've been wondering. Swallow hard. "You didn't really . . . ?"

She glares at me. "You really think I'd cut someone's eye out?"

"Yeah, I figured . . . sorry."

We don't talk much for the rest of the lab, other than a few mumbled remarks like, "I think I found the pharynx." But I keep staring at her hands. I want to ask . . .

No. I can't. What would I say? Girls scratch people all the time. She probably uses nail hardener, or has really strong keratin. Or better yet, dead worm skin is probably really fragile. Exactly! I can even test that.

The next time Catherine has her head bowed and is scribbling away at our lab work sheet, I jab my thumbnail into the pasty worm carcass, to see if I can chop its head off. But my nail is too short and blunt; I end up squishing it.

Ugh. I have to close my eyes and think of puppies to keep from throwing up.

"You done playing with that?" Catherine says.

"Heh . . . finished."

"Good." She gets up to turn in the worm and our work sheet, and I wipe my thumb on my jeans, totally ill and convinced that I smell like zombified worm flesh.

Out of the corner of my eye I sense a scuffle; I hear a girly yelp and then the air crackles, fills with the scent of burned grease and Robitussin. The Burnout next to Darla convulses before slumping down on his desk, face-first into the worm tray.

I hope I'm the only person who saw her stash that inhaler.

The teacher pulls her earphones out of her ears. "Did he just have a seizure?"

"He's been asleep the whole time," Darla says. Her face is flushed and she's breathing heavily.

This girl is INSANE!

Not to mention a terrible liar.

But no one calls her on it. I am so, so grateful for that right now.

When Catherine comes back, she sniffs the air; makes a horrible face. Then: "Hey, he's mouth-to-mouth with that worm. You owe me five bucks. That counts as eating it."

What?! "No, it doesn't!"

I don't bother to check my wallet—I know for a fact that I don't even *have* five bucks. My mom only gave me enough to buy a drink for lunch. And I am NOT drinking from the water fountain at this school.

"You never specified he had to swallow it," Catherine says, smirking like she's got me.

What, now she's a rules lawyer? Two can play at that game.

"Our bet was whether he'd eat it to get high," I say. "He's face-first in that tray because Darla electrocuted him with her inhaler, *not* because he wanted—"

"Excuse me?" Catherine looks at me like I'm even more retarded than I was that night at Roast.

"I didn't mean to say that," I backtrack, not meaning to say that either. Then I laugh. "Hahaha, how would an inhaler electrocute someone? Heh . . . heh . . ." It gets less and less believable and more and more pathetic. But she's totally not paying attention to me anymore.

Catherine's eyes narrow to slits. Her nose twitches every few seconds like an angry rabbit's. Darla must sense the heat of her stare, because she pulls the collar of her parka up to hide her face.

"Holy shit," Catherine says as it suddenly clicks. "'Darla'—is that my stalker?"

"Your stalker?"

"Yeah." Catherine's bristling—the hairs on her arms are perked right up. "She's been coming to the coffee shop where I work for weeks. She's always staring at me, or taking pictures of me with her cell phone . . . she's obsessed. And it's freaking annoying, but whatever, it's a coffee shop, weird people come in sometimes. I could even deal with her stupid questions about 'my feelings' and 'do I feel different, like I don't belong sometimes'—because at least I could ignore her. But now she's at my school? What the hell??"

Her lips pull back over her teeth.

Oh, crap.

Darla, you do not want this girl to look at you the wrong way—let alone make you the target of her white-hot fury. I am so, so sorry for throwing you under the bus so I could save five dollars. It was an accident and I will try to make it up to you. I think all this in Darla's direction, as a kind of silent apology in case Catherine rips her face off before I can calm her down.

"It's probably just another girl named Darla. That's a pretty common name. Nowadays." I shrug. Smile.

Catherine grimaces. "Were you dropped on your head as a child?"

Distraction is my best defense right now. Like tanking in a MMORPG, taking all the damage so your weaker allies can do their thing without getting smashed. And maybe run away.

"Sooo . . . bread, huh?" I gesture to the package of Wonder Bread on our table. "Sliced bread—gotta love that. That's why people are always saying stuff is 'the best thing since sliced bread.' Were you gonna make toast? Toast is awesome."

"You're an idiot," she says.

And then the bell rings. Saved! I gather up my books and proceed to drop them, trip, and sprawl out on the floor in front of Catherine—"Oops! Sorry, sorry!"—so that Darla has a chance to haul her scrawny butt out of danger.

Catherine regards me with so much scorn she could totally scorch toast with her eyes. "Uh, see you at lunch?" I call after her. She shoves past me and doesn't bother to turn around.

The friend count stays firmly at one.

LUNCH USED TO BE the highlight of my day. I'd sit
with my friends, chill, eat whatever nutritious meal
my mom packed for me without worrying that someone
slipped a razor blade into my sandwich, and I'd copy
Henry's math homework so I didn't have to do my own.
But now? It's sad to say this, but I'd rather be in class.

It's like anarchy central in the cafeteria. Here, the students are free to roam and attack whomever they want.
Without a teacher to actively ignore, their focus is entirely
on chaos and mayhem. Which, you know, I might enjoy if
I were totally unhinged.

Did I mention that adult supervision is almost nonexistent in the cafeteria? The music teacher and the
math teacher are standing next to the garbage can, making
sure nobody misses and throws their trash on the floor,
trading stories about the times they've knocked naughty
students unconscious by clocking them with a yardstick.
(Okay, so I'm making that part up. But I wouldn't put it
past them.)

Are they paying attention to us? Noooo, not really.

I unpack my lunch (turkey sandwich, Oreos, apple) and

wave when I spot Darla. She bustles through the crowd, her huge backpack sagging behind her.

"Hi!" She grabs a seat next to me. "Looks like we both survived!"

"About that . . ." I cough. "You know Catherine? In our science class?"

"The, uh, your lab partner?"

Darla slurps extra hard on her juice box—a sure sign that she's hiding something.

"Right. Well, she kind of thinks you've been stalking her. And she wants to eviscerate you."

The extra-loud slurping has now turned to choking. I pound her on the back (lightly!) and she coughs it up.

"Don't worry—I think we can call a truce. But I have to know what's going on. Do you have a crush on her or something?"

"Ohmygod*what?!*" Darla squeezes her juice box and apple juice sprays into my eye.

Tingly. Ow.

"No, I don't have a crush on her!"

I wipe my eye with the back of my hand. "Well, whatever's at the root of your stalkerish behavior, it's making her uncomfortable. I think we need to work on your social skills."

"But—I'm not stalking her! I'm trying to get to know her better! So that we can, um . . ." She peers at me, almost meekly. "I'm not sure if I can tell you yet."

"Yet?"

"We have to be friends first, so you don't think I'm a freak."

"Darla?" I give her a look. "You're wearing an 'R.I.P. Marie Curie' shirt and size sixty-two jeans. Anything you tell me can only improve things."

"Not necessarily," she mumbles.

"All right, look: you think about it. I'll be right back. If you want to tell me then, you can. If not . . . well, we'll talk about something else."

I get up to buy my drink, keeping alert as I approach the graffiti'd Coke machine: prime lunchroom real estate. The overprivileged Bonecrushers hold court there. I've already seen them slam one kid against the wall and steal his lunch money, but mostly they use this time to refuel.

Today they're focused on their . . . uh, arts-and-crafts projects? I guess their history class had an assignment where they had to build models or something. One of them constructed the Colosseum out of Popsicle sticks. Big Dawg baked and frosted a cake shaped like the Sphinx (although it looks more like a dog). He keeps yelling at his friends not to eat it, knocking their hands away when they try to swipe some frosting.

How . . . educational.

I slip my money into the Coke machine, push the only button that isn't broken, and wait for that satisfying *clunk-thump* that means a frosty drink is on its way.

Nothing.

"Check out my diorama," booms a proud voice behind

me. It's Butch, the ten-o'clock-shadow guy from my Reme-dial English class. He's the biggest dumb-ass of all: at fif-teen he's like six-foot-two, two hundred pounds. Plus he's already been arrested for driving drunk without a license, which is as good as being royalty in his crowd.

"Dude, you already showed us."

It's midafternoon, so by now Butch is rocking a partial beard. He strokes it like some wise guru as he says, "Miss Watson's gonna love it. Look at the tiny elephants."

"Get it off the table—put it on the floor by Big Dawg's cake."

I press the button again, wait for my drink. Still nothing.

So I try the coin-return button. Wait for the reassuring jingle of my money being returned.

Nope.

Press it again.

There's a line of kids behind me. One of the Thugs is getting antsy. "Are you almost *done*, holmes?"

This stupid machine ate my money.

I don't have another dollar-fifty. My mom only gives me exactly what I need, and my allowance is ancient his-tory, confiscated for the next eight hundred years to pay for the damages to Henry's parents' car.

"In a minute," I say. I'm getting agitated now—I *hate* when vending machines steal my money. And to top it off, some of the girls behind me, for whom a Diet Coke is, like, their sole sustenance, are threatening to cut me. So I'm in a hurry; I grab the machine by either side and start shak-ing it. I mean, everyone does that. It's totally expected.

And then I look down. And see that, um, the Coke machine?

Is no longer touching the floor.

I panic and drop it, jump back like it burned me, but the machine hits at an awkward angle, tips to one side, and *BOOM!* Slams onto the floor with a rumble, snap, *SMOOSH!* Cake frosting squirts out the side, and the Sphinx's ass is sticking out like the Wicked Witch's ruby slippers. The rest of it?

Demolished.

It took down the Popsicle-stick Colosseum, the Hannibal-crossing-the-Alps thingie—the whole row of Bonecrusher history projects, lined up on the floor next to their table.

"MY DIORAMA!!" Butch bashes his seat to the ground. "I'm gonna kill you, Pirzwick!"

He lurches toward me like a drunken Frankenstein. His man-boobs are trembling beneath his Budweiser T-shirt, his ruddy face is burning, and I can smell his breath from here. Sausage, my death—nice combo.

"Uh, sorry guys," I say, moving to put some distance between the Bonecrushers and me. "That thing just fell. I don't know what happened."

"You just signed your own death warrant!" Big Dawg says. "It's onnnnn, Pirzwick! It's ON! My mom spent all day baking that Sphinx!"

"To be fair," I say, climbing over a table backward and stumbling over a chair and a tuna sandwich and almost falling on my ass, "this isn't fifth grade. You're supposed to do your own homework. So maybe this is—"

"You're gonna get cut!" some girl says, flipping a switchblade out of her purse. "You broke the Coke machine, bitch!"

"—justice," I finish. Crap. How am I supposed to get out of this?

I look around for Darla, like: yo, Taser girl, a little help here? But she's not the one who comes to my rescue. No, it's Mr. Nerdly, the math teacher—armed with a yardstick—who grabs me by my collar and drags me out of the fray.

"Calm down, people!" he shouts, in his nasal tough-guy voice. "This is a cafeteria, not a cage match. Get back to your seats!" He's still holding my collar. Thanks, but I can stand upright by myself. I wriggle away and he shoots me a dirty look, menaces me with a shake of the yardstick.

Back at my seat, I manage to squeeze some juice out of my apple. Okay, actually, I obliterate it by crushing it with my fist.

"Are you okay?" Darla says.

Yeah—I'm gonna pretend she didn't notice. I'm sure her friends destroy fruit all the time. "Fine," I say, wiping up the pieces with my lunch bag.

My heart's racing. I don't want to get into a fight here. I don't want to lose my cool and snap, then pay for it later—with 120 years of incarceration.

When the bell rings, I try to make a swift exit, but Butch and his bonecrushing posse are waiting for me by the door.

"We'll finish this after school," Butch says. "And if you

punk out and don't show . . ." He crunches his knuckles in his fist. "You'll regret it."

He doesn't even wait until the teachers are out of earshot to threaten me. Mr. Nerdly's right there by the door, busy chewing on his thumbnail, then pulling his hand back to examine it, like magic marshmallows are growing out of it instead of fungus. What is this guy's purpose? Seriously?

"Fine," I say. "Whatever." It's not like I'm afraid of these guys. But how am I supposed to put an end to this? Show up and let them pummel the crap out of me? Call my mom and get her to pick me up in the middle of it, so I look like a little kid?

Not cool.

One last threat and a clumsy throat-slitting gesture, and Butch and his posse are gone. I breathe. Exhaaaale. Three more hours until I have to deal with that crap.

As I push through the mass of messed-up students, my eyes catch Catherine's. She's studying me. No idea why. Maybe because she already suspects I'm an idiot, and today's spectacle just confirmed it?

I nod like, "hey," and keep going, moving with the wave of delinquent students into the hall, where the clang-and-bang of lockers meets shouts of, "Ha! You're gonna get your ass kicked!"

I shrug it off, try to look tough—but honestly? I'm posing hardcore. Because that's *exactly* what's going to happen.

TWENTY MINUTES AFTER the last bell, when the
buses have pulled away and most of the adults have
jumped ship, I'm standing on the run-down baseball field
behind the school, surrounded by the more bloodthirsty
half of our screwed-up class. Some of the kids are clinging to the metal backstop, the rest are spread out along the
foul line, chanting:

"Fight! Fight! Fight! Fight!"

Butch and Big Dawg and the rest of the Bonecrushers
are closing in. They're wearing huge toothy grins—they
don't look like they *ever* get in fights with anyone who
could actually hurt them. For a second I'm tempted to
change that, put a stop to their bullying by showing them
what it feels like.

But that would open up a whole other set of consequences.

Before Butch has a chance to "bring the pain," Darla
tries to stop the inevitable. She climbs to the top of the
bleachers and starts waving her cell phone (which now
has a blinking antenna poking out of it) like it's a conductor's baton. "Listen up!" she shouts. "You'd better make

yourselves scarce, because a *ginormous* robot is about to bust out of those trees and *kill you all!*"

I wince.

A few heads turn toward the wooded lot that borders the school. Curiously, like, *eh, a giant robot?* A bird chirps.

I guess this would be a good sucker punch moment, if I was going for that.

Wind rustles the leaves, but no robot head emerges. The toy-loving cons quickly lose interest.

"I mean it! It shoots laser beams!"

Nice try, I mouth, giving her a double thumbs-up—right as a huge fist appears in my peripheral vision.

I dodge out of the way; it's not my instinct to be a punching bag.

But I'd better learn. Fast.

Butch jams his knuckles deep into my stomach, uppercuts me; he's wailing on me with these big fat clumsy combos, and I'm taking every hit, doubling over and acting like it hurts—like it's supposed to. Like I'm normal.

But every punch lands with the intensity of a Nerf arrow. It's like being in a vicious pillow fight, only more confusing, and scary, because up close their faces are brutish and stupid, flushed with glee as much as rage. They're getting off on "teaching me a lesson." Talking trash with their perfect teeth shining in my face.

A year ago, this assault would've had me on the ground with two swollen eyes, blood oozing from my nose and mouth. I would've winced at every kick to my broken ribs.

And the grand finale, the moment that would finally signal "enough," would come when I had passed out half dead.

That's what they expect—I can't believe I almost forgot that.

I'm still on my feet, fake-groaning but bouncing back every time. This could go on indefinitely, until these idiots get tired because this beat-down turns into cardio. And that? Might prompt someone to think about this.

So I wait for the next blow—a pathetic kick from Big Dawg, who can barely get his meaty leg off the ground—and I take a dive, choke on all the kicked-up field dust, curl into the fetal position, and let them kick the crap out of me.

I bite down on my lip to try to squeeze some blood out, squint through a dust cloud to see if they're buying it, and—

Whoa.

I must be . . .

Imagining this?

There's a black figure above me on the backstop, on the part that hangs over home plate. She's crouched like an animal, tangled hair hanging down like a ghost in a horror movie.

She springs, pounces; flings herself through the air.

Catherine. Death from above.

"Oh, shit! Move, move!"

The Bonecrushers hustle, banging into each other in their haste not to be her target.

I roll onto my side just in time to see Catherine slice

into Big Dawg. She barely pauses before she launches herself at her next victim.

Meanwhile, Big Dawg can barely speak. The front of his jersey has five long slashes in it like a bear attacked him. Dark red blood is starting to seep through. He touches it with one beefy finger, then he screams, hauls A across the field and through the parking lot and finally into the street, where he just keeps running until he's out of sight.

There's a mad rush to safety then. This might be a school full of badasses, but nobody wants to *really* get hurt. Even the hardcore thugs who supposedly take a bullet every other weekend don't want a piece of Catherine.

I don't want to get in her way right now, which doesn't explain why I'm still lying here, sucking blood off my lip as the Mary Janes hurry past us shrieking, and the cornered Bonecrushers are offering up their next homemade Sphinx cakes in exchange for their lives. I'm totally neglecting my own safety.

I'm thinking.

It's impossible for a human fingernail to slice through flesh like that. *Impossible*—just like lifting a car before you're old enough to drive it. Or flying. Or getting the crap kicked out of you without a single bruise to show for it.

Cherchette's voice pierces my head: *Surely you suspected you weren't the only extraordinary person in the world.*

Catherine shakes her hair out of her face, scrunches her nose, and flicks her fingers like she's got something gross on them. Then she blinks and it's like she's coming back to herself, shifting from an ultraviolent hurt machine to your typical antisocial girl. With, uh, anger issues. I guess.

The field is even more of a mess than it was before. Smears of blood stain the dirt, and the faint smell of Bone-crusher sweat sours the air. Darla's standing where first base should be, shifting her backpack from one shoulder to the other, nervous-tick style. I wish she would run.

Catherine turns her attention to me at last. "Were you just gonna let those freaks kill you?"

"I'm a pacifist," I say, and cough.

"More like a masochist. Even Gandhi would've kicked those guys in the nuts."

I pause a moment to picture Gandhi delivering a swift kick to Big Dawg's balls. "It was no big deal," I say. "But, uh, thanks for saving me."

"Don't expect it to happen again. You're lucky I was hanging around."

"Hey, yeah." I smile, as I realize: "You waited for me. You knew this was gonna go down, so . . ."

She spits on the ground. "Like hell! I had detention."

"HA!" Darla claps her hands over her mouth, but it's too late: the laugh is out. Catherine pivots, nails upturned in a bring-it gesture.

"Something funny, stalker?"

"N-no! Just . . . the idea of you actually showing up for detention . . ."

"Yeah, I'm sure you know a lot about me. Like what? Where I live? Where I work? Where I'm gonna bury you *after I rip your throat out?!*"

. . . .
74

I grab Catherine around the waist as she lunges for Darla, claws primed for homicide.

"Move!" I shout. "Now!"

Darla spins on her heel and runs, backpack clanking like nobody's business.

"Get your hands off me!" Catherine's thrashing around so fiercely she's breaking a sweat. "Let go of me or I'll—"

"I don't want to fight with you. I'm making sure you don't do something you'll regret."

This is going to be bad. This is going to be *so bad*. Unless she wears herself out and is too tired to slay me, those nails will be slicing through my throat the second I let go.

"You need to calm down," I say. "Or get a scratching post or something. Darla isn't—"

BAM!

That was the wrong thing to say.

The back of her skull is rock hard. Ow.

"She wants to be friends with you but she doesn't know how."

"I don't *need* friends," Catherine growls. "And I'm not looking for some stupid *support group*."

"You've already got one, whether you like it or not." I take a deep breath, prepare to get skull-slammed in the nose. "Me."

She laughs. "Oh yeah? Why's that?"

"You have to ask?" I let her go; spring out of the way in case she comes after me. "We, uh . . ." I try to remember how Cherchette put it. "We share a special bond."

"Tell me you did *not* just feed me that line."

"It's not a line—it's true. We both have powers!"

All my frustration, my hope, spills out in that moment. I feel like I just handed over my future and now I have to wait to see what she'll do with it.

I count my heartbeats. They're thudding in my head like a metronome, marking the split seconds she spends staring at me, her expression wide-open and exposed. Scared.

And then it's gone. Catherine closes up. Turns on her hate face.

"Powers," she says. "Wow. You really are retarded."

Great. I finally tell someone the truth about me, and she acts like I'm insane.

"Don't be like that. We can—I mean, I need someone to talk to about this. You do, too, right?" I'm grasping, following her as she steps back, claws at the ready. She's *not* interested—I'm only making it worse. But I can't let go.

I saw it in her face. I *saw* it.

"Why would I want to talk to a delusional freak?" She practically spits the last word. Steps around a tangled clump of branches like a dancer navigating a stage. Doesn't even look at them.

"Because." I take a deep breath. "You know I'm not delusional. And maybe you're this badass tough girl, but I doubt you have all the answers. Do you even know why we're like this?"

Something more than ferocity flickers in her eyes. Does she want to know? Does she *already* know? Whatever it is only lasts a second.

"Don't *ever* mention this again." Catherine stalks away and then toward me, jabs a claw at my face, razor-sharp nail an inch from my eye. "And if you start spreading lies about me, I'll kill you. That's a promise."

"Why would I tell anyone about you?" I throw my hands up. "Haven't you been paying attention? I have as much to lose as—"

She screams. Clenches her fists so tightly I'm afraid her hands will bleed. "You don't want me to do something I'll regret? Then *get out of here*! Get the hell away from me!"

I bow my head and bite my tongue. Leave, like she asked me to.

But I'm not giving up.

8

I **SPEND THE** whole walk home kicking rocks in the road and cursing. I'm pissed at myself for ruining my first shot at superpowered friendship, for just plunging in without a game plan. First impressions count for a lot; first forced confessions are even trickier. I should have thought of that, should have remembered how freaked out I was when Cherchette approached me.

By the time I get to my street, I'm worked up to the nth degree, somewhere between angry (because I'm a moron) and ecstatic. Yeah, I screwed up—but I found someone *extraordinary* today. All I need is another chance.

Catherine will chill out once she realizes I'm not her enemy, and then . . .

Um, why is there an Aston Martin in my driveway?

I circle that beautiful creature like a jackal who just discovered a dying zebra and can't believe his luck. Did my dad lose his mind and buy an Aston Martin to soothe his midlife-crisis-having heart? Like: "I'll be damned if my son's going to bankrupt us, I'll do it myself"?

The car's totally immaculate: no crappy gym bag in the

back, no dirt ground into the carpet. Leather interior, ice-blue paint job—this is a car for James Bond, not my dad. I keep looking over my shoulder, like the rich dude who broke down in our driveway will be back any second, and is gonna bitch me out for touching his car.

I tear into the house, yelling, "Dad! Did you buy an Aston Martin?" I think about warning him that my mom's going to kill him, but I want him to take me for a ride first.

The last person I expect to see is Cherchette. She's on her hands and knees in front of our TV, all tangled up in electrical cords and A/V cables. She's wearing leather boots and a tight white skirt with a slit up the back. *I, um, yeah.*

I think I should be freaked that she broke into my house but I'm a little more confused than that. "What are you doing?"

"Avery." She gives me this weird pouty look that totally clashes with the severity of her face. "I wanted to finish before you arrived, but this machine is not working. Now you've ruined your surprise."

"Surprise?" This definitely still counts as a surprise. I did not expect to see this woman in my living room.

"I bought you a video-game system. You don't have this one, do you?"

I shake my head. "I don't have one at all. My parents are like cave people."

Slight exaggeration, but still: my mom acts like having at-home access to video games will ruin my chances of going to college, turn me into a serial killer, and ensure that I never get a girlfriend because I'll be too busy propositioning hookers in Grand Theft Auto. Never mind that every other guy I know has one, and they're fine.

"Ah. Well. We know that entertainment must evolve, just like everything else." Cherchette winks at me conspiratorially. "Would you help me to get this working, Avery?"

I don't have a game system, but Henry has three of them, and whenever he slept over he'd pack at least one in his backpack and we'd hook it up in my basement. Should be easy.

I'm untangling the monstrous octopus of cords, amazed at the mess Cherchette made, when she starts apologizing. "I understand that things went badly the other night. I didn't intend that. I don't blame you if you're angry."

"Why would I be angry?" I rip open one of the plastic packages with my teeth. "Because you set me up and almost got me arrested?"

"Yes, I suppose I deserve that." She sighs. "But I had to see what you would do, Avery. You insist on putting yourself in this 'hero' role, and while it has been on a small scale . . . I had to see how you would react if a more dangerous situation presented itself."

"And?"

"And I am worried."

Cherchette's kneeling next to me on the carpet, and a cloud of cold wafts off her, like when you stand in the refrigerated aisle in the grocery store. The air in my lungs feels like winter.

"The 'criminals' you encountered were carrying unloaded guns. If you had interfered in an actual robbery, you would have been killed."

"Maybe," I say, shivering. My fine motor control's shutting down. I have to try twice to plug in one of the cables. "Maybe not."

A buff space marine appears on the screen, his boot balanced on a dead alien's armored back. I'm watching the shiny graphics of my new game, but my mind's replaying the moment that gun got shoved in my face. Staring down the barrel, sure that I could make everything right. Not knowing the threat was never real.

"I want you to understand these things before it's too late. You have a wonderful gift. I don't want it to end up hurting you."

The game's theme music booms like a moody opening salvo.

"Is it working? Wonderful!" Cherchette claps her hands. "Now we'll play." She gives me controller one and keeps the other for herself. "Be careful not to throw the controller at the screen, Avery. I read about that—it will break." She sounds concerned, which strikes me as absurd. I mean, she set me up to go toe to toe with two thugs in an antiques shop—wasn't she worried about me breaking crap there?

"I'm not going to put a hole in my parents' TV. Don't worry." I choose the cooperative mode; skip the intro and vanquish the first few enemies while Cherchette examines her controller.

"How do I do this?"

"Uh, just hide behind something. Or mash some buttons; you'll see what they do."

"He won't stop jumping!"

"Try a different button. If you keep hitting that one, you're going to keep doing that." I try not to laugh as Cherchette gets vaporized by an alien, then sputters in shock that the alien was cheating.

We play for a while longer, Cherchette displaying some very dramatic poor sportsmanship, and then she tells me she has to go.

"But I will be in touch. And"—she reaches down and pats my head, sends a chill down my spine—"I've settled your bill with the antique-store owner. He'll refund your parents' money shortly. So don't worry about that."

"Really?" I can't help it; this goofy smile takes over my face. My mom and dad might even let me out of that crappy school if the owner says he realized it was an accident or something. "Thank you! It was . . . a lot."

"I will always take care of you." Cherchette drapes this little fur cape over her shoulders, and gazes at me like . . . I dunno, like a proud parent or something. Her eyes narrow when she smiles, just a sliver of blue shining through, but the skin on her face remains as smooth as always. Like a watchful statue's.

"See you soon," she coos.

As soon as Cherchette leaves I yank all the cables out of the TV, bundle my new game system in a blanket, and run upstairs to hide it in my closet. Time flies when you're having fun with a morally suspect ice goddess—my parents will be home any minute! I run back down and tear the box up, cram it into the bottom of our garbage can, and even dump some nasty leftovers on top so my parents are less likely to find it. I'm washing splattered spaghetti sauce off my hands when I hear the garage door open.

Five, four, three, two . . .

"Sounds like you're doing well at your new school, kiddo."

My mom clicks in after him, doing her "happy" walk (definitely different from her "angry" walk). "I got a call from your school today." She's smiling. What the heck could this be about?

"Uh, you did?"

"Assistant Principal Carmine said it's remarkable how well you're adjusting."

Principal Carmine? The only Carmine I know is Darla.

My dad sets down a paper take-out bag. "Your mom was so thrilled she even stopped to get Chinese food."

"Thanks. Awesome." I peek inside to see what she ordered. Mmm—it smells so good. I pry out an eggroll and bite into it.

"Ms. Carmine said you stopped a fight today."

I almost hack up my eggroll.

My mom's bustling around, all proud, setting the table. "It seems your instincts aren't *all* bad. She said you managed to talk two known bullies into not fighting each other, and sitting down and *discussing* their problems instead. Can you believe that?"

Uh, noooo.

No one under eighteen would believe that. But she's talking to my dad now, not me. Chattering on about how being in an environment "that lacks traditional peer pressure" and where I don't have to worry about "being cool enough" (did she really just say that??) is allowing me to have a positive effect on the other students.

I empty a whole quart of beef and broccoli onto my plate. "Do you mind if I take this into the den? I need to do some work on the computer. One of the kids I helped today wants me to IM him to talk about his anger issues. That okay?"

My mom blinks, a little surprised. "I guess so."

"Thanks!" I call out. I'm already gone. Logging in and hunting down Darla Carmine—the freaking craziest girl I've ever met. My mom's not mad at me anymore, which is a good thing, but Darla still has some explaining to do.

Me: *hey there assistant principal. lie to my mom much?*

Carmine314: *I do what I can. :) how'd it go w/Catherine?*

Me: *not good not horrible. she sends her love.*

Carmine314: *lol yeah I bet. are you writing this from the hospital?*

Me: *intensive care of course ;)*

Time to move in for the kill and ask a real question. Deep breath.

Me: *so help me understand something. what's ur place in all this?*

Carmine314: *??*

Me: *stalking catherine, enrolling in our school—why? what's in it for u?*

A new window pops up, this time with Nate's screen name. I haven't heard from any of my old teammates since I hung up on Henry the night of his birthday. Now the most detested of all my friends (past and future) wants to talk to me?

natethegrate: *still sulking? ;) u should call h it rily hurt his feelings u didn't evn get him a prezzie 4 his bday some freind lol*

I'm still trying to respond with something more eloquent than F*** Y** when motor hands gets his next line out.

natethegrate: **hands u tissue* dry those tears Av lol is it tru ur at that loser skool? u fit in so well ther*

I grit my teeth. Yeah—you're hilarious. You could go on all night, right? I click over to Darla's window.

Me: *sorry my a-hole ex-friend is harassing me. give me something good to say.*

Carmine314: *in response to what?*

I copy and paste Nate's hilarity and send it to her.

Me: *I need to get him back w/o sounding pathetic.*

Carmine314: *can't you just ignore him?*

Me: *NO!!!*

Carmine314: *hmm all right . . . do you want me to hack his MySpace & wreak unimaginable havoc?*

Me: *YES PLEASE*

Carmine314: *he's going to love his new My Little Pony layout so much he won't even mind that his password's changed & he can't take it down.*
Me: *ur awesome* :D
Carmine314: *np that's what friends are for* ;D
Me: *gtg but 1 more thing . . .*
Me: *do u have catherine's address?*

9

TONIGHT'S FLIGHT HAS a purpose. I take a few slow
breaths, pushing the air as deep into my lungs as it'll
go, till it's like I'm filled up with sky. And then I push
off, with every ounce of strength that I have. I will myself
higher, higher . . .

A branch catches my sleeve and bends upward, scrapes
the length of my arm until I rise past it and it snaps back
down.

And then I'm free; I'm past the tops of the tallest trees
and into the crisp, cold air, doing my best to navigate by
landmarks that I can see from above, by the patterns I'm
learning.

Catherine lives in a more rural part of town, where the
houses range between neat but old and totally run-down. I
land in a field and then check mailboxes until I find hers:
11605, the word *Drake* stenciled on the metal in faded
white letters. There's a rusty blue pickup truck propped
on cinder blocks in the front yard. The tailgate is down
and a few cats are curled up in the back. A black pickup
truck sits parked in the driveway but the cats seem to
avoid that one.

Other than the occasional twitch of a feline tail, it's totally still out here. A television flickers through the front window, the only light on in the house—and I can hear what sounds like sports announcing, the muffled roar of the crowd. But there's no sign that anyone's awake. Looks like I'm safe.

Or not.

I'm halfway around the house when a skinny thirty-something guy in jeans and no shirt comes out. He's carrying a bulging garbage bag, muttering that the whole place smells like cat urine.

Mr. Drake doesn't notice me. He's too busy wrestling with the bag of garbage, trying to cram it into a metal trash can—but the bag's too fat to fit. He keeps trying to force it and getting pissed. Until finally it rips.

Bottles, cans, and all sorts of refuse tumble out. Catherine's dad kicks the trash can with his bare foot and almost trips over it—then starts kicking the individual pieces of garbage, cursing.

In the middle of all this, a small black cat with a white patch over its eye tiptoes toward the mess and starts lapping at a crumpled food wrapper, speedy and nervous, like it knows it's in trouble if it doesn't get its fill and get out of there—but the cat's not fast enough. Catherine's dad's foot shoots out and catches the cat under the ribs, sends it flying. "Damn cats!" he yells. He picks up a stray bottle and hurls it in the cat's direction, then storms into the house.

I count to sixty to make sure he's not coming back, then

pick my way across the yard, searching for the cat so I can check if it's okay. No luck at first—but then I see it dart out from under a drainpipe. It runs along the back of the house and leaps at an open first-floor window.

As if on cue, Catherine appears and plucks the cat out of the air, curls its body into a *U*, and cradles it against her chest. Kisses its nose.

A weird smile spreads across my face. She caught that cat perfectly—almost like she knew it was going to be there. *And* she's being nice to it. So I wonder:

Does she have a psychic bond with cats?

And, uh, if so . . . is night vision part of the equation?

I squat down but it's too late: two sets of glowing eyes lock onto me like freak-seeking missiles. Catherine uncurls the cat and lets it drop; vaults over the windowsill like a ninja. Nice!

But, ah, I don't have much time to admire her moves—seeing as how she's coming toward me with a tonight-you-die look on her face. Scrambling backward like a crab, I experience a moment of agility envy. She's in my face before I have a chance to say hello. Claws bright white in the moonlight.

Catherine grabs my throat with one hand and shoves me back.

"Stop!" she angry-whispers. "Just stop!"

My skin tingles where one of her nails scraped my neck. I expected her to scream at me, to blow up like she did at school. So this . . .

"All of you—*stop!*" Catherine's voice is raw and on the

verge of breaking. Her words explode like a burst of air, the sound just barely attached.

All of you?

Who? Darla and me?

"I'm not here to spy on you," I say, afraid she'll stop listening if I don't explain fast enough. "I'm no danger to you. I swear. I'm just like you and—"

"You think I haven't heard that before?" She scrapes her knuckle across her eyes in two fierce motions. And I stop.

"Who have you heard it from?"

My heart beats into my throat and crowds the word out. *Who else is there?* I want to offer Cherchette's name but my voice won't cooperate.

"No one," Catherine whispers. "Just leave me alone."

We're quiet for a moment. I'm not sure what to say to break down this wall between us. Catherine's probably unsure how to get me to leave.

I wish there was a foolproof way to do this. Like when you're little and you want to win someone's friendship, so you give them your best-loved toy. One sacrifice and the person looks at you differently.

Maybe I can still do that . . .

"I'm sorry," I say. "I'm freaking you out and that's not what I want—I just want to be your friend. And maybe that's totally ridiculous to you, and you want me out of your life and I'm going to have to deal with that. But give me one more chance to prove it to you. And then . . . I'll leave you alone. We'll talk about this on your terms or not at all. Deal?"

She rubs her eye with the palm of her hand. "Like I have a choice?"

"Catherine . . ." I sigh. "This isn't easy for me either. Just give me a chance."

I close my eyes, because I can't look at her when I do this. This is like the most private thing I have. The biggest secret I've ever held. My best-loved toy—the one that has the most potential to destroy me.

Fists clenched, I push upward—everything in my body focused in that one direction. Up. *Up.* A bullet cutting through the air. *Visualize it.* Forget that you have an audience. Forget how much is riding on this.

Up.

It's colder, smoother. I'm slipping through the sky now, arms outstretched to take it all in. Stars in my eyes.

You have to lose something to gain something.

You can't expect someone to trust you if you don't trust them.

When I look down Catherine is so small she blends into the night. I can't see her expression, don't know if she's calmed down or if she hates me more than ever.

I hope I'm making the right choice.

THE NEXT MORNING in the car I'm nervous as hell. The ball's in Catherine's court now—I promised I wouldn't bother her. But what if she never speaks to me again? And all of this is just . . . over?

"Avery?" My mom turns her head at a stoplight to check on me. "Are you all right? Are you afraid of someone at school?"

"Um." I'm afraid of *everyone* right now. How am I supposed to tell her *that*? "Not really." I squirm in my seat. "I'm okay."

"Because . . . You know we only want what's best for you." She sips her iced coffee, keeps her lips pressed together awhile afterward, like she's thinking. Jiggles the plastic cup, so the ice sloshes around. "Last night I was so happy you were doing well at your new school . . . but maybe you don't belong there. I mean, bullies, fights every day? Some of the kids might be jealous of you if you start doing well and getting attention from the other students. Your dad and I don't want you to get hurt."

Bingo! This is my golden opportunity: parental self-doubt. Say the word and I'll be out of there, safe and comfortable in my old school. Where, even if my friends hate me, at least I *know* people.

So why don't I?

"They're all talk," I say, and shrug. "I have, um, this dissection lab in science today. We're cutting up a worm and I feel sick about it. That's why I'm being weird. Sorry."

"Yuck." My mom shudders. "I think I missed that day when I was in school."

After that she's all smiles and conspiratorial "ew" moments, confident that she's doing the right thing. I wish it was that easy for me—my mind keeps drifting back to Catherine, to the look on her face that I *couldn't* see last night. Where do we stand now?

Once my mom drops me off, my worries switch gears. I haven't been in the building more than five seconds when Darla races up to me, grabs my arm, and drags me into the girls' bathroom.

Three Mary Janes are posing in front of the mirror doing their makeup. When they see me they freak; one of the girls loses control of her eyebrow pencil and it shoots wildly up her forehead, so that she's suddenly cartoon-angry, one eyebrow slanted to the extreme. "This is the *girls'* bathroom, you freak!"

"Get out!"

"Sorry—the following conversation is classified," Darla says. "You'll have to complete your beauty routine elsewhere." She fires up her inhaler and zaps the wall-mounted hand dryer with a bolt of electricity. It starts sparking and smoking and the Mary Janes run out like . . . uh, like girls who just saw Darla set a hand dryer on fire. I knock it to the floor and stomp on it till it stops sparking. Darla digs this purple, hockey-puck-shaped device out of her backpack and slaps it against the center of the door. As soon as the purple disk makes contact, two spindly metal arms shoot out from either side, and tiny drills at the end of each arm quickly bore holes into the cinder-block walls, effectively securing the door. The purple disk lights up and the air fills with the noxious smell of lavender.

"We're in trouble," she says.

Um—there's a barricade-slash-air-freshener on the bathroom door. *Obviously* doesn't even begin to cover it.

"I should have predicted this!" Darla rages, pacing back and forth in front of the sinks. "Yesterday was so *Catherine ex machina*, so unexpected, so perfect—it was all I could think about when I got home. Because either she jumped in because a rumble is her equivalent of a food fight, and she didn't want to be left out—or she *is* capable of caring about others and working with them! That means we can still reach her! I was so excited I didn't stop to consider the consequences.

"Fool! And you call yourself a great mind!"

"I never—" I start. But then I realize she's talking to herself. Cool. So I didn't have to understand any of that. "Um . . . what's the problem?"

"Big Dawg's mother got involved," Darla says. "Maybe you noticed that personalized football jersey he was wearing? They're ridiculously expensive, and now that it's ruined his mom is *livid.* She's adamant that someone be punished for it. I don't think Big Dawg named names, but cutting stuff up is Catherine's specialty. The office is definitely going to try to pin it on her."

"Damn it." I stomp on the dryer once more for good measure. She was sticking up for me. "We can't let that happen."

"Exactly. Catherine's record is already a mile long. This could be the offense that puts the final nail in her juvie coffin—so to speak. It's not her fault that she has, umm, unusual weapons at her disposal."

I raise my eyebrows. Darla coughs and barrels forward. "I have a plan. It's not the most *brilliant* plan, but there's a seventy-two percent chance it'll work. Just . . . one of us has to take the fall, and the other has to be a witness and back up everything that person says. Are you a good liar?"

"Darla? If lying was a sport I would letter in it, go to state, get a college scholarship, and be a first-round draft pick."

Darla blinks. "Sports metaphors—not my thing. Is it safe to say you mean yes?"

"I mean 'hell yes!' Let's do this."

⚡⚡⚡

Ten minutes later Darla and I are sitting in the office, waiting for our meeting with the principal while the secretary jams out to her iPod and works her way through an early-morning bowl of Cookie Crisp. Catherine just got called down over the PA system and Darla's busy adding the final touches to my costume before she arrives: I've got two three-pronged hand rakes (apparently they're called "cultivators" in gardening circles) strapped to my hands, and Darla's securing them with duct tape and boxing wraps, winding them around and around until I effectively have claws.

This is so not going to work.

I want to bury my head in my hands so that no one passing the office will know the moron-claw loser is me— but I'd probably gouge my eyes out with the rakes. "He's not going to fall for this."

"Shh—I told you to practice saying 'snikt.'" Darla pins the boxing wraps so that they're snug around my wrists. "It's all about the delivery. Now, let's rehearse your story."

"Out loud??"

"Yes! You have to practice now so you don't choke later. Trust me—I'm a master of disguise."

I groan. Darla is the worst chameleon ever. And I'm taking advice from her? "Maybe you should do this, then."

"No way. It's already a given that you'll lose half your arm hair when I rip that duct tape off. No reason we should both suffer. Besides—you'll be great."

I'm still grumbling when Catherine slouches into the office, a crumpled hall pass in her hand. Smiling awkwardly, I cross my arms over my chest and try to hide the claws under my armpits.

"Deny everything!" Darla stage-whispers at Catherine. "Trust us! We've got you covered!" She's nodding like a bobblehead and double-thumbs-upping like there's no tomorrow. Reassurance with thousand-volt cherries on top.

"Like I would do anything else," Catherine mutters. She leans against the wall, red-rimmed eyes flitting between the secretary's desk and the principal's door. "Can I get this over with?"

The secretary's music is cranked so loud that her earphones buzz like eager insects; her eyes are glued to the blog she's reading.

Catherine tosses her crumpled hall pass into the secretary's half-full cereal bowl. It floats in the milk for a sec before the secretary hurriedly spoons it out.

"What is wrong with you brats?" she sputters.

"I *said*, 'Can I get this over with?'" Catherine points at the principal's closed door. "You called me down here."

The secretary shuffles some papers on her desk, stops muttering under her breath long enough to send Catherine in. She narrows her eyes at us. "What do you two need?"

"We're here to see the principal about yesterday's unfortunate incident," Darla says. "He's expecting us. We checked in about ten minutes ago?"

"Hmm, that's right. Try to behave yourselves."

We smile like angels and she warily puts her music back on.

"Okay, now let's practice!" Darla says. "Last chance! We're down to the wire! Here—I made you a cue card." She hands me a three-by-five card with my lines written on it in tiny letters.

I clear my throat. "I . . . sometimes like to role-play."

....
97

Darla nods excitedly like, *go on*.

"I pretend I'm Wolverine from the X-Men. Yesterday after school I was practicing martial arts moves on the baseball field . . . and I . . . I imagined I was surrounded by Sentinels." Every word is painful. "Those are the robots that, um, try to destroy the X-Men. I was fighting them when Big Dawg and his friends showed up, and I show remorse accidentally—"

"No! You're not supposed to read the part in parentheses!" Darla swats my arm. "You're supposed to 'show remorse'!"

"Oh." I fake a few sniffles, but it sounds like I have something caught in my nose. Not convincing. ". . . Big Dawg and his friends showed up, and I accidentally hit Big Dawg with my claws when I . . . did a, uh, spin-kick-double-claw-strike combo." *What??* Where does Darla get this stuff, Street Fighter? "I thought I was all alone. I didn't realize he was there until I had hurt him and it was too late. I am so, so sorry. I'm so sorry. Cries."

No—wait. That part's in parentheses. I'm supposed to cry??

Darla makes an annoyed sound. "Could your eyes be any drier? I thought you said you were a good liar."

"I said I could lie; I never claimed to be friggin' Shakespeare—agh!!"

A stream of fiery liquid shoots out of Darla's wristwatch and sprays me in the face. An unbearable burning sensation rages in both my eyes. Thick, mucus-y tears are flowing down my cheeks, snot's bubbling out of my nose like a volcano.

I hear a door click open, the polyester swish of our principal's thighs rubbing together.

"Start saying 'I'm so sorry, I'm so sorry'!" Darla hisses. "Here he comes!"

"Mr. Pirzwick? Ms. Carmine? You have something to tell me?"

"I'm sorry," I blubber, wiping my nose and eyes with an open palm and spreading snotty tears all over my face. I snort when I should sniff and a blob of mucus explodes in my hand. If I wasn't myself I would throw up right now. "I'm so sorry."

"He didn't mean to hurt anyone," Darla adds.

"I was the one who scratched Big Dawg on the baseball field," I say. "I'm so sorry. It was an accident. I was . . ."

Um. I would like to refer to my cue card right now, but I can't see.

"Role-playing," Darla hisses.

"Pull yourself together, Mr. Pirzwick." Someone stuffs a tissue into my hand and I do a quick wipe job.

"I like to role-play and pretend that I am, um, Wolverine. From the X-Men. These are my claws." I do a few karate-style swiping moves and end in a decent approximation of a fighting stance. Wipe my eyes again since they're still churning out tears. Catherine's mouth opens and stays that way.

"Mr. Pirzwick, come into my office before you hurt someone else."

I fumble for my cue card and follow him in. Darla's bouncing on her seat, grinning like a carnival clown. She holds up a piece of paper that has NOW: 82% CHANCE OF SUCCESS! written on it in thick black marker.

I'd like to hold up a piece of paper that says, WTF, I THOUGHT YOU WERE COMING WITH ME! But I don't have one of those.

Wish me luck.

AT LUNCHTIME I GIVE DARLA THE VERDICT.

"You're not even suspended?" she squeals. "That's awesome! It was the tears, wasn't it? See, I hesitated to spray you at first, but it turned out to be a genius move—"

I stop her with a glare that would wilt lettuce. My eyes stopped watering hours ago, but the pain and humiliation of being a human snot-cannon will last forever.

"Yeah, it was weird . . . the principal seemed almost sorry for me. We had a long talk about how I can't let my delusions take over my life. Then he rearranged my schedule so that I have Reality Management last period." Darla needs that class more than I do, but whatever. Catherine was deemed innocent, which is what really matters.

I scan the cafeteria for some sign of her, but I guess she's lying low. I wish I knew what she was thinking. Are we cool now? Or not?

All's well in the rest of cafeteria land: the Burnouts are gagging on NyQuil and ecstatically inhaling Sharpie fumes; the Thugs are freestyling; the Mary Janes are lavishing love on their Nintendogs.

Big Dawg and Butch and the other Bonecrushers are camped at their regular table, next to the out-of-order Coke machine. They must be feeling pretty Zen after having their asses handed to them—they're busy playing paper football, ignoring the multitudes of potential victims. They haven't even stolen anyone's lunch money yet.

Maybe we *did* make a difference.

"I think it's time I was totally honest with you," Darla says. She squirms uncomfortably, like telling the truth causes her physical pain. "I'm not actually a juvenile delinquent."

"You're scaring me. What's next? The earth is round?"

Darla sticks her tongue out. "Okay, so maybe that's not a huge shock. But you asked me what I'm doing here, right? What's in it for me?"

Darla slips some fake psychological evaluations and doctored school records from her backpack. "At the risk of sounding like a complete maniac: I infiltrated the school so I could get closer to you and Catherine. I created a fake criminal background for myself—mostly shoplifting and stealing my nana's painkillers—because I thought if I had street cred it would help you trust me. I thought you were a badass."

I smile. "I *am* a badass."

"No, but, like, a real one. Anyway. You're probably wondering why I'm interested in you and Catherine, since we don't appear to have much in common."

"It's crossed my mind."

Darla sucks in a breath. Holds it a few seconds before

releasing it in an anxiety-filled rush. "I think you should meet my friends. I can't explain everything here, but you guys have a lot to talk about. Stuff most people wouldn't understand. We're getting together Friday night at Sophie's house. Sophie's the girl who lent you her cell phone at Roast."

"I remember her." Of course I do.

My heart's hammering. It's not hard to read between the lines—I *know* what Catherine and I have in common. Is Darla saying that Sophie has powers, too?

How does she even know about us?

I want to ask her—my brain's swarming with questions. But school doesn't seem like the right place to get into it. Terror squeezes my stomach, mixes with the hopeful-nervous flutter of butterflies. This could change my whole life.

"Oh," I say as Darla jots down Sophie's address on a piece of paper. "Um. What time?"

"Five or so. Her parents have some dinner thing, so we'll have the place to ourselves. You should invite Catherine, if you get a chance. I'd do it myself but I'm trying to respect her space. She kind of hates me."

"Yeah . . . Me, too, I think. We'll work on that."

"Oh! I almost forgot!" Darla slips a gift card out of her wallet and slides it across the table. It's black with a picture of a purple robot on the front, and the exciting words TWO DOLLARS! coming out of the robot's mouth, cartoon speech-bubble style. "This is for you."

A two-dollar gift card? What store even sells those? I

turn the card over to get an answer, but the opposite side is blank. There's no trusty magnetic strip or string of numbers or fine print telling me where and when the card can be used. Darla must sense my disappointment.

"Um, it's not *really* a gift card," she says. "You did know that, right?"

"Yeah, of course." I roll my eyes. "It's a, um . . ." I turn the gift card upside down, trying to figure out what it's supposed to be. No clue.

"Think of it as an e-book reader, only more compact," Darla says. "You can keep it in your wallet or wherever, and hopefully no one will try to steal it, because who wants a two-dollar gift card, right?" She grins. "It's a way for me to send you top-secret files without fear that they'll be intercepted—it's a zillion times more secure than e-mail or IM. The screen is on the back of the card, and it will only function while *your* left thumbprint is pressed to the robot's head. If someone tries to look over your shoulder while you're reading, take your thumb off the robot and the screen will black out. Right now I've only uploaded my personal file, but my friends have created files, too. I'll send you those as soon as I think you're ready."

"Your personal file? Like . . . your permanent record?" I give her this confused look.

"No, silly. It's everything I think you should know about me—since I already know a lot about you. It evens the score." She smiles. "Just drag your finger down the screen to scroll. And make sure you read it today; the file's set to auto-corrupt in sixteen hours."

Why am I not surprised?

"Thanks," I say, slipping the card into my backpack.

The rest of the day seems to fly by. Even Reality Management isn't as bad as it could be. While the rest of the class is role-playing the proper way to behave in a restaurant, I'm spaced out in my own world, wondering what Sophie's power could be. And since Darla said her *friends* need to talk to me, who else did she mean? That guy in the trench coat—Nicholas? I'm pretty sure he doesn't like me, but I've never met another guy with powers. It would be sweet to have a friend to watch sports with *and* talk powers with.

When the final bell rings, I rush to my locker—like if I hurry, everything will happen faster. Friday seems like a million years away, now that I know these other kids are out there. How are they coping? Do their parents know? I'm so busy going over the possibilities, I almost don't notice the word *thanks* scratched into my locker door—until Catherine bumps me to get my attention.

"Hey," she says. One corner of her mouth is turned up in an almost smile. "That stunt you pulled was pretty dumb. But it was cool of you."

I shrug, like I do cool, stupid things all the time. "No problem. I hope to live it down one day."

Then, since she's not saying anything, and awkward silences are poison to new friendships: "So, um, do you want to maybe hang out Friday? There's this party thing I'm going to, and . . ."

"Another party? Are the Pokémons invited?" She's teasing me, though—I can tell. "I can't. I have to work Friday."

"Okay. Well, what about Saturday?"

Catherine shakes her head. "I work all weekend."

Right. I wonder if I should ask her straight out if she's blowing me off. But then I have this other, crazier thought: what if she's doing what I used to do, claiming she has to work when she's really going around town in amateur-vigilante mode, trying to make a difference in people's lives?

Um. But Catherine actually *has* a job. Whereas I never had an extra-credit science project to do. Or any of the other projects I claimed to be working on.

"Well, maybe when you're free sometime." This is awkward as hell. It's like asking a girl on a date, only it's *not* a date. And it's worse than that, because there aren't a ton of fish in the superpowered sea. So if I screw this up . . .

"I'm not really free ever."

"Ever?" I stare at her, maybe a little too intensely, looking for an explanation or something. Because—ever?

Catherine breaks eye contact, turns her attention to some gum on the floor. "Anyway, I have to go. I'll probably see you if you stop by Roast. I'm usually there."

She leaves me wondering what that was all about. And what else I don't know about her.

Darla Carmine: MY STORY

If you're reading this, you've reached the inner circle of Darla Carmine. (Just so you know, that's kind of a big deal.)

Ready?

FACT: Being a genius isn't easy. (Okay, well, technically it is easy—it doesn't take any effort. What I mean is that it's hard to find people you can relate to. And I would've put this in a footnote but Sophie told me that most people don't like reading footnotes, so I'm trying to cut down on that.)

I was born to do great things, and I quickly discovered that I was pretty much alone in the attempt. When other kids were busy building mud pies and eating paste, and picking their noses and trying to wipe their "discoveries" on me, I was dabbling in robotics and adapting Gibbon's *The Decline and Fall of the Roman Empire* into a coloring book version I hoped my peers could appreciate.

It was the first of many disappointments.

As I entered school and became more ambitious, my lack of real friends became even more frustrating. I had so much I wanted to share with people! What's the point of making exciting discoveries if you have to keep them to yourself? It would be like Newton discovering gravity and then not telling anyone about it, which leads me to my own personal Zen koan: If a genius doesn't leave behind a legacy, does her brilliance really exist?

I refused to believe I was destined to lead the life of a lonely, eccentric hermit. All I had to do was put my mind to the problem and work out a solution. If I couldn't attract kids with my genius, I would infiltrate their playdates and bring my genius to them. Surreptitiously, of course.

So, in the pursuit of true friends (who I hoped would one day become kindred spirits), I willingly engaged in inane activities like dressing up Bratz dolls, and pretended that a jolly fat man squeezing down a chimney (with a sack of toys, no less) made logical sense. And all I asked for in exchange was a chance to play them music from Wagner's *Ring* Cycle so I could teach them about leitmotifs, which I thought were pretty awesome. Baby steps, right? But that sort of compromise was beyond the seven-year-olds in my neighborhood.

Meanwhile, I was zipping through school at light speed. I thought things would change once my classmates were high schoolers—intellectual equals at last! They were almost adults, so I automatically assumed we'd have stuff to talk about. But my teenage classmates were too engrossed in dating drama and unrequited-love angst to listen to me rhapsodize about the latest robotics news. And at that age, the only boys I didn't think were gross were dead scientists—and it's not like I wanted to *kiss* those guys. [No offense, Niels Bohr.] What could I really contribute to the lunchroom gossip?

Regardless, I persevered. I kept telling myself that *one day*, I would find a place where I fit in. I would find my people. And I had plenty of time to refine my technique.

Thanks to my dad's job, my dad, my nana, and I moved around a lot. Every new city offered me the opportunity to reinvent myself and learn from past mistakes. Instead of lecturing on topics no one else cared about, I started to study potential friends and try to find common ground—like, if they were into a certain type of music, I'd listen to it at home and see if maybe I could like it, too. And, okay, *obviously* that didn't always work, but it didn't turn people off as fast either.

Once I graduated from college [that was last year— so yes, you can stop worrying about how this crappy school is going to affect my transcript], I stopped being so defined by my genius. It was still a huge part of who I was, but since I wasn't in a classroom, I wasn't the weird prodigy girl anymore—I was whoever I wanted to be. I could hide my genius until I was ready to reveal the truth—without the risk that people would judge me before they got the chance to know me.

I met Sophie at an ice-skating class. I noticed she liked Japanese toys and manga and stuff, so the following week I brought in some Hello Kitty key chains I'd bought in Japan, and showed her that a lot of Japanese cities have their own special Hello Kitties—something I'd always found interesting. It started off simply, but now she's my best friend.

I met Nicholas because he lived down the street and our dads knew each other, and we bonded over a mutual love of strategy games. (Granted, I used to prefer chess, but now I'm all about rolling dice and crushing his orc army.)

They're amazing people. They're part of that bigger, better world I feel like I was born to be a part of. They have their own "specialties" that make them different, like me . . . and, like YOU. (Don't pass out. Please. I'm almost finished.)

I want to have adventures. I want to make an impact and be remembered. I don't want to be the tree that falls in the forest and doesn't make a sound. And I feel like I'm finally in the right place.

Looking back, it seems like all those years of trial and error and rejection were preparing me for this. Like it's kismet. And since I haven't had a lot of friends, the ones I do have mean a lot to me.

I guess what I'm trying to tell you, Avery, is that I consider you a friend, too. I know this is a lot to take in, and you're probably freaking out a little and wondering if you can trust me with *certain things that will not be mentioned, even in a top-secret document [!!],* but I promise I'll never let you down. Cross my heart, hope to ~~die~~ wake up one day as brain-dead as Big Dawg [infinitely worse than death], stick a needle in my . . . er, you get the idea.

See you Friday!!!!!

I'VE BEEN STRESSING about this meeting all week, my mood swinging back and forth. One minute I'm excited, pumped to meet other kids like me (finally!); the next minute I'm sweating bullets. I *want* friends, I don't want to be alone—but what if Darla's friends don't want me?

And I like Darla, but I barely know her—even with all that top-secret file stuff. What if I open the door and she's suddenly bald and sitting in a wheelchair with a plaid blanket on her lap and her massive cranium is throbbing like a telepathic strobe light? What if her crappy disguises were merely tacked onto a truly *excellent* disguise, and she's not who I think she is at all??

Okay. Calm down. Time to call for backup.

Hiding behind the fountain in Sophie's driveway, I punch in the number for Roast—conveniently added to my speed dial this afternoon, in case of an emergency freak-out. I try to make my voice as deep as possible, so that whoever answers believes me when I claim to be Catherine's dad.

"It's Avery," I say when she picks up. "Sorry to bother you. I need some advice."

"About coffee?"

"Not exactly. I'm meeting some other kids today who have um, unusual abilities. Hint hint? And I'm freaking out. I don't know what I should do or say or if I should even go through with it. What do you think?"

Classic-rock music fills the silence. The growl of a blender crunching ice assaults my ear.

"Are they for real?"

"Yeah. I mean, I think so."

"I don't know. It's kind of suspicious. I'd probably skip it."

"Even if they seem—"

She curses under her breath. "I have to go. Some kid dumped a pack of chocolate muffins on the floor and is smearing them everywhere. It looks like a giant crap streak."

She hangs up. Okay, really—what did I expect? That she'd wish me luck and volunteer to go with me? In my dreams, maybe.

I'm still behind the fountain, trying to force a fearless smile onto my face so I don't look like I'm about to pee myself, when the front door opens and Nicholas storms out.

This is what I hear before the door slams:

Darla: "You can't just invite someone else without clearing it with me! That wasn't part of the plan!"

Sophie: "There are other people on this team besides you, and if you would ever take the time to *listen* to their ideas, maybe it wouldn't be such a shock when—"

SLAM!

Nicholas is hurrying down the driveway, so I fake an untied shoelace to seem less creepy. "Oh, hey," I say, popping up from behind the fountain. "Everything all right in there?"

His hands are plowed into the pockets of his trench coat. His eyes flicker. For a second I think they're lit from within, like cool blue Christmas lights. But. Um. That's impossible.

"Yeah. Fine. I just can't deal when people argue. I get too agitated." He's taking deep breaths, like you do at the doctor's office when they've got a stethoscope pressed to your back and all you can think about is breathing. "I don't recommend going in to play peacemaker—neither one of them is going to budge. Feel like walking? I need to calm down."

"Walking's good," I say.

Damn. His eyes *are* glowing. Does he have laser eyes? I wonder if Darla told them what I can do. How much does she even know? You could draw a few conclusions from my hero moment last summer, but does she know I fly? I've been pretty good about keeping that feat to myself. Catherine knows, but she barely talks to *me,* let alone the rest of the human race. I doubt she'd spill my secret to her "stalker."

"So, when you say 'agitated,' how big of a risk is there that laser beams will shoot out of your eyes?"

Nicholas squeezes his eyes shut. "I don't have laser eyes. The light is a symptom." He's grimacing, half hunched over like his appendix is about to burst.

"Are you okay? Do you need me to get Darla?"

"There's nothing she can do. But if I stop answering you, because I can't hear you? Promise me you'll run."

"Why? What'll happen?"

"My senses go into overload right before . . ." He winces. "Um, hang on." Nicholas crosses his arms over his chest and hurries around the side of Sophie's house and into the backyard. I follow him; he keeps running until he falls to his knees and starts gasping.

I edge closer, my boots sinking into the soft earth. "Nicholas? You okay?"

Nicholas is hugging himself, bent all the way forward so his forehead almost touches the grass. He looks like he's about to start puking, but nothing comes out.

Crap. I have no idea what to do. I don't even know what I'm dealing with here.

The wind starts to pick up.

"Nick!" I shout. "Can you hear me? Hang in there. I'm going to—"

The backdoor opens. I hear the thud of bare feet on wood and then Sophie races past me, dressed for summer in shorts and a tank top, plastic cherry earrings bobbing back and forth.

"Don't!" I say, feeling about as pathetic and panicked as a person could possibly feel. Do I stop her? "He said to run if he gets like this! Not to—"

"I know what he says!" Sophie shouts back. She hurls herself at Nicholas, wraps her arms around him from behind, and yanks his trench coat open. The trees in the yard start to tremble, branches waving in the sudden wind. Leaves and buds are torn from their places, sucked toward Nicholas like he's the center of a tornado. Leaves cling to him, flutter across his body like panicked butterflies—and then they disappear *into him.*

I move for a better look—and that's when I see it.

There's some kind of *vortex* raging in his chest: dark and swirling like liquid night. Nicholas's shirt is flapping up around his neck; the vortex stretches in a jagged diamond shape from his belly to his collarbone, churning like a maelstrom. Sophie's arms are clamped across his chest; she gives a little yelp, but she's not being drawn into it—not like everything else around him.

"What can I do?" I shout. I trip closer, the pull of the vortex tugging me forward.

"We need something big! Something to sate it!" Sophie turns her head, blinking against the grit that's being sucked toward Nicholas. "The patio furniture! Can you throw a chair so it lands in front of him?"

And not hit them with it? Crap, I don't know; I don't have super aim.

I grab a wrought-iron chair from the patio and hurl it into the air, aiming to overshoot them by about twenty feet, since I don't know how close it needs to be—but it never gets a chance to land.

Sophie shifts her arms from Nicholas's chest to his shoulders, uses her body weight to pull him back so that his vortex is pointing skyward. The chair rockets toward him, shrinking and warping as it gets closer, until it looks more like an arrow than a chair: paper-thin and wavy and surreal and then . . . *gone.*

The bright blue light in Nicholas's eyes starts to fade. The vortex quiets, spins away to nothing. I wipe the grit from my eyes and I see his ribs heaving, skin covering them instead of a living storm.

"Did I hurt anyone?" Nicholas blinks and finally starts to look around him, his eyes gradually focusing on us. "Sophie, I could have killed you! What were you thinking?"

"I wasn't going anywhere if you weren't. I'm just glad you didn't suck my earrings out before I got sticky—I just made these." She fingers the plastic red cherries dangling from her ears, seemingly unfazed. Then she flashes a smile at me. "Hi, Avery. Have you been here long? I guess this is more of a demo than you were hoping for."

"Um, yeah . . . it was pretty intense."

She grins. "There's pizza inside. I don't know about you, but watching Nicholas almost destroy us always makes me hungry."

I feel myself flushing—totally stupid. Didn't we almost die here? Why am I so fixated on how cute she is? "Thanks. Pizza's great."

Nicholas is quiet. He's trying to close his trench coat, but most of the buttons are gone. Sophie's bouncing around, telling me how happy they are that I came today, and how much fun we're going to have. But Nicholas can't let it go.

Destruction, absorption—whatever his power is, he can't control it. He looks haunted by what just happened, even though the only casualty was a chair from Sophie's parents' patio set.

I wonder, looking at him, what else he's done.

⚡〰️〰️

Sinking my teeth into a slice of pizza piled high with glistening pepperoni, I listen to Darla admit she was wrong—for probably the first time in her life. Well, according to Sophie anyway.

"I'm sorry we caused you to flare up," Darla says. "We shouldn't have been arguing like that."

Nicholas, who's sipping chamomile tea (Darla says it has a calming effect), shrugs. "It's not your fault. I need to keep it together better. I was already on edge because I was nervous about today, and—"

"And hearing that Jacques was coming didn't help. I understand," Darla says. "Sophie shouldn't surprise us like that. I am totally in agreement."

Um, end of apology? And who's Jacques?

Sophie laughs in disbelief. "Noooo, he was nervous about Avery. You kept making it sound like Avery was this hard-ass who would beat us up if we looked at him wrong."

"I am," I say. "I'm totally gonna beat up all of you as soon as I finish my pizza. Darla first." I chomp into my slice. "You better keep feeding me if you want to live."

Darla humphs and resumes picking the onions off her pizza and wiping them on her plate. "That was *before*. Obviously I told them you were okay once I got to know you."

"So . . . is it out of line if I ask what happened back there?"

Nicholas shakes his head. "No, you should know. So you know that I mean it when I tell you to run. *All* of you." He shoots a pointed look at Sophie.

She rolls her eyes. "I'm not helpless. I happen to be well adapted to your particular death trap."

"My power is . . . unstable. And dangerous. You saw the vortex, right?" I nod, and he goes on. "It's dormant until I lose my emotional equilibrium. If I get upset, or angry, or overly nervous, it activates. The vortex starts absorbing things until it's satisfied and I finally calm down. Sometimes it wants a little, sometimes a lot—but I don't know *what* it wants, or why it does this. I don't know how to stop it. When I try to resist and keep my coat closed so there's a barrier, it hurts like hell. All I can do is try to get away from people before I give in."

My lips part with a question: *Have you ever absorbed a person?* But it's too personal, too cruel to ask if the answer is yes. I silence myself with another bite.

"I don't know what happens to the things I absorb. Only that they don't come back. So maybe they become part of me. But I think I destroy them." He's staring into his tea, knees up in front of his chest—to form a barrier, I guess, since his trench coat is open.

"There's no proof of that," Darla says.

"No proof of anything else either."

"You know what we need?" Sophie says. "Some music to cheer us up." She springs to her feet and Nicholas groans.

....

"If I hear any more J-Pop I am going to become *very* unstable."

"Hmm, yes, what might help—some soothing Norwegian death metal? Nice try, Nicholas." Sophie scrolls through her playlists. "I don't think Nordic screaming helps your mood any."

"We should play 'In the Garage'!" Darla says. "It's only the best song ever!"

"It's only your anthem," Sophie says. "I think you've heard it enough."

Sophie settles on some bubbly pop that appears to have Nicholas attempting to strangle himself with the string from his chamomile tea bag, and we settle down for the rest of our confessions.

"Demo time for me," Sophie says. "Avery, will you help?"

At her instruction, I carry a stepladder in from the garage and prop it against the wall. Sophie climbs up, flings her clothes off so she's only wearing a bikini (whoa), and leans back so that her whole body is touching the wall—arms at her sides, pointed toes still braced against the top of the stepladder.

"Okay, now pull the ladder away."

I just blink at her. "You'll fall."

"Gee, I didn't think of that." Sophie rolls her eyes in this goofy way. "Just do it."

Prepared for the worst, I yank the ladder. And miraculously, Sophie stays exactly where she is. It looks like . . . do you know that amusement-park ride where you're inside this big cylinder, and everyone braces themselves against the wall and the thing starts spinning faster and faster until centrifugal force sticks you to the wall, and then the floor drops and you're still stuck?

That's what Sophie looks like: just chilling, in no danger of falling. She slides her feet up one at a time until her knees are bent and her feet are flat against the wall. "Welcome to the most useless power ever," she says, and laughs. "I'm sticky. Well, when I want to be. And sometimes when I don't—it's not perfect."

"Bad*ass,*" I say. "You should be a bull rider. You'd totally kill."

Sophie starts laughing so hard she unsticks partway and starts to fall off the wall, then gets hold of herself and shoves off, lands in a crouch. "I'd have to ride in booty shorts. My parents would love that."

She climbs back into her clothes, dusts off the paint flecks that are still attached to her skin. Flops down on the couch and takes a big swig of water, letting the mouth of the bottle stick to her lower lip before she pops it off again and grins at me.

"Avery's turn," Darla announces.

Great.

All eyes are on me and I have no idea what to show them. Flying would be the most impressive thing I could do, but I'm almost positive they don't know about my flight yet, and I'm not sure I want to reveal that on the first day. I mean, there are secrets, and then there are *secrets.* Besides, flying indoors is too creepy, like opening an umbrella in the house. Breaking stuff is out of the question, and I'm not going to risk denting whatever expensive car is in the garage.

"Um, well, you guys already know what I can do, right?"

"Yeah, but show us!" Sophie says, her eyes glittering. "Do something awesome."

Oh, no pressure there.

Finally I get this picture in my head: an old-fashioned strongman, carrying a girl on each arm. Sophie and Darla are sitting on opposite ends of the couch. Perfect.

"You might want to go sticky," I say. "Darla, prepare your grappling hook."

I squat down and heft the couch onto my shoulders, careful not to tip it too far in either direction. When I'm sure I've got it balanced, I lift the couch over my head and take Darla and Sophie on an elevated tour of the living room. It's a stupid, show-offy thing to do, but it was either this or rip a phone book in half.

Nicholas scrambles out of his seat to pull the curtains shut.

Sophie giggles. "I need to be carried around like this all the time. Like Cleopatra."

"That would be a total waste of Avery's potential," Darla says. "That's why we need robots. And robots at least have laser cannons attached to them. Unlike couches."

Um, okay, Darla. "So, you have a robot in your living room instead of a couch?"

"No," she scoffs. "I have one in my workshop."

I'd give her a skeptical look if I wasn't holding her over my head. "Workshop?"

"She means the shed in her backyard," Nicholas says. "Ninety percent inventions, ten percent lawn-care supplies. She doesn't want her dad going in there anymore, so I always get roped into mowing their lawn. Be careful you don't get tricked into joining the club."

"It's a small price to pay," Darla says. "My workshop is where the greatest technological dreams of this century become a reality."

"Ooh, show him the boomerangs you made for me!"

I manage to set the couch down without breaking anything, and Darla unzips her backpack and dumps out four shiny boomerangs, ranging in color from jet black to fire-engine red. "They look like toys so no one will suspect anything. But they're capable of doing serious damage. This one"—she holds up a black boomerang with a bomb graphic on the front—"is a bomb boomerang. It detonates on impact."

"Mega-bomberang!" Sophie cheers.

"Er, no." Darla winces at the cutesiness, like Einstein might overhear and take away her scientific-seriousness badge. "We're still working on the names." Darla goes on to show me a white boomerang that explodes and covers the target with a sticky, gluelike substance ("gluemerang!" according to Sophie); a silver boomerang with a ninja-star graphic ("ninjarang!") that doesn't explode, but is designed to cut through hanging ropes, wires, etc.; and a red boomerang that bursts into flame on impact.

If you're playing along at home, that would be the "flamerang."

"These are just prototypes," Darla says. "I have tons more in development. There's some other stuff I want to show you, but it's locked up in my workshop. Like my *Darlar*! It's like Kevlar, only better: lightweight, bullet-proof body armor that is also impact-repellent and cute-looking. Well, that's the plan, anyway—I'm not finished with it. And . . . oh!" She perks up suddenly, like she's just thought of something. "There's a concussion grenade I really want to try out, but it's hard to test it because I *personally* can't risk a concussion, and it's hard for anyone else to tell me what the experience was like, since they'd be concussed directly afterward, but see, you, on the other hand . . ."

Nicholas makes a quick "noooo, don't do it!" gesture behind her back.

"I'm kind of . . . um. I'll have to think about that."

We fall into a five-second awkward silence while Darla puts her boomerangs away, and my stomach tenses up, like things are about to get weird now. I mean, we just revealed our powers to each other—and our techno secrets, in Darla's case. That's a lot of secret sharing for people who barely know each other. There's got to be some back-lash, right?

It's not like that at all.

Sophie brings more drinks from the kitchen, and we go back to this hyperactive version of normal: talking about our parents, school, our lives; how much Nicholas hates the pop music blaring from the speakers, and how he's going to change it the next time Sophie leaves the room. I polish off the rest of the pizza before getting up to do my lousy Wolverine impression, while Darla tells them the story of what happened in the office. Sophie laughs so hard she's almost crying; Nicholas cracks a smile and just shakes his head.

"I'm glad that wasn't me," he says. "You know you *can* say no to Darla, right? She'll try to make you believe you can't, but it's not true."

Darla socks him in the arm. "Lies! Don't tell him that!"

Sophie and Darla are in the middle of telling me how they met in an ice-skating class and bonded as the class freaks (Sophie would stay in the locker room half the time, because her power was out of whack and she couldn't change out of her street clothes because they were stuck to her—or the opposite would happen, and she'd be tromping into the parking lot in full figure-skater regalia, ruining her skate blades on the concrete because she couldn't unstick long enough to get them off. Darla, meanwhile, was taking the class because her dad forced her to get out and do something non-gadget-oriented, but she was afraid she'd get hurt, so she skated in a snowsuit, like a puffy snow-angel marshmallow . . .) when the doorbell rings.

Sophie bounds over to the door. "That's him!"

Darla prides herself on being a master of disguise, but she's pretty easy to read: she is *not* happy. Her eyebrows are scrunched in an angry *V*. Nicholas jabs her with his foot. "Lower the obvious quotient a little."

"I know, I know, but I'm so *mad.* Jacques is as close to the enemy as it gets. What is she doing bringing him here? When *Avery's* here? Is she nuts?"

"Mind filling me in?" I ask. My foot's tapping, my nerves have gone from pumped to screaming like fingernails down a chalkboard, like don't-go-into-the-basement-alone, the-killer-is-calling-from-inside-the-house! Primordial warnings you don't ignore.

Or, you know, I could be overreacting, responding to Darla's tendency to exaggerate.

Nicholas starts: "Jacques is . . ."

Before he can finish, Sophie leads her guest into the room and we all clam up. He's lagging a step or two behind her, platinum-blond hair in his face, diamond stud earrings in his ears.

It takes me all of two seconds to recognize him.

Jacques is the guy with the Jaguar. Casanova with a driver's license. And . . . superpowers?

I feel about as tense as Darla looks. Sophie's friend or not, I don't want him here. I don't want to see her hug him hello, or laugh at anything he says that I'm *sure* won't be funny . . . and I definitely don't need a demo of his badass force-field-invisibility-bulletproof-better-than-mine powers.

His eyes travel the room until they land on me—and lock. Sizing me up, like we're having some kind of stare-down.

Sophie's hugging his arm, her face brighter and cheerier than it was after my feat of strength, or silly charades.

"Everyone, this is Jacques. Jacques, these are my friends Darla, Nicholas, and Avery."

We all *hello* him in return.

"Pleased to meet you," Jacques says coolly.

I remember his accent from when I first heard him outside Roast, remember thinking it was an unfair advantage—because don't girls always fall for exotic accents? But as it has time to sink into my consciousness, the odd rise and fall of his speech hits me like a steel pipe.

He sounds like Cherchette.

MY MIND'S POUNDING along with my nervous-tapping fingers: *Cherchette, Cherchette, how old is Cherchette?* She looks . . . not so much young as ageless: like she's lived, but the scars have stayed on the inside. She's like a perfect portrait, trapped in time. A white marble statue.

Is it possible she has a teenage son?

I watch Jacques while Sophie babbles on, getting him up to speed on things I'd rather he didn't know about—if there are even any secrets anymore. If he's Cherchette's son, does he know what *she* knows? He definitely looks like her: same pale skin, piercing blue eyes, bloodless lips. I don't worry about being caught staring, because Jacques's eyes haven't left me since he got here. His gaze digs into me, eager to unearth something ugly, or weak. I don't know—I've never had anyone look at me that way before.

The shiver running down my spine cranks itself higher. Feverlike chills assault my body in waves, getting stronger the longer Jacques stares at me—and there's no break. I grab a blanket off the back of the couch and wrap it around my shoulders like a cape. Try to think: *summer, barbeque, heat wave,* like he's not getting to me at all.

No one else is reacting to Jacques like this. Darla's oblivious, wound up in a tight ball of frustration, a twitchy fake smile on her face. Nicholas is politely listening to Sophie and nodding at all the right times, but at one point our eyes meet and I feel like he recognizes that something isn't quite right here.

"You know what would be an awesome team-building exercise?" Sophie says abruptly.

"Team-building exercises usually involve a team," Darla says before she can finish. "I don't recall Benedict Arnold being on our *team,* so the point is moot."

The two girls glare at each other. Nicholas squirms in his seat. I sense a girl fight on the horizon. Time to get him out of this.

I get up, dragging my blanket cape behind me like it's a fashion statement, not a necessity. "Sophie, do you have any macaroni and cheese we could make?"

"Macaroni and—umm, didn't you just eat like a whole pizza?" She tilts her head, waves of hair tumbling onto her shoulder, totally confused. Jacques snorts, like I'm this disgusting glutton and now he has a legitimate reason to despise me.

"Yeah, I promised Nicholas I'd show him my secret recipe."

Sophie shrugs. "Check the cabinets."

"Cool. Onward, Nicholas." I gesture dramatically with my cape, and thankfully he has the sense to follow. I figure Darla can hold her own out there—Jacques is the one who should be afraid.

We raid the cabinets and I bang a bunch of pots and pans around, doing my best to create an inconspicuous wall of noise. "What the hell?" I say. "Who is that guy and why does he look like he wants to kill me?"

"Jacques Morozov," Nicholas says. "Sophie met him a few weeks ago. I guess he's like us, but his pedigree has Darla freaking out. She thinks his mom is evil incarnate."

"Evil incarnate?" Uh . . . that's a bit harsh.

He sighs, tears open the macaroni-and-cheese box. "Has a woman named Cherchette contacted you?"

What do I say? Should I lie? Is that the best way to start a new friendship?

"Once," I say, hoping a half-truth is better than no truth. "You?"

Nicholas nods. "I don't know if she said the same stuff to you, but she basically offered me a place with her, like she has this powered-kid sanctuary or something, and she claimed she could help me get my power under control so I wouldn't hurt anyone."

"And Darla thinks that makes her evil?"

Nicholas digs the powdered-cheese packet out of the box, sets it neatly beside the stove, and opens the fridge to find whatever else we'll need. "It's a combination of things with Darla. Natural caution, competitiveness, paranoia. But I'm sure she'll tell you all about that, whether you want to hear it or not."

Actually, I do want to hear it. I'll take any input I can

get, even if it's a little biased. "And what do you think about Cherchette?"

"It's hard to say. It's not like anyone else has shown up and offered to help, you know? So I'm inclined to think her intentions are good, since, I mean, she must know how hard it is, having powers and not knowing what the hell's going on. What did Cherchette say when you met her?"

"Same stuff." I don't mention breaking the thug's hand and smashing up the antique shop. I concentrate on filling a pot with water, focus on the stream. "So . . . what did you think of her offer? Is hurting people something you worry about?"

I want to say what I've never said, except in a screwed-up rush of emotion to my parents after my last wrestling match—and they misinterpreted it, they thought I was being too hard on myself: *I hurt someone. I messed up and I hurt someone. And it could have been worse. One day, it could be so much worse.*

"How could I not worry about it?" He takes a deep breath. "I fight so much with my dad. He doesn't get who I am at all, and I'm afraid that one day he'll get in my face and I won't be able to get away from him in time. My vortex will activate and I won't be able to stop it."

"Wow," I say, before I can think better of it. "That sucks."

Nicholas laughs. "I know, right? Darla keeps telling me that great minds can triumph over anything—the great mind is Darla, if she hasn't made that abundantly clear yet—but it's not that simple. She thinks I can train my power and learn to control it, but the only way to train it is to purposely use it . . . and there's too much room for error. It's like testing a nuclear bomb to find out what it does. Yeah, you'd end up with answers, but maybe you're better off not knowing. At least this way it's still speculation, that I destroy things because some part of me wants to. If I ever really tap into that, and find out that deep down I'm a monster . . ."

He repositions the flaps of his trench coat, folds his arms over his chest. "Would you want to know that about yourself?"

"I feel like I'm still figuring that out." My voice comes out weak and I clear my throat. "I've done some things that make me wonder that, too. It was never because I wanted to hurt anyone—I just couldn't control it. It's like I have to relearn everything. And when I'm worked up—scared, or even feeling competitive or whatever—I don't think. Stuff just happens and then you're left with a bunch of broken pieces, and there are no rules to tell you how to handle it."

"Exactly," Nicholas says. "That's the thing Darla doesn't get. There *are* no rules. She wants to help us make them. But I feel like I might be opening Pandora's box if I try to tame my power. I'd rather just suffocate it."

We're quiet awhile, watching the water boil, dumping in the dried macaroni, and stirring it around. I wonder what he means by "suffocate it." How do you stop your power without stopping yourself?

I hear music coming from the other room—not sunshiny, girly pop but hard, raucous metal. The lead singer's voice sounds like it's being filtered through a lawn mower. Not quite Sophie's style.

"Sounds like they migrated," Nicholas says. "Darla's probably blowing off steam. Come on—before she head-bangs herself to death."

I turn off the burner and we head out to the living room, where Darla is standing on the couch, hands poised for air guitar, thrashing like mad.

"Careful." Nicholas grabs her shoulders to steady her. She already looks woozy. "You could hurt someone with that giant brain of yours."

"Good," she mutters, sinking down into the couch cushions. "I hope it gives Jacques a concussion. I would've zapped him but I knew Sophie would never talk to me again if I did."

Nicholas pats Darla's head, casually petting her hard-rocking hair into place and soothing her at the same time. She's fidgety, but I think she's calming down. Well, as much as is possible for Darla.

"Where'd they go?" I ask.

"Basement," Darla says. "Sophie has a sewing room down there. She wanted to show Jacques the costume she made for him."

"He . . . uh, he wears a costume?"

"I don't know if he'll actually *wear* it," Nicholas says. "Sophie made one for all of us. I think she did some sketches for yours. She wanted to get your okay first."

"I don't trust him!" Darla sputters, springing away from

Nicholas's hand. She folds her arms behind her back and starts pacing. "His mom is an evil megalomaniac pod person with no soul who thinks she knows *everything*—"

Nicholas raises his eyebrows at me mid-rant. "Sound familiar?"

"FYI, Nicholas, I am not an evil pod person with no soul."

"Um, about this evil thing . . . does anyone want to explain that to me? Or is this just part of crazy-exaggeration happy hour?"

"He knows about Cherchette," Nicholas tells Darla.

"She offered you the same deal?" Darla asks, shocked for a sec before I nod and she shouts, "I knew it! Didn't I predict this? I knew, I freaking *knew* she would come for you! And you have to ask me why she's evil??"

"Uh, apparently," I say, running through a whole list of dastardly villains in my head. "Unless she eats babies and wears a skeleton mask and I just haven't figured it out yet."

Darla takes a deep breath and sits down, all stern like she's prepared to school me. "Avery, seriously—what kind of person shows up out of nowhere and tries to lure kids away from their parents? Murderers, pedophiles, and psychopaths. Normal people do not do that. Just because she didn't offer you candy and tell you your mom was in the hospital, then ask you to get in her car so she could drive you there, doesn't mean she has good intentions."

"Yeah, but she has powers," I say. "She's proven that. And she's a little weird, but so are we. I doubt she wants to carve us up in her basement. She's probably just trying to help, like she says."

"If she really wanted to help, she'd arrange to be a liaison with your parents, and give *them* the info they need to help you. Not take matters into her own hands and make you, like, lie to your mom and dad and disappear from their lives forever. *That* is evil. It's exerting waaay too much control over you guys, when what you really need is practice—not some creepy, ice-sculpted villainess running your lives for you."

"That does sound kind of evil," I admit. "But I still think you're totally wrong."

Nicholas presses his palm to Darla's head to calm her before her eyes can pop out. I'm getting the impression that *wrong* is like the dirtiest word you can use when it comes to Darla.

"What kind of liaison is she supposed to be? Look at the X-Men and Professor Xavier. He invites superpowered people to live with him at his school because he's trying to help them learn about their powers. He can't exactly pop into the X-Jet and make house calls whenever a new crisis erupts, so he brings them to where he is."

"Yeah, but in that case, the parents still know where their kids are," Darla points out. "Everything about Cherchette is shrouded in secrecy."

"My freaking power is a secret!" I say. "Are you saying I should tell my parents about it?"

"No! That would be a horrible idea! You're missing the whole point! Do you know what I've been able to find out about Cherchette, other than what I've learned from Nicholas? Next to nothing! Her life is so tightly guarded that it's like she doesn't exist. Meanwhile, she seems to know *everything* about you guys. Doesn't that scare you?"

"Darla also hates that Cherchette even knows about us in the first place," Nicholas says. "She doesn't like anyone having the same secret intel she has."

"Speaking of that," I say. "Darla, how *do* you have all this information? I mean, Sophie and Nicholas I get, but as for me, and, um . . ."

"Catherine?" Darla fills in. "Catherine was easy. Once I knew that people with powers existed, all it took was a combination of my excellent observation skills, and an awareness of the trouble she was getting into. I used to hang out at Roast way before I started 'stalking' her." She adds finger quotes that I'm sure are for my benefit. "It's a good place to study. And Catherine plus a freshly mopped floor is an amazing sight. Her balance is *un*real. Plus, have you ever noticed that she punctures stuff with her nails, without meaning to? Like, cuts her skin or scratches the tables with just a casual touch? I could go on, but I think you've seen the rest for yourself."

I nod, remembering the carnage when Catherine tangled with Big Dawg. "I mean, but do you think it's obvious? Because I know she doesn't want to be found out. None of us do. But if *you* could figure it out . . ."

"No way." Darla shuts that down, sure as sure can be. "I had to know what to look for. And once I knew that powers existed, any and all 'amazing feats of adrenaline' had to get a second look. Like a guy your age lifting a car? Nice *Today* show interview, by the way. Very heroic. I'm surprised you didn't get a girlfriend after that."

"Uh, thanks," I say, wondering how I'm supposed to take that, and whether I should be creeped out that she probably has files on my love life.

"The point is, I have a reason for knowing about you guys. *And* I'm not methodically hunting kids down."

"*Or* enrolling in their schools and adopting different personas to try to befriend them," Nicholas says. "That would be insane."

Darla throws a pillow at him. "Remind me why I haven't replaced you with a robot?"

"No clue." Nicholas grins. "Because you're lazy?"

Darla howls and stomps on the couch, hurls the last remaining pillow at Nicholas. I wonder if she's flirting with him or if she's just being overly dramatic. Maybe both.

"Is she about to turn into the Hulk?" I ask.

"Yep." Nicholas grabs Darla and flips her over his shoulder so he can carry her down the stairs. "Let's check on the dynamic duo. Sophie has an Xbox and a pool table in the basement, so we should be able to find something to do without killing each other. Right, Darla? Can you behave or do you need to live in upside-down world a little longer?"

"The blood is rushing to my brain," Darla says. "You're *only* making me stronger!"

"Looks like dizzier," I point out.

We troop down the stairs and enter a subterranean playground. While the rest of the house is decorated in this deliberately stuffy style (lots of breakables and expensive furniture, paintings of landscapes and flowers), the basement is a bastion of cartoon violence—with some girly, glittery stuff thrown in. Posters of Captain America and Supergirl share wall space with fashionista manga girls. A Ping-Pong table has been reborn as a plastic battleground: toy-size Master Chief leads an army of cutesy Japanese trading figures, Disney princess dolls showing off their right to bear arms (um, since when does the Little Mermaid wield a submachine gun?), and G.I. Joes against a legion of alien grunts—with Godzilla bringing up the rear.

My fingers itch with the desire to pop Cinderella's head off and stuff it into Godzilla's open maw so it looks like he's eating it.

But I resist. I'm competing with a guy who has a driver's license and wears jewelry—I doubt he does stuff like that.

Nicholas dumps Darla onto a pile of beanbag chairs. "You want to check on them?" he asks me. "The sewing room's back there. Sophie probably wants to show you her costume sketches anyway."

Nice. More semi-alone time with Jacques. I bundle up in a blanket toga and matching cape (yeah, there's a style for you) and lumber over to the sewing room. Fingers crossed that I don't get turned into a Popsicle.

I hear them before I see them.

"... tonight it's a dinner party. No big surprise there," Sophie says, with an eye-roll kind of tone. "They're never here. And I guess it's convenient sometimes but I wonder if they even remember they *have* a kid, or if they just think they hired an underage housekeeper."

Jacques laughs awkwardly, sort of stiffly and politely. "I doubt they think you are their housekeeper. But I know what you mean. My mother is frequently away . . . always with something more important to do. People to meet. You know."

"The worst thing is when they're actually here and we're eating some kind of gross macrobiotic takeout and my mom will have the nerve to be like, 'Oh, remember Snitzi so-and-so? She's editing her school's newspaper now!' And it's like, oh, I'm sorry—is there some journalism ambition I'm supposed to have that you never told me about? Or do you just like knowing what other kids are doing and not your own?"

"Their priorities are warped," Jacques says. "They are so busy looking elsewhere, they don't realize how special you are."

Sophie giggles. "Thanks, Jacques. That's sweet. Okay, enough of my whining: arms up? Ooh, it looks awesome! Not that we'll even have a chance to *wear* costumes. Darla's being so bossy lately . . . and if she doesn't want to include you, it's gonna be like this constant war with her . . ."

"Even so, thank you. I like it very much."

Jacques is standing with his arms way out at his sides while Sophie makes adjustments to the motocross-looking costume he's wearing: it's pearl white with armored plates on the knees, elbows, chest, and back, and a silver snow-flake emblem on the chest—like where Spider-Man has a spider and Batman has a bat. Sophie's got a row of pins pressed between her lips, but she still manages a grin when she sees me.

"I don't know if I can compete with *that* costume," she says.

"I figured I could be blanket-toga man. You like the look?" I do a model spin, confident that while Jacques might be cooler than me (literally), he can't rock a ratty blanket like I can.

"I'm impressed," Sophie says. "But if you want to see the sketches I did for you—you know, just so you can see how inferior they are . . ."

"Bring 'em on."

She sticks a few more pins in Jacques and dismisses him to get changed, then watches over my shoulder while I flip through her sketchbook.

The amazing Avery costumes range from old-school spandex to Jacques's motocross-inspired look. I have my choice of logos, too: a badass eagle, a clenched fist, a sil-houette of a strongman, and a star. Not every design is to my taste, but they're all really well done. "Wow," I say. "You do art, you bull-ride, you teach your Barbie dolls guerrilla warfare. You're like a Renaissance girl."

She pokes me in the ribs, but she's totally smiling. "I do not bull-ride. Want to see mine?"

She flicks through a rack of costumes—all skimpy or

with cutouts and mesh panels to take advantage of her power. Some are sparkly figure-skater-style numbers, covered with sequins; others are sleeker and more practical. There's even a spandex jumpsuit for Darla: purple with orange racing stripes. "So she can fit into her mecha better," Sophie explains.

"Mecha?"

"Umm . . . it's like this giant robot Darla built to ride around in. Have you ever seen Gundam? Almost like an armored bodysuit but bigger, because it has a cockpit."

"Wait—for real? As in, she really built this and it works, it's not just papier-mâché or something?"

"Supposedly it works. I haven't seen it do much." She whips out her measuring tape. "Enough stalling! Drop the toga, blanket man. Time to surrender your measurements."

"Foiled!" I curse. "The Fleece Gladiator is no more."

Five minutes later Sophie has all the numbers necessary to start work on my faux-fur-and-vinyl catsuit. (Kidding—we'll save that one for Catherine.) Back in the main part of the basement, Nicholas and Darla are engrossed in a game of Rainbow Six. Darla keeps yelling, "Go go go!" then grumbling when her character gets blown off the map.

"Darla has the hand-eye coordination of a sloth," Sophie informs me.

"That's all you need when you have a shotgun," Darla says, teeth stabbing into her bottom lip, deep in concentration as her character slinks around the screen. She somehow manages to blast a hole in an enemy who's nowhere near her. "Yeah! Check out my boomstick!"

Jacques is lounging on one of the couches in the corner, idly surfing the web on his expensive cell phone . . . but of course he flashes a frosty death glare when *I* show up.

Making an effort to ignore him, I pull a bar stool up to the Ping-Pong table and start messing with Sophie's battlefield: switching sides so that Master Chief is massacring the cutesy trading figures, and the Disney princesses join forces with Godzilla. The G.I. Joes overturn an alien grunt and use it for cover, biding their time until a clear victor emerges. I figure the more chaos I create, the more likely Sophie is to spend her time chastising me—time that *won't* be spent cozying up to Jacques.

Sophie scolds me, right on schedule—but I only get a few minutes of her attention before Nicholas begs me to take Darla's controller, and Sophie curls up on the couch and starts showing Jacques some pink-haired manga girls she drew.

I concentrate on sniping virtual terrorists so I don't have to see them whispering together. I'm glad I don't have super-senses; I seriously don't want to know what they're saying. Much more satisfying to invent a conversation for them.

Sophie: You should be nicer to Avery. He's cute and his power is awesome.

Jacques: You're right. I'm so ashamed. (weeps)

Okay, even I don't believe that.

Eight-thirty rolls around and Sophie hustles us out; her parents are supposed to be back at nine and she's only allowed to have two people over. We trade numbers and IM names and Nicholas and I make plans to hang out sometime. Darla thanks me for coming and says (out of earshot of Sophie, of course) that our next meeting will be better because Jacques will absolutely *not* be invited—and she tells me I should be excited, because she has awesome plans for us. Sophie promises to retire my blankets to the bad costume hall of fame. And then—and this is the best part—she hugs me good-bye on my way out. Yeah, she hugs everyone else, too—but that's not the point.

When I fly home through the dark, flying feels more like floating than it ever has. I'm everything in the world, all compacted into one person, vibrant and pulsing and alive. Every thought, every feeling, every wish, every dream.

I can still feel Sophie's skin, the way she stuck to me for a second when she hugged me. I close my eyes and see Darla's maniacal smile, the weird joy she got from bringing us together. I hear Nicholas's laugh, when we were commiserating about how sometimes our powers are more powerful than we are, and how it's hard to know how to deal with that.

Every single one of us has secrets. Only now we have them together.

Something's starting here. I can feel it.

Sophie Miller: ORIGIN STORY

NOTE: *The following account was written by Sophie Miller approximately six months after her power manifested, and delivered to Darla Carmine in exchange for two explosive glitter boomerangs and one box of giant-size strawberry Pocky. Let the records show that Sophie demands bribes, unlike Nicholas.*   —D.C.

I envy people whose powers sort of make sense when they first show up. That wasn't the case with mine at all.

Flashback to the class trip at the end of eighth grade: fifty prep-school girls swarming an amusement park, pairing up by twos in the buddy system, finally free from our hideous uniforms. I could still pass for *mostly* normal back then—I always had too many toys dangling from my backpack, but I never did anything out-and-out freakish, like brag about getting a Killtacular in Halo. So I guess I made an acceptable replacement for girl number four in our class (on the popularity scale) when she came down with mono and number three needed someone to ride rides with.

And it was like . . . back then I just didn't say *no* to people. I thought there was still room for me in that world—or that there could be, if I got serious about "real" fashion instead of sewing my own stuff, and . . . you know. I'm sure there's a list somewhere.

How was I supposed to know that that was the day I'd become a freak for real, with everyone watching? That I'd be branded as *that girl* like I was too bizarre for words?

It's all the fault of the Phantom Loop: a metal roller coaster that spirals upside down twice, for people who get their kicks cheating death—and who have way more faith in engineers than I do. Set me at the edge of a cliff, and I'm fine; I'm not afraid of heights, because I trust myself not to take that extra step. What I *don't* trust are machines—kind of funny considering my best friend's robot obsession, but it's true. Don't give me a so-called safety harness and start telling me about physics and expect me to feel secure.

Unless you're one of the three most popular girls in my ridiculously insulated prep school: then I guess all you have to do is tell me to shut up and stop being a baby, and I'll do whatever you want. When Liza, Hannah, and Riley want to ride the Phantom Loop, you do it—no matter how sick the thought makes you. What's a little death risk compared to being an outcast?

We waited in line for over an hour. I was sweating the whole time, trying to be accommodating and friendly and normal so they'd like me, and so maybe I could be the fifth wheel to their foursome, and get invited to sleepovers and to the mall and parties, and eventually I'd catch their popularity like a virus, and I wouldn't sit in my room wondering why my supersocial parents were always out at parties and functions and I hadn't inherited *any* of that grace—because I was usually alone.

It totally didn't matter that I was bored and zoning out in the presence of the Queen Bee trio, that I wasn't into the boys they liked or the music they listened to or the celebrity gossip that made their worlds go 'round. They were extending an "it girl" apprenticeship to me like a golden ticket, and I knew I'd be stupid not to take it.

My body had other ideas.

As soon as I sat down and locked the safety harness into place, I was seized by terror: this was it, this was real. It was like someone flipped a switch in my brain. Anticipating the ride had been bad enough; now that I was two seconds away from the slow creep up the hill and the nightmarish plunge *doooown*, my eyes welled up and I clenched them shut to keep the tears in. No such luck—I was crying all over myself. I dug my nails into the bar so I wouldn't gouge Riley's arm when my fear ratcheted up to killer levels.

Terror is hard to explain. Like, for some people, a roller coaster is just a ride, and they'll never see it as anything else. It scares you a little, but it's fun to be scared, so it's a rush. Not for me. We started inching up the hill—*click, click, click, click*—closer and closer to going over. Riley was trying to calm me down: "Relax! Nothing's going to happen! Open your eyes!"

My shirt was pushed up in the back a little, and my back and my thighs stuck to the plastic seat, drenched with sweat from the heat and from panic. I was praying under my breath—and then the clicking stopped. For an instant, we were poised on the edge of a precipice. Pure and total silence.

And then my stomach dropped. My heart rose into my throat. I screamed, the rumble and the speed battering my head against the restraints as we tore around the track, flipping upside down in tight, spiraling loops, our screams rising to a crescendo just as, breathless, we pulled into the loading station.

The whole trip took less than a minute. I wiped my eyes, grateful to be done with it. Riley grinned at me. "See, that wasn't so bad."

Our safety harnesses unlocked and lifted automatically, and everyone began to disembark. I wanted to be out of there like lightning, racing down the ramp and on my way to the Dodge 'Ems, or the carousel—something I could trust.

But I couldn't move.

My legs—mostly bare in a pair of shorts that had crept up when I sat down—were stuck to the roller coaster seat. The next group of riders was starting to board, and the couple waiting for my row to empty out stood to one side, eyeing me with annoyance. People were staring. Liza, Hannah, and Riley waited awkwardly at my side. The ride operator made his way toward us.

This was like a felony, in it-girl world. We were too cool to be this kind of spectacle.

"Come *on*," Hannah hissed impatiently. "Get out already!"

I gave a weak smile, but panic was setting in. My bottom half literally felt like it had bonded with the roller coaster—like I'd sat in Super Glue and it dried. Shifting even a millimeter was impossible.

My eyes spilled over when I tried to speak. How was I supposed to explain this when *I* didn't know what was happening? The ride operator asked me what the holdup was. He had a sympathetic face, so I played the last desperate card I had: crying-girl-with-a-simple-request. I apologized; I told him that I rode the Phantom Loop last summer with my grandpa, and that he wasn't with us anymore, so I was kind of emotional, and could I ride one more time? Please?

The thought of going through those loops again nauseated me—and the stupidity of the lie made it worse. Liza, Hannah, and Riley made it clear they thought I was a mess—and that they wouldn't be waiting for me when I got off. Minutes were ticking by and I still wouldn't budge, so the ride operator finally gave in and I had to go through the whole nightmare again. Terrified, sick, panicked—three more times total before I became so emotionally exhausted that I unstuck. Eight upside-down loops. I stumbled down the ramp and threw up in the flower bushes next to the "You Must Be This Tall to Ride" sign.

After that, I was worse than "not normal." The Queen Bees spread the word: I was a head case, mental patient, schizo freak. Unfit for it-girl consumption, I withdrew into myself even more. At school the next year, instead of trying to fit into their boxes, I entertained myself drawing hot manga punk boys, princesses with plasma rifles and Gothic Lolita ruffles. At home I honed my first-person-shooter skills, read about parkour, and started practicing stunts (don't laugh!), using my stickiness (now that I knew what it was) to give me an edge. I sewed my first costume. Met Darla and Nicholas: people who got what I was about, who didn't expect me to be exactly like them and wouldn't want that anyway.

I turned into a freak—and it saved my life.

I'M BACK ON A SCHEDULE: all work and no play. The video games Cherchette bought me are buried in my closet, untouched.

I do my homework during school hours, typically while the teacher's busy breaking up a fight. Sit at the back of the class whenever possible so I'm more likely to see a chair coming if someone throws one at my head. Participate in Reality Management just enough to make sure Principal Arnold hears about my progress and feels like he made the right decision.

I brainstorm with Darla during lunch about how we can make an impact; what's our next move? She promises she has awesome plans for us—like actual *missions*—and I don't doubt that she'll pull us all together, but she needs help figuring out what we might realistically be able to do. How can we help people in our city—not just as individuals, but as a team—and maybe get in some powers practice at the same time?

I also make a daily attempt to lure Catherine to our table with treats: neon-pink marshmallow rabbits, some over-priced cookies I swiped from my dad. (It doesn't work.

The only day I manage to convince her is when Darla's absent.)

I spend an hour after school at Roast, drawing patrol routes on a city map in different colored markers, starring points of interest in between pestering Catherine, showing her my plans whenever she has a chance to sit down.

From four-thirty to six-thirty I hit the streets, following a different route each day. I stop by the elementary school, the local park, the soccer field, the mall—almost wishing for a flash flood or a freak volcanic eruption to force my hand, to make me show people what I can do. Instead I find some kids lobbing rocks at ducks in the park, and use the threat of my fist to teach them a lesson about animal cruelty. Their moms aren't too happy—but I bet the ducks are.

I break up a fight outside a burger place: two girls not quite ready to stop tearing each other's hair out. I get between them and get a slap to the face for my efforts.

By the time I get home and eat dinner, fend off my parents' prying questions with a folder full of finished homework, I'm exhausted. I take a shower, watch a movie or sit at the computer for a while, IMing Darla, Sophie, Nicholas—whoever's on. I scan the police blotter, wondering why I'm never in the right place at the right time. I sleep for an hour or two, wake when the house is silent.

Then I fly. For hours. Soar through the sky until three in the morning, always unwilling to let go, to return to earth and be grounded, heavy, like everyone else.

Afterward I lie in bed, staring at the ceiling, cold sweat drying on my skin, a silver-and-white business card held loosely in my hand. My powers have made me this whole other person. My dreams are different, my needs are different—but I can only be myself 10 percent of the time. Maybe less. And even so, I'm still hiding.

Lying in the dark, I wonder what it would be like if I lived somewhere where *this* was life, all the time. Where everyone was like me.

I don't even know the reality of living with Cherchette. I mean, hell, there's the problem of *Jacques* being there, and freezing all the time—that's a pretty big negative. It's ridiculous to even contemplate it.

But . . .

What if it isn't?

In the morning it starts all over again. Until Darla makes good on her "I've got awesome plans for us" promise, and Friday nights get a whole lot more intense.

———————

On Friday night, our secret identities are three masquerade masks (two silver, one pink) and one black knit ski mask.

"Take your pick," Sophie says. "Except for the pink one—that's mine."

We're gathered just off the park's beaten path, five amateur crime fighters suiting up in the moonlight, ready to catch the mugger who's made this park his personal purse-snatching ground. Nicholas dives for the ski mask so I'm stuck with silver, making me costume twins with Jacques—who's here, despite Darla's attempts to keep him out of this. He's dressed for a night of fine dining followed by the opera or something, and looks more like a disgruntled matador than a superhero.

"I'm good," Darla says. "Got my mugger-bait costume right here." She pulls a hot pink velvet tracksuit on over her clothes. The butt says RICH BITCH in gold embroidery. All the price tags are still attached and she quickly tucks them inside the waistband, then finishes her disguise with an enormous Louis Vuitton purse—it's almost big enough to be a suitcase.

I give her my best mind-boggled look. "What do you carry in there, a tiny horse?"

"Temptation!" She gives the purse a hearty shake so it jingles. "All the change I could find in my house. It's noisier than dollar bills."

"And really not suspicious at all," Nicholas says.

"The mugger will fall for it. Trust me," Darla says. "If he was smart he'd be an investment banker—he wouldn't be robbing joggers in the park."

Sophie nods in agreement, buckling her utility belt over her snug figure-skater-esque costume, and double-checking her row of boomerangs to make sure they're all in place. She has a new sparkly pink-and-red one that gets extra-special attention. She must be eager to try it out.

"Everybody ready?" Darla says.

We fan out and head for our positions. Nicholas hangs back, camouflaged by the shadows. He and Darla got into an argument in Jacques's car, about how his power isn't good for anything so she shouldn't try to invent good uses for it, etc., and Darla came up with this "last resort" plan: if the mugger has a gun and it looks like he's going to use it before we can disarm him, Nicholas will get his vortex going and absorb it.

No offense to Darla and her genius intellect, but that's idiotic. We all know Nicholas can't direct his power with any accuracy, and panicking him with the idea that he *might* have to use it is only going to make things worse. I pulled him aside when we arrived and told him not to worry—if there was a gun, *I'd* handle it. I have armed-bad-guy-takedown experience.

Riiight. We all know how *that* went.

Sophie and I are stationed in trees at different points along the jogging path, equipped with binoculars and miniature communicators (comprised of a plug-in ear-piece and a tiny microphone that attaches to your mouth like a fake lip ring). "Anything?" I whisper.

There's a soft crackling in my ear. "Not yet."

I push the leaves out of my way, watching for Darla to round the bend. The jingling precedes her: a bunch of coins clanging together and then thumping en masse like a fist against the bottom. I bite my knuckle to keep from laughing.

Darla hums as she jogs. She pops her bling-encrusted thumb up as she passes my tree. The jingling grows faint and then louder again as Darla rounds the half-mile path for the second time, face flushed but her smile intact. By the third lap, there's still no sign of the mugger. Darla's flagging. That purse looks as heavy as her steps, and she's not exactly a track star.

"Pace yourself," I murmur into the mike. "It doesn't have to look like you're into it; just that you're here. This could take a while."

"Or forever," Nicholas says. "Maybe this is his day off. I'm ready to go if you guys are."

"No way." Darla's rough breathing breaks her sentences into pieces. "I calculated. This is. An ideal time for. Him to strike again. We're not leaving."

She's probably right. Hell, there's a Jag in the parking lot; if the mugger's here, he *knows* he's got a rich victim on his hands. Hmm. Unless . . .

"Unless he's stealing Jacques's car," I say.

I think I detect an exotic curse in my earpiece. First word I've heard from him all night.

"My bet is on both," Sophie says. "Much easier to get the keys from the owner than to break in, if—whoop!"

My earpiece hums with a weird, staticky shuffling. A crash. Then—

"Sophie?" I rattle my speaker around, which just makes it fall out. As I'm struggling to get the bee-size device back in place, I see Darla careen around the bend, hauling ass like she's twenty feet from the finish line and there's a rampaging grizzly behind her.

A black-clad guy—dressed kind of like me, actually— is tearing after her in sneakers and Adidas pants, rapidly closing the distance. I leap from my perch, soles making contact just as a slick of ice shoots across the path. The mugger's feet fly out from under him and he slams onto his back, hard.

Sophie's charging toward him from the opposite direction, hand on her utility belt, her eyes on the prize. She's closer, but I'm faster—and I'm not taking any chances. The mugger could have a weapon.

I dive at him, pinning his arms. We both go sliding— *BOOM!*—right into the wake of a glitter-and-pepper-spray explosion. Sophie's shiny pink-and-red boomerang lies next to us, devoid of its irritating contents. It's the last thing I see before my eyes tear up and start to burn like a thousand skunks peed in them. I'm coughing, my spit thick and disgusting, struggling not to claw at my throat, wipe my eyes—or even try to *move*—because I know I'll just slip on the ice, and I need to keep this guy stationary.

"Ohmygod, Avery!"

I take that as an apology.

There's enough glitter on my body to keep Big Dawg's arts-and-crafts class happy for a year. I'm hacking up gobs of bitter, sparkle-filled saliva. *Ptoo!*

"We've got it under control!" Darla says. "Just a few more seconds."

While the team waits for the pepper cloud to clear, I keep the mugger on the ground. He's fighting me, cursing between bouts of wheezing, but he's no match for my strength or three years' worth of wrestling skills. Then his body starts to get cold—and my temperature plummets, too.

"What the hell is Jacques doing?" I grunt.

Ice boy deigns to speak to me for the first time all night. "Lowering his body temperature so he'll stop struggling."

"Great idea!" Sophie chirps. No "Nice takedown, Avery," I notice.

I grind my face against my sleeve, try to wipe some of the mess away so I can see what's going on. Sophie and Darla are binding the mugger with rope, securing the trap with an elaborate knot. Red and pink glitter specks freckle their faces: a Valentine and chili-pepper supernova. Nicholas is standing clear of the chaos, shaking his head at us, baffled or amused or both.

Now that the mugger can breathe again, he's suddenly inspired to utter more than four-letter words. "F-freaking maniacs!" he says, shivering in his rope straitjacket. "Who does this shit?"

"You would've gotten away with it if it wasn't for us meddling kids," Darla says.

Once the mugger's pretty much hog-tied, I carry him to one of the park benches and we tie him to that, too—then call the police from an ancient pay phone. Jacques pulls the Jaguar out of the lot and takes it to a preplanned meeting place to wait for us, and Darla, Sophie, Nicholas, and I watch from a distance while police apprehend the mugger. His face matches the sketch Darla saw in the newspaper (give or take a hundred pounds of glitter), so they know they've got their guy. Although *how* they got him remains a mystery.

"Sorry I pepper-sprayed you," Sophie says, after we're done trading high fives, now trooping down a side street on our way to rendezvous with Jacques. "It was an accident. I launched that boomerang before I even saw you."

"Don't worry. He's used to it," Darla says. "We're helping him develop an immunity."

Unreal. I give Nicholas my what-the-crap look and he shrugs.

"You can't argue with genius. I mean, if Einstein said that, you'd just take his word for it, right?"

Darla jabs him with a glitter-flecked elbow. "Wiseass. Anyway, I'm proud of us. We did an awesome job."

"We really worked together," Sophie says. "Even Jacques. You have to admit he was the MVP tonight."

Um, *what*ever. I try to keep my grimaces to a minimum, for Sophie's sake. Yeah, maybe he was sort of useful—if you think freezing your own teammate is ethical, which I don't.

Luckily Darla has even less self-restraint than I do.

"Sure," she says. "He lulls us into a state of complacency, posing as a helpful member of the team—only to betray us in the end. I know how this stuff works. If anything, tonight has only served to show me how dangerous he is."

"You're impossible," Sophie grumbles.

"The real lesson is this," Darla says. "You guys don't need anyone to teach you about your powers. You can learn in the field, through action. We can set up training scenarios, too—I'm already working on some 'bots, I'm just short on parts right now—but imagine all the kick-ass stuff we could accomplish! It's like, you learn best through doing, and what better way to create an environment ripe for innovation than for you guys to put yourselves in positions where people need you? Where your powers can do actual good?"

Nicholas has been quiet the whole time she's been talking. Now he snaps like she's hit a nerve. "What good am I supposed to do? Hurt people? Kill them?"

"No," Darla says. "No! See, that's what I'm saying— you might not even know *what* you can do until someone needs you, and your body responds."

"My body's a hell of a lot more responsive to outside influences than anyone else's," Nicholas says. "That time at Sophie's house, when you guys were arguing and I had a flare-up—what was that? Was my body going to end the conflict by destroying one of you? Is that how it works?"

"No!" Darla's getting frustrated; words are failing her, but it's like she's determined to prove Nicholas wrong. "I mean if someone really needed you—"

"You think there's a difference? It's still a reaction. What, my body knows best sometimes and other times it's chaotic? One day it's a savior, the next it destroys someone?"

"Don't get excited," Sophie murmurs, rubbing his back. "Come on, you don't want to get angry and then—"

"You're failing at your own logic game, Darla." Nicholas's forehead is damp; his eyes spark with light. He runs his hand across his brow, takes stock of what's happening. "I have to get out of here."

He hurries across the street, leaving the three of us behind. Shocked. It's almost eleven; we don't exactly have the most reliable bus system, and it took us at least twenty minutes to drive here.

"How are you going to get home?" Darla calls after him.

"I'll figure something out!" he shouts, cutting across an empty mini-mall parking lot. Litter flutters in his wake.

"Avery, you have to go after him," Sophie says, once he's out of sight.

"I will. Just let me walk you guys to the car."

Darla's eyes are scrunched and unhappy. She's soldiering on with her fists clenched, like she wants to punch something. "What was I supposed to tell him? That he's a lost cause? No! I don't believe that!"

"Nicholas just . . ." Sophie bites her lip. "He needs more time. He'll realize . . ."

"What if he doesn't?"

"He will. We'll put our heads together, all right? We don't just give up."

"I know." Darla sighs, her whole face pulling down, distressed. "I just feel like Nicholas and I keep having the same fight, and it's getting worse."

"I'll talk to him," I say. I'm walking faster now, hoping Sophie and Darla will follow my example and pick up the pace. I want to get them off the street and into the relative safety of the Jaguar before too much time passes and I lose track of Nicholas altogether.

When we get to the dark and deserted scenic overlook, Jacques unlocks the car doors and gets out. "Where's your friend Nicholas?"

Sophie lets out a long sigh, blowing glitter off the tip of her nose. "He ran off. We were talking and . . . he got upset."

Jacques is convincing—you have to give him that. His icy model face thaws a little, so that he's wearing a concerned expression. Almost like he genuinely cares. "Do you want me to drive around and look for him?"

"We don't need your help," Darla growls, flinging herself into the backseat, her body an angry tangle of hot-pink velvet tracksuit. "He'd be fine if your mom wasn't filling his head with lies and making him stupid promises."

"Stop it!" Sophie hisses. "Jacques didn't do anything!"

"Yet!" Darla hisses back.

"Um, I've got it covered," I say, almost—but not quite—feeling bad for Jacques. "I saw where he went. I'll take a look for him and see if I can get him home."

Jacques nods and slides into the driver's seat, like he's relieved to not have to deal with us anymore tonight. Sophie squeezes my hand.

"Good luck, Avery. I know you can do this. I have faith in you." Then she pops up on one foot and kisses my cheek, totally out of nowhere. It's odd—it's the opposite cheek from the one Cherchette kissed the night I met her, but my face burns with almost the same intensity: fire instead of ice.

"Thanks," I say.

The Jaguar peels away, and I swear it comes *this* close to running over my foot.

Not that I would feel it. I'm in a daze for a sec—then I snap out of it. My body goes on autopilot: I have a mission.

I have to find Nicholas.

• D. CARMINE • FILE #00373

Nicholas Brighter: ORIGIN STORY

★ SECURITY LEVEL: Top Secret

★ CATEGORY: Autobiographical Account

NOTE: *The following account was written by Nicholas Brighter approximately three and a half months after his power manifested, and delivered to Darla Carmine in the interest of furthering her research.   —D.C.*

I try not to put down roots when we settle into a new town, because I know before long we'll have to move again—but I can't help it. People and places stick with me; I close my eyes and I can picture them perfectly, with this weird sort of longing for the lives I never got to finish.

I remember playing war with my best friend in Florida, trampling the cilantro in my mom's garden while we shot each other with my older brothers' paintball guns—and I can still see the movie theater where I got my first kiss like it's painted on the back of my eyelids. I get nostalgic for the house on the cul-de-sac in Virginia, when Brock and Jake still lived at home, and alternated torturing me with being the best brothers you could ever have. When they weren't tying me up in a sleeping bag and leaving me hanging from a tree in the backyard (true story), they'd take me to the beach or to get ice cream, and they'd let me ride in the back of the truck with my dog.

Back then, I was free to explore and build forts and play my guitar (badly). If I wanted to roam the woods for hours with my dog, Boots, looking for goblins or orcs behind trees . . . no one really minded. My dad was so busy obsessing over my brothers—their grades, how much time they spent benched or on the field, and whether they'd be admitted to the Academy—that I barely entered his radar.

Sometimes I wish I could go back, return to a place where I was just *myself,* not an inferior successor to Brock and Jake. I wish my family could've settled somewhere, instead of moving to a new state just as high school was starting, when all the cliques are pre-formed and airtight and if you're new and you're a little unusual, there's no room to squeeze in.

"So make room," my dad would say—like it's that easy. I don't have the commanding personality he has; or Brock's physique, girls falling all over him and guys giving him respect; or Jake's charisma, always making everyone laugh, fitting in wherever he goes. When you have someplace to disappear to (for me it's music), it's easy to just do it. To not make that extra effort so people notice you, so they *want* to get to know you.

The only reason I even met Darla is because my dad knows her dad through work. We clicked; she was will-ing to try things I was interested in, and she was full of

life and craziness, always ambitious: scheming, inventing, creating. I taught her the rules for Warhammer, this
tabletop strategy game I like, and we'd go to war in my
basement for hours.

My dad hated it; still does. "Why do you have to
coop yourself up like a vampire?" "Go outside; throw
the ball around." "You hang around girls all the time,
you're gonna turn into one." Jake and Brock were away
by then; Jake in the Academy, Brock serving in the U. S.
Navy. And married! My oldest brother's life was set
up perfectly, exactly what my dad wanted. Only he
couldn't be satisfied—because he wanted that for *all*
of us.

With no other guy in the house to micromanage,
he turned to me. It started to irritate him that I was a
"loner," didn't want to watch the game with him, and
so on. I'd play my guitar, and he'd make fun of me for
wanting to be a "rock star"—almost like if he picked
at me enough, I'd lose interest and just live his life
instead.

The stress was building. I spent more hours tossing and turning than actually sleeping; and when I did
sleep, I woke up drenched in sweat. I'd crawl out of bed
to go through my old photo albums, amazed by pictures
of myself smiling, or acting goofy with old friends—
what had happened to that kid? I'd curl up with Boots
on the floor, like he was my rock instead of my dog.
He was loyal. He was the one friend I'd never had to

leave behind when we moved. He knew me; he stayed with me.

I always liked hugging Boots—he was kind of old by then, but when we first brought him home, he was almost as big as I was. I used to hang on to him, burying my face in his fur when I was upset, and I guess I never grew out of it. My dad would've hated that if he'd known—that I was a teenager and still crying into my dog's fur.

All I wanted was to be somewhere else—*anywhere* else—but especially a place that felt like home. I felt like I would die if I had to stay here.

One night my dad's friend stopped by with his perfect teenage son: strong, athletic, confident; looked you in the eye when he spoke to you. I was messing around on my guitar and my dad forced me to come out—then spent the whole time ragging on my clothes, my hair, and laughing about what a wuss I was. Like he could somehow separate himself from his freak son by pointing out everything that was supposedly wrong with me. All in good fun, of course.

By the time they left and I got back to my room, I was crying so hard I couldn't breathe. Boots was licking my face at first, and then he started whining, but my ears started to buzz with this high-pitched drone and I couldn't hear him anymore. My field of vision closed off; everything around me got fuzzy and gray. Pain pierced my chest, like something was breaking inside.

I hugged Boots tighter, like he could fix me. Like it wouldn't hurt as much if I wasn't alone.

I should have pushed him away. Thrown something, screamed even, so he'd leave me.

But I didn't know.

Before I could make sense of the strange suction, the pain, the papers flying off my desk like they'd been swept up by a whirlwind . . . Boots was gone. He warped before my eyes; folded up into a tiny sliver of his former self and vanished. *Into me.*

I absorbed him. I destroyed him.

I was in denial at first: Boots was gone, but maybe he ran away. Shouldn't that be more possible than, than— *what happened*? I roamed the neighborhood searching for him. I asked neighbors, strangers, whether they'd seen him.

A week or so passed. I was in the basement, arranging my Warhammer figures into armies, listening to my parents "discuss" me upstairs, their voices traveling through the vents. How I was never like this *before:* sullen, uncommunicative, possibly depressed. Their speculation made me sick—Boots might be *dead*. What did it matter why I wore all black or didn't talk to them anymore?

I contemplated running away—but where would I go? Did I think I could move in with Brock's family? I was slamming my Warhammer figures down when my vision started to fade again. A jolt went through me— the way I imagine it feels to be hit with a defibrillator.

I seized the table; clutched my chest with my other hand.

I didn't know how to react when my hand sank into nothing, into cold chaos that smelled like smoke, into a vortex that tore my body in half.

My Warhammer figures were swept up almost instantly: dull blades that pelted me like bullets, until my entire collection had disappeared and the vortex exhausted itself.

That night was the end of my denial. The beginning of my dread. Somehow I had imprisoned something evil in my body—I was as wrong and terrible as my parents thought. Only worse—because who could imagine something as twisted as this? When I met Sophie via Darla, and later Cherchette . . . I realized there was more to it. I wasn't evil so much as *changed*. But knowing that doesn't make up for anything I've done. It's only a matter of time before someone else I care about becomes a victim.

Cherchette calls my power *extraordinary*. I call it unforgivable.

Sometimes I wonder . . . why I can't just absorb myself and be done with it.

THE KID WORRIES ME—I don't think I'm being a bad friend if I say that. He's going through all this stuff that I can only *try* to understand. I've got my own personal darkness, but Nicholas is trapped in his—and I'm afraid I'm not good enough to show him the way out. If a genius like Darla and somebody as positive as Sophie can't make Nicholas see himself as something more than a destructive force, how am I supposed to?

By the time I catch up to him, he's sitting outside a convenience store with his back to a bright red soda machine that lights up the night. The way he's slouched there in his trench coat, with his face damp and that vague look of despair on his face, it's almost as good as a neon sign asking the cops to pick him up.

"You figure on getting a ride from the POPO?" I say. He doesn't even crack a smile at the lame slang attempt, which is eerie—I thought for sure I could lighten the mood a little. I try a different tack. "Your dad's kind of a hardass, right? You sure you want to do that to yourself?"

He rolls his head against the soda machine. Bangs it once, startling me. "How long do you think this can last, Avery?"

"Last? You mean your power?"

"Just . . . this state of instability. How long can it really go on like this?"

"I don't know," I say. "But I'm sure it'll get better. I mean, even your voice is screwed up for a while before it changes. Your body just has to adapt. And . . ." I'm fumbling; I feel so ill-equipped to talk about this. What the hell do I know?

"I mean, you're not the only one who screws up. I broke a guy's arm wrestling last season, but . . ." I swallow, flashing back to the gunman in the antiques store. "But it doesn't mean I'm going to maim people for the rest of my life."

"No . . ." Nicholas says. "But hurting people is—for you it's like an unfortunate side effect. For me, that *is* my power. I destroy things."

"As far as you know," I remind him.

He coughs out a bitter laugh. "Yes. As far as I know. But since no other option has presented itself, that's what I have to think about every time it activates and something disappears. Not very comforting when that 'thing' is alive."

"Yeah, but . . ." Damn it. I'm so far out of my league. I don't want to say the wrong thing and be the one to push him over the edge. And when I try to put a positive spin on his situation, I almost feel like I'm disrespecting him, like I'm lying to his face and we both know it. Even though I'm not sure that's true . . . "You could use it for good, too. Once you learned to control it. You could . . . um, protect the environment by absorbing trash and . . . cutting down on landfills?"

I wince. Now that it's out of my mouth, I realize how idiotic that sounds.

"Thanks, Avery. I feel so much better." More bitter laughter, like he's halfway to breaking down. "With that to look forward to, I don't know what I'm worried about."

"Sorry," I say. "I'm not good at this. That didn't come out right."

"That's because there's nothing else to say. You know it and I know it. It's not your fault." Nicholas shrugs and stands up, his face void of emotion, like he doesn't care anymore—which worries me more than his prelude-to-crying face.

"Come on," he says. "We might as well get out of here."

By the time we ring the bell at Nicholas's house, it's after midnight. I know he either has a key or snuck out earlier and left a window open, but he doesn't seem to care about subterfuge. It's almost like he's daring the night to blow up in his face.

His dad opens the door in sweatpants and a NAVY FOOTBALL T-shirt, towering over us, his mouth wide and disapproving. He's *nothing* like my dad. Mr. Brighter is six-four or six-five and barrel-chested, with a dark, weathered tan: the kind of guy who eats steak for breakfast. My dad's like a totally different species: mild-mannered, eats chocolate ice cream and plays along with game shows, wears actual plaid pajamas.

I'm used to placating angry moms, not dads—but Nicholas's jaw is set. Looks like I'd better learn how, fast.

"Do you have any idea what time it is?" Mr. Brighter's voice is low and gravelly, like a gym teacher from hell.

"Yes. Yes, we do, sir. Sorry for disturbing you. It's my fault we're out late. Nick was helping me TP our coach's yard. It's, like, a tradition on his birthday. The whole team does it, so it was kind of like . . . an initiation."

"Team?" Nicholas's dad barks—like he found the word in a bowl of alphabet soup and just chomped it in half.

I take in his NAVY FOOTBALL T-shirt, versus Nicholas's antisocial all-black trench coat. I'm no Darla "Einstein" Carmine but I know conflict when I see it. You know why? My dad bird-watches. I've lived this from the other side.

"Yeah, the football team?" I say. "I've been trying to talk Nick into trying out next year. I think he'd be a killer QB."

If Nicholas had laser eyes, my brain would be leaking out a hole in my head in a sizzling stream of ooze right now.

"Huhn," Mr. Brighter grunts. "Coach must love you bastards. Supposed to rain tomorrow morning. Gonna be a bitch to clean up that toilet paper."

I laugh. "We'll probably get roped into helping if we don't want to get benched. He's got to look at it with pride, though: teamwork at its finest. Although I don't know if his wife's as impressed."

"Doubt it." Mr. Brighter cracks a rough smile, probably flashing back to his troublemaking days. "You two ready to crash yet? I'm getting sick of standing here."

"Yeah, thanks," I say quickly.

Nicholas and I shuffle in, kick our shoes off in the entryway.

"You need sleeping bags? Camping stuff's in the basement," Mr. Brighter says. He snorts and then clears his throat. "I'm going to bed." Nicholas's mom makes a brief appearance, half asleep and wearing a puffy robe. Waves and then disappears into her room.

We raid the kitchen for Cheetos and ice-cream bars and soda, then carry our loot to the unfinished basement: all cinder-block walls and exposed ducts, a cement floor with a scrubby scrap of carpet placed seemingly at random, a weight bench and heavy bag. Posters of sex-bomb girls busting out of their bikini tops are taped up next to the weight bench, for inspiration.

Nicholas rips the Cheetos bag open along the seam. "You know how much worse it'll be when I *don't* try out for football now?"

"Dude, you have to live in the moment when you lie," I say. "I can't worry about everything adding up for the future—I needed to get your ass out of the fire *now*."

"You don't even *play* football," Nicholas goes on. "Didn't you used to wrestle?"

"Uh, yeah," I say. "And if your dad had been wearing a wrestling shirt, I would've milked that instead. The point is: if I'd left it up to you, you'd be getting your ass chewed out and I'd be walking home right now, using my mad lying skills to break into my own house."

Nicholas sighs and paces the floor. Not sure if I'm getting through to him yet, but at least he's calming down. I hunt down the Brighter clan's musty camping gear and unroll two camouflage sleeping bags, set them up next to our little junk-food altar so the melty ice cream bars are within easy reach. Stop a sec to admire the artwork.

"Those are my brother's posters, by the way. Before you say anything."

"Sure. That's what you tell Darla, right?"

He shrugs. "I don't have to explain pervy posters to her. We're just friends. Unlike some people."

I throw a handful of Cheetos at him. "Subtle. No, really—is it that obvious? Did Sophie say anything?"

"I don't know if I'd be able to tell if she did. Sophie likes everybody."

"Even soulless ice boys." I make a face.

"You ever wonder why Jacques never talks about his mom?" Nicholas says suddenly.

"Um, no. Do you hear me talking about my mom?"

"It's different. Cherchette has powers. She's the only adult we know who does, and she has years of experience—she's probably mastered her powers by now. She knows what we're going through, and what we still have ahead of us. She's the only person we might actually be able to turn to for advice. And she's invited us to *live* with her, you know? We're all in this together somehow . . . so it's weird that it never comes up in conversation when he's around.

....

173

Sometimes I've wanted to ask him stuff, but I knew Darla would freak out."

"What exactly do you want to know?"

He shrugs. "I just want another point of view. Cherchette says she wants to help us, but I still don't get why it's so important to her. And Darla's good for digging up dirt, but—"

"Dirt?" I raise my eyebrows. I can't believe Darla's been holding out on me.

"It's probably blown out of proportion." Nicholas picks up the melting ice-cream bars, tosses them in the trash. "She found out that Cherchette's parents died of exposure—they froze to death during a blizzard. It's a little suspicious, considering her powers . . . but that doesn't mean Cherchette killed them. Maybe it was an accident."

I nod, thinking it over. "Maybe that's why she wants to help us." Was Cherchette out of control once, too? Does she feel, like, a bond with Nicholas because of that?

"Maybe." Nicholas drags an extra blanket out of the closet and sets it on top of his sleeping bag. "I just wish there was some way to know without leaving everything behind."

That makes two of us. How many times have I lain in bed and had that same thought? It's complicated, though—because I have friends now. Real ones, people who are important to me and who make me feel at home in the middle of all this weirdness. And so running away now would be like leaving one sanctuary for another, in a way.

I crawl into my sleeping bag, worn out from tonight's excitement. Nick's seriousness is making me nervous. I'm not ready for him to leave us, to even consider it, really—so I try to distract him with a joke. "Well, I know what you'd be missing if you did leave: more awesome superteam missions. Plus if you left, Darla would be so mad she'd build an evil robot clone of you and send it to kill you."

"That's old news." Nicholas yawns and switches off the light. "My evil robot clone is in the closet. He's tied up with electrical tape."

"Uh . . ."

"Don't worry. He probably won't escape. But if he does, you can fight him off, right?"

I close my eyes and burrow deeper into the sleeping bag, grumbling incoherent threats into my pillow ("I'll kick that robot's ass . . .") as my body relaxes and my head grows heavier.

Before I know it, I'm waking up in the dark, my muscles stiff from sleeping on the floor, bleary-eyed and confused. It takes me a few seconds to remember I'm in Nicholas's basement.

I check the time: 5 A.M. Time for me to leave if I want to sneak into my room successfully. I nudge Nicholas awake so he can let me out. Rain's already pounding down, blurring the windows. I sprint through a few soggy backyards on my way to a more secluded takeoff spot. The streets are deserted, and my body aches to be off the ground. I haven't flown in over twenty-four hours.

I push off; shoot quickly into the rumbling, black-gray sky, crossing my fingers that I don't get taken out by a sudden lightning bolt. My clothes are drenched, weighing me down. It's not a huge hindrance, but it's annoying. I don't feel graceful, powerful; I feel like the earth is trying to shackle me. It makes me that much more determined to stick it out.

By the time I get home and get cleaned up, the rain's hammering in earnest and I've got my second wind, fueled by the memory of last night's rush. We were *heroes* last night—and it's only going to get better. I'm running on next to no sleep, but I'm way too energetic to be cooped up in the house. I want to share it with someone.

"What are you doing up?" my mom says, surprised.

I shrug, like I'm up to greet the sun every day of the week. (Well, most days I am.) "Seizing the day?" I pop her toast out of the toaster and butter it and even shake cinnamon and sugar on it. She watches me with a wry smile—she knows I want something. But I don't think she minds. "Can I get a ride somewhere?"

"What? The company here isn't good enough?"

"It's too good. I don't want to overdose on you guys and start to take you for granted."

"Uh-huh." She shakes her head with a smile, amazed to have such a charming son—I'm sure. "All right. Where is it you want to go this early in the morning?"

The one place that's open: Roast.

CATHERINE LOOKS SHOCKED to see me when I flag her down. I'm like the only person here not reading the paper or doing the crossword puzzle. I spill my drink on the table so she has an excuse to come over.

"I can't believe you're missing Saturday cartoons for me," she says.

"You're just that special."

She rolls her eyes, wipes at the tiny juice puddle with slow, exaggerated circles. "So what's up?"

"I think you should become a hero with me."

"Hmm . . . I'm sorry, did you save the world while I wasn't paying attention? Stop a meteor from crashing into the earth or something?"

"You really don't read the paper, do you?"

"Apparently not the one that follows your escapades. Spill your juice again?"

I lean in, lower my voice as I dribble more OJ onto the table. "Remember I told you I met some people? With powers? Last night we got together and caught that guy who's been mugging joggers in the park. Like, we used our powers as a team and took him down."

"He saw you?" she hisses. "He knows that you can fl—"

I hold my hand up to stop her. "No, not that; nothing that couldn't be explained some other way. I just restrained him, and then . . . um, this other girl used a weapon, and this one guy created some ice and cold effects, but there's no way the mugger can prove that. The ice melted; there's no evidence."

"Ice?" She stops wiping. Squeezes the rag in her fist.

"Yeah. That guy's a freak, though; don't worry about him. Anyway . . ." So I tell her how it went down, embellishing some stuff and skipping the part where I got pepper-sprayed. "I want you to be part of it. Like, it's incredible—but it's not the same without you."

"I don't really play well with others." She's back to wiping now, head down and hair hanging over her face— but the tops of her cheeks are pink. A chink in her armor? I aim for it.

"You don't have to play well with others—you're a bad-ass army of one. Just think of the others as backup. And besides, you play okay with me. I could be your trusty sidekick."

She laughs. "Oh yeah, you're really sidekick material."

"If you hated the team, you could stop." She's not saying "absolutely not," so I push on. "It wouldn't mean revealing yourself to anyone new, if you're worried about that. They already know about you; they've known about us longer than we've known about each other. That's why Darla was always bothering you: she was trying to get close enough to invite you without freaking you out."

"Darla's part of this? What's her power? Annoying anyone within a fifty-foot radius?"

"Nooo, Catherine. She's the brains of the operation. The organizer or whatever. But her friends Sophie and Nicholas are like us. You've probably seen them here with her."

Catherine wrings out her juice-soaked rag, then knocks the rest of my juice over so that the floor next to my table becomes a slippery danger zone. "Be right back." I jog my foot nervously until she returns with a mop, pushes it around as aimlessly as ever.

"So what's the point?" she says finally. "Besides entertaining yourselves? I don't really have time to goof off. I have plans."

"Like what?"

She scrunches up her nose like I just asked her what color underwear she's wearing. "Since when do I tell you stuff like that?"

"Um, since we're friends? I know that's a weird concept for you, but you *can* tell me about your life."

"None of your business," she says. "Hurry up and answer my question. This floor is freaking spotless. I need to get back to work."

I sigh. I don't intend to go home anytime soon, and now I have to buy another juice while I wait for her to go on break. That might not seem like a huge deal, but my allowance has been put on hold for, like, the next eight hundred years—and getting money the way I've been getting it (selling my old toys for chump change to the entrepreneurial eBay kids down the street) is just embarrassing. This friendship is getting expensive.

"The point is camaraderie. Teamwork. Proving that we have a purpose, that we can do more than just cause trouble. Will you at least think about it?"

"I didn't say I wouldn't think about it. Just don't get your hopes up." She glances over her shoulder to survey the damage: the messes that have built up while she's been talking to me. Two well-dressed women around my grandma's age creak up from their table, leaving behind a mountain of muffin crumbs. Catherine swears under her breath and sets her attitude to *stun*.

I buy another juice and sit down to watch her. Even hunched over a broom, or angrily scrubbing frosting off a tabletop, she's as fluid as water. Every motion seems effortless. But it's like watching a dancer in a trap. A tiger in a cramped cage.

When I force myself *not* to fly, it's like a part of me is paralyzed: my body can't move the way it's meant to. Catherine's the most graceful person I've ever seen—but she's always skulking around, forced to hide what she can really do.

I want to see her in action again. I feel like, how could that not make her feel better than she does right now?

TWO DAYS LATER I'm patrolling after school, eyes peeled for vandals, wishing I wasn't alone—or that I at least had an intact cell phone so I could harass my friends and try to get one of them to join me. I'm contemplating using a skuzzy pay phone when two mango-scented hands cover my eyes. A warm body bumps me from behind.

"Surprise." In another moment she's in front of me: the dark-haired Victoria's Secret–looking girl from the antiques store. Cherchette's . . . assistant? She points to the ice-blue Aston Martin a short way behind us, creeping along at five miles an hour. "Time to go for a ride." She grabs my hand, treating me to a lush, full-lipped smile. "It's not optional."

Leilani escorts me to the passenger's side and practically shoves me in. Cherchette's platinum hair is hanging loose on either side of her face. She's wearing dark, wraparound sunglasses and her head is tilted away from me. The whole atmosphere is weird, uncomfortable. I can't bring myself to say hello, or even to ask where we're going. Classical music plays on the radio. The digital readout identifies it as Sibelius.

We drive through the neighborhood slowly, steadily. Passersby gawk at the car, but Cherchette doesn't speed up; she sticks to the exact speed limit until we reach a long stretch of road: a rural sort of highway that doesn't get a ton of traffic. I'm pretty sure it leads to Catherine's house, and the connection makes me shiver. But I don't bring it up. Cherchette's never mentioned Catherine, and vice versa. As far as I know, they don't know about each other—and as ambivalent as I am about Cherchette's recruitment scheme, I'd like it to stay that way.

Cherchette crunches to a stop on the gravel shoulder. "Would you like to drive?"

I roll my head to one side, staring out the window at an empty field, waiting for Leilani to answer. Then I realize she's asking *me*. "I don't have a license."

"I'm not a police officer." Cherchette smiles—oddly, because she's only turned toward me partway. "You can drive a bit. Like when you are a child and your parents give you a sip of wine. Just a taste."

Yeahhh . . . my mom was about as likely to give me alcohol as my dad was to kick me in the face. In other words: not gonna happen. Besides, my mom doesn't drink anything that's supposed to relax you. For her, it's coffee all the way.

"Would you feel better if I instructed you?"

"Um." I take a second to think about this. If we get pulled over because I'm weaving all over the place, I'm in deep trouble. But if I drive slowly, and I'm careful, it'll probably be okay. How many chances am I going to have to get behind the wheel of a car like this?

"Yes," I say. "Yeah. I definitely want to." I unfasten my seat belt and clamber out of the car to switch sides with Cherchette. She's moving slowly, one pale hand keeping her hair close to her face, but the wind picks up and lifts it at the crown, revealing a fresh set of stitches at her hairline: tiny Xs caked with dried blood. She smiles awkwardly and smoothes her hair down as we pass each other. My eyes drift to the ground-up stones at my feet.

Once we're buckled in, Cherchette gives me an improvised driving lesson, most of which is unnecessary. It's actually *not* that hard to drive in a straight line. After a few moments of adjustment, I'm rolling down the road like James Bond in my Aston Martin, getting comfortable in my leather throne, easing up on the steering wheel. I could get used to this.

"You like it?" Cherchette says.

"Yeah, it's awesome."

"Go faster, then. No need to drive like a senior citizen."

I press the pedal down carefully, watching the speedometer creep higher as Cherchette urges me on. Past seventy, eighty . . . and then I start to get nervous. It feels too good when the car speeds up. Like flying. I could never fly this fast.

"What are you afraid of?" Cherchette says when I start to slow down.

She spins the volume dial on the radio. An orchestra booms from the speakers and the gas pedal sinks under my weight, soft as butter—to hell with finesse. It's like the music is the soundtrack for this moment, and I need to live up to it. Speed equals euphoria.

The road is straight with the occasional slight curve— easy. Traffic is so minimal it's easy to forget that we're not alone. But when a pickup truck heads toward us from the opposite direction, I instinctively hit the brake. Slowing down, until—

Suddenly the road shines like glass. Sunlight glints off the newly icy street, and before I can react, the car starts to spin out. I swear and slam on the brakes, jerking the steering wheel to send us spinning sideways into a ditch. Dual air bags erupt. Low tree branches scrape the windows. Leilani gasps, almost hyperventilating in the backseat.

"Variables," Cherchette says. "That's what you should be afraid of." She sighs pleasantly and bats at a deflating air bag. "You can't plan for them. What you need is to be properly prepared for them."

"How the hell was I supposed to be prepared for that?" I'm struggling to get my breathing under control. Struggling not to scream at her.

"I encouraged you to drive faster precisely to see if you would do it. It's your own responsibility to make wise decisions. You could have killed someone just now."

"Christ," Leilani mutters. "Feel free to leave me out of your test next time."

"A car is a weapon," Cherchette continues. "And *you* are a weapon, Avery. Equally deadly. The difference is that drivers are required to be licensed. There are rules, and potential drivers must practice with an experienced adult.

It's foolish to learn to drive on your own; no one does that, dear. Shouldn't you take your training as seriously as the average person seeking a driver's license?"

My heart's still racing from the near collision. My muscles are locked in the past, braced for impact, adrenaline saturating my blood like poison. I don't know what to say to her. It was dumb of her to egg me on like that, but I'm the one who listened.

"My offer still stands, you know," Cherchette says. "I could make you into something remarkable. More special than you already are."

I knead my forehead in frustration—I can't believe I'm about to ask this. "If I took you up on that . . . what would it mean for me? Would I have to leave home forever? Would I be able to see my parents?"

"Why don't I let you speak with Leilani about that? She can tell you better than I can."

I climb out and push the banged-up Aston Martin out of the ditch, tempted to walk home and leave this screwed-up scene behind. But I can't; I need to know what else is out there. Because Cherchette might be a little crazy, but she's not lying when she says I'm a weapon. Dangerous, deadly, and totally irresponsible.

Cherchette drives us out of town, to a novelty ice-cream place with picnic tables out front and a giant plastic cow on the roof. The last time I was here was in elementary school, after a big baseball game—the whole team went to celebrate. It's weird to be here now. Everything seems smaller.

"So what can I tell you?" Leilani asks, when we sit down at one of the picnic tables. Her hands are folded, pert and businesslike.

The sun sinks into me, chasing away the chill. It's a warm spring day, but we're the only customers outside. "Why'd you do it? What made you leave home and . . . your friends and everything? Was it fear?"

Leilani digs into her sundae, tips the spoon so the hot fudge oozes back down. "Not fear. Need. I needed my life to make sense, and without Cherchette, it didn't.

"I'm a shape-shifter. You know that, don't you? Well, can you imagine what it's like for me when *my* power is out of control? I don't have to worry about hurting anyone, exactly . . . but it's much harder to hide. I used to look at myself in the mirror a lot—you know, pouting, posing. I guess I was a little in love with myself. I wanted to know what everyone else saw. If one expression was more flattering than another. And then . . .

"One day there was a shift. My features blurred—and then they were back. Only I wasn't myself. One eye was lopsided. My nose had twisted, like I was staring into a fun-house mirror. And then I blurred again, but it was like my skin was melting this time, like wax molding itself into a different shape. My face was in flux and I couldn't control it; I didn't know what was happening.

"I broke the mirror. I covered my face with my hands, but it was even worse then—because I could *feel* the changes as they occurred. How could I be hallucinating if I could feel my face reshaping itself?

"I finally flipped. I went into the bathroom with a paring knife, ready to slice the excess skin off my nose, force my left cheekbone to go back to the right size. I was prepared to completely mangle myself, take my eye out so I wouldn't have to look anymore. Just thinking about that time makes me shaky. Like I could go back to that again." Her lips tremble as she tries to laugh it off. She slides a perfectly manicured nail along the edge of her eyelid. Pauses.

"Right. I know I sound crazy—but that was honestly how I felt. My mother came into the bathroom then; I must have been hysterical, holding the knife up to my face like that. I don't even think I could see myself anymore at that point; I couldn't focus on anything. She took the knife away from me and I told her my face kept changing, that I needed it to go back to normal; I had to fix things before school tomorrow. I would just cut off the bad parts. I asked her if she would help me. If she wouldn't let me do it myself, would she help me . . ."

"Damn," I say. "I can't even imagine how horrible that must have been. It's scary just listening to you talk about it."

Leilani shivers. "I know. My parents took me to a therapist, who diagnosed me with body dysmorphic disorder, which is where you perceive things as being wrong with your appearance, completely irrationally, to the point where you become so obsessive about it that you can't function. They put me on medication, which drove my emotions up and down and backward and only made things worse.

"And in a way I suppose I was lucky that my power had a kind of defense mechanism, where it didn't manifest in front of people. But at the time I wanted it to so badly, because everyone thought I was crazy and *I* thought I was crazy, and I needed someone to witness it and tell me I wasn't. Someone who could explain it to me. And that's when I was fortunate enough to meet Cherchette."

"So you really did need her," I say.

"More than anything. I honestly think I'd be dead without her. I don't think I could have gone on that way, not understanding what was happening. But she explained and she told me about 'powers,' that there were others like us, and that my features were changing because I was a shape-shifter. That it would be an asset if I could take control of it. I could become anyone I wanted, anonymous or famous. An impostor or myself.

"She taught me how to focus so I wasn't so anxious, fluctuating all the time. And then we worked on more productive shifting—changes that would be *my* choice. She's a funny motivator." Leilani smirks, twisting her hair around her fingers. "Once she took me on a whirlwind tour of all these designer clothing stores and wouldn't let me buy anything; she told me it was pointless, because I could shift into something couture if I wanted to. She's a doll. I love that woman more than I love my own mother."

"Wow. That's, um, a seriously good endorsement. So . . . you left home, though. What do your parents think? Do they know about you?"

"No. I couldn't tell them. They already thought I was out of my mind—you think telling them I had superpowers was going to change anything? I wasn't able to *show* them, at that point. And, after talking to Cherchette, I wasn't sure it would be best for them to know."

"So you ran away and they have no idea what happened to you? Isn't that kind of harsh?"

Leilani gathers her dark, sleek hair into a ponytail and flings it over one shoulder. "Even if it hurts them now, it's not like their grief will be permanent. This way I can go home when I'm ready. And I will—one day. They'll have their daughter back, and I'll be healthy. Prepared to play with the cards life has dealt me. I can't imagine what any parent would want more—even if it hurts for a little while."

I think of Nicholas—how he's afraid he'll hurt his dad. Kill him, even. How disappearing for a while—working through this stuff—could be beneficial. Scary, maybe, and unusual, but . . . isn't all of it? Superpowers don't come with an instruction manual. You can't get a college degree in taming your deadly vortex.

"Make sense?" She swirls her spoon through her ice cream—mostly melted now.

"Perfect sense."

Her face lights up like a sunset, warm and gorgeous and perfect—even if parts of her are manipulated, or fake. The way she feels about this is real.

• D. CARMINE • FILE #00495
Catherine Drake: FUTURE TEAMMATE?
★ **SECURITY LEVEL:** Top Secret

★ **CATEGORY:** Observation & Tactics

Powers I've confirmed with 94% Certainty: Extreme agility and balance; razor-sharp fingernails (aka "claws"); may exert some influence over feral and domestic felines. Others??

Status: Extremely resistant to friendly overtures!

Primary Personality Traits: hostile, unfriendly, confrontational, suspicious. However, I have reason to believe that there is more to Catherine than those unpleasant attributes (case in point: the Big Dawg offensive), and that with the right combination of persistence, ingenuity, and alternative fashion choices, I can break through that wall and earn her trust.

Tactics to gain her trust and friendship: 1] Proclaim shared interest in her favorite musical group/performer. UPDATE: Failed to engage. Must up my game! Thoughts: Maybe my exterior is too geek chic? 2] Try out "goth" look (aka "Operation Paint it Black") so that she sees me as a kindred spirit and is not immediately dismissive of my attempts. UPDATE: Failed. Unless an angry scowl is the goth equivalent of a friendly smile?? RESEARCH THIS! 3] Hack her account at the library and check out the last five books she returned. Casually bring them with me next time I go to Roast. Attempt to engage her in conversation about them; she'll be surprised we have so much in common, and will quickly feel at ease! UPDATE: Still traumatized by her reaction. Will write more later. *wibble* 4) Compose a heartfelt poem that subtly interweaves suggestions of powers ("more than meets the eye") with themes of not belonging. End with the idea of the outsider finding his/her people. Genius! So far I think my problem has been that I'm too obvious. Catherine is a connoisseur of subtlety—no need to hit her over the head with these ideas. I can't believe I didn't think of this before . . .

UPDATE: Avery's help may be required.

LIFE IS GOOD. The mysterious mugger-capture got its own article in the paper (the glitter was a source of bewilderment for everyone involved), and Catherine and I are acing science. I stuck our latest A-plus lab report on the fridge to show it off, and my parents almost passed out.

"Maybe he *has* been studying at the library," my mom said, gazing adoringly at the gaudy "Great Job!" sticker. "I thought he was looking at porn."

I sighed dramatically at her and went back to polishing the gold stars on my Remedial English quiz.

So things are good—but not perfect. And they're not even *close* to perfect for some of us. Which is why Darla and Sophie and I are meeting secretly at Sophie's house: to figure out how to help Nicholas. I've got a mix of ideas in my head already—one of which I'm afraid to bring up, since I know it'll spark a firestorm of genius-grade ferocity.

Darla and Sophie are crowded together on an over-stuffed white couch, Darla's sparkly laptop bridged across their knees. They're staring intently at the screen, leaving me with a view of the bling-encrusted backside, custom decorated with rhinestones mosaic'd into the shape of Hello Kitty's face.

"Two problems," Darla says, holding up two fingers. "Not just Nicholas. Catherine, too. She's as susceptible as anyone."

"Susceptible to what?" I say.

"To Cherchette's nefarious promises," Darla says. "Duh."

I nod like, *oh yeah, of course;* meanwhile bile's creeping up my throat. Because Cherchette might be Nicholas's best option—and I have to make Darla see that.

"Cherchette hasn't met with Catherine," I say. "I'd know. Catherine would've told me."

"Maybe not yet," Darla says. "But she will. And when she does, Catherine has to know that there are people she can count on. I know she acts like she doesn't need anyone—but nobody's *that* tough. In a moment of weakness, she could totally go over to the dark side."

"Ohmygod, it's *not* the dark side." Sophie commandeers the track pad and starts scrolling. "And Cherchette doesn't contact everyone. You should know that."

"In a way she does. She sent Jacques after you."

"Cherchette had nothing to do with that," Sophie mutters. "Trust me, she's not interested in me. I'm on her reject list."

My head snaps up. "Reject list? What the hell is that?"

"It's a list," Sophie says, raising her voice uncharacteristically, "of all the known powered kids who don't serve any purpose, who are basically losers, aren't worth bothering with, et cetera. End of story. Any more questions?"

"She has a list of all the kids?" Darla says. "Why didn't you tell me that? How many—"

"I don't know!" Sophie shakes her head fiercely, blond hair flying. Then squeezes her eyes shut and sinks back into the couch. "Sorry. I just think it's unfair, being judged like that. She doesn't even know me."

"Did Jacques tell you about the list?" Darla says. "Did he tell you anything else?"

"Umm, if you want information from him, why don't you try talking to him, instead of over-the-top yelling at him and accusing him of stuff he's never done?"

The girls steam for a few minutes, stubbornly web-searching in silence, trading control of the mouse and the keyboard. I zone out staring at Hello Kitty's rhinestone face, wondering why Cherchette would keep a list of so-called rejects. It doesn't make sense. Would Cherchette really do something that corrupt and calculating? She says she wants to help us. And when you want to help, you look for people who *need* help, right? You don't divide them into heroes and zeroes, then turn your back on anyone who doesn't rank.

"It's probably not a reject list like you're thinking," I tell Sophie. "You're like the most well-adjusted person I've ever met. It seems like Cherchette focuses more on screw-ups, kids whose powers are out of control and who'd be lost without her."

"No such thing," Darla says. "Neither you nor Nicholas actually needs her help. You just have to believe in yourself and be willing to work through the hard parts. There are pioneers in every field—it's not like Cherchette even has the same powers as you guys. Do you think Marie Curie was like, 'let me wait for someone else to teach me about radiation?' No—she was hungry for knowledge and she dove in headfirst."

"Yeah, but Nicholas's power has serious consequences," I say.

"So does studying radiation," Darla says. "Hello, cancer."

"Okay, I'm sorry, but that's like the worst argument ever."

Darla shrugs. "I stand by my point. In this world, you've got leaders and innovators, and then you've got the people who follow them. You have *superpowers,* Avery, and so does Nicholas—shouldn't it be obvious which category you fit into?"

I want to tell her about Leilani—to explain that sometimes you need a mentor. I mean, come on: Obi-Wan, Gandalf? Shouldn't this be part of Darla's frame of reference?

I want to tell her that when you're a living weapon, it's irresponsible to go around blowing stuff up until you learn how to stop. But I can't think of how to say that without sounding brainwashed. Darla's convinced that Cherchette is evil incarnate.

"Soapbox time is over," Sophie says, pastel-pink nails

tapping the keyboard. "Can we get back to business, please?"

"We need a mission the whole team can take part in," Darla says. "Something that makes Nicholas feel useful, so he's not just tagging along. Once he realizes he can help people, not just hurt them, I'm hoping he'll stop being so hard on himself."

"He's relentless," I say. "I mean, I've done some messed-up stuff, too, and I feel bad about it. But Nicholas refuses to forgive himself. He's dealing with a force beyond his control. How can anything it does be his fault?"

"We've tried telling him that," Darla says. "With zero success. Which is why showing him is the only option we have left."

Well, not the only option, I think.

"Nicholas is more than just his vortex," Darla says. "He's a good person; he cares about people and animals—just like Sophie is more than her stickiness. She's loyal, and she has a good heart—that's what really makes her strong."

"Aww." Sophie reaches over and hugs Darla. "Darla's getting mushy."

"Anyway," Darla says, "Nicholas has another power, too. He claims it's just a coincidence—but normal people get lost. Nicholas never does. If he's been somewhere before, he can *always* find his way back. Ever since he was little. It's like he has an internal compass or something. His sense of direction is infallible."

While Darla's been talking, Sophie's been biting her index finger, grinning in anticipation. "You guys, I think I found something." She turns the laptop toward me so I can read the headline.

LOCAL SCOUT TROOP STILL MISSING AFTER 24 HOURS

"Bingo."

I'm busy," Catherine says.

"Not after ten you're not." I point to tonight's closing time on Roast's hours-of-operation sign.

Catherine's avoiding me, latching onto any excuse to hang around here longer—rinsing out mugs, refilling the cinnamon shaker, scrubbing fingerprints off the glass dessert case. Like there aren't three other industrious workers just dying to get their hands on those jobs.

"You're afraid to do something heroic," I say. "You're afraid you'll like it, and it'll interfere with your I-hate-the-world persona."

Catherine sprays my shirt with glass cleaner—totally uncalled for. She could just *ask* me to leave. Not that I would, but . . .

"Maybe I just want to get home and sit down. I've been on my feet all day; I'm not exactly in the mood to hike through the woods in the dark. Besides—those kids probably fell into a gorge and are dead by now. Let the park rangers sort it out."

"That settles it," I say, stealing her spray bottle and

tossing it behind the counter. "I'm kidnapping you. You are so unbelievably cold—you need some good, old-fashioned altruism to warm you up."

Altruism: see Darla's vocabulary. Also: selflessness.

I drag Catherine out the door and none of her coworkers stops me; one girl even smiles. They probably think it's cute that scowly Catherine has a "boyfriend."

"You're so getting eviscerated."

"I'm so not," I say. "You're gonna send me a thank-you card, handmade with little cats drawn on it, because tonight's your lucky night." I haul her down the street to a blacked-out parking lot and lift her into my arms like an oversize baby. "You're going where no girl has gone before. Without an airplane, that is."

"Oh, hell no!" Her eyes go wide and she does this scramble-struggle thing that's totally ineffective, since I've got a firm grip on her already—there's no way I'm letting her fall.

"Calm down; this is totally safe. On three. One, two . . ."

Her claws sink into my arm as we take off and I stifle a gurgle of pain. *It's just like getting ten rabies shots at once,* I try to tell myself, putting on a brave face for Catherine's benefit.

The wind picks up and everything below us gets smaller: empty parking lots become black squares, streets curve like snakes, and tiny lights glimmer everywhere. I bully my way through air currents, try to keep the turbulence to a minimum. Catherine's got her head buried in my shirt, her claws taking up permanent residence in my flesh.

"Don't you want to look?" I ask. "When are you going to experience this again?"

"Hopefully never!"

"You're the one who complained about being on your feet all day."

Her threat to eviscerate me gets carried away by the wind, replaced by a shriek as I dip lower, eyes narrowed to pick out our meeting spot: a deserted picnic area bordering the state park. I told Darla I'd be flying in (that was a hell of a confession), and she signals me with a flashlight so I know where to land.

As soon as my boots touch down, Catherine wriggles loose and curls into a protective crouch. I think she'd kiss the ground if she wasn't worried about getting a mouthful of muck.

"Eeeeee!" Sophie squeals. "Avery, you *have* to take me up sometime. Like, right after this." She tries to help Catherine up, but the cat-girl is rooted, unwilling to be any closer to the sky than she has to. "Are you okay? What was it like to *fly*?"

"Um, you're bleeding," Darla tells me. Good thing she's an inventor and not a doctor—I don't think she reacts well to flesh wounds. In the glow of the flashlight, she's looking sickly pale—but it might just be the dark red of her flannel lumberjack shirt contrasting with her geek pallor. Because yep, ever the master of disguise: she's dressed like Paul Bunyan. Knit hat, flannel shirt, jeans, boots, and a trusty robotic blue ox—she's all set for a night of search-and-rescue and/or logging.

(I'm kidding about the ox. Maybe.)

"Catherine got a little excited on the way over," I explain. As my eyes adjust to the artificial light, I take in the scene: Nicholas is loading bottled water and a first-aid kit into his backpack. Jacques is aloof, fixated on his open hand, icing his fingers one at a time, then thawing them. The Jaguar is parked on a slope, mostly hidden by a black tarp and some overhanging tree branches.

Oh, and Sophie? She's outfitted in a black neoprene leotard and ballet flats, with a camouflage hoodie as her token nod to wilderness survival. That and a sparkly utility belt.

"We have to be careful," Darla says. "The official night search party consists of fewer searchers than the one during the day, and they'll be keeping to trails so they don't lose anyone—but they *are* out here, and they're not going to be happy if they find us. Our best bet is to plunge into the forest itself—if the scouts are lost, that's probably where they are. Also, be aware that the search-and-rescue teams have dogs who will sniff us out no problem, so we need to steer clear of them if we want a shot at saving these kids."

Catherine scowls. "I hate dogs."

"How do you intend to locate the scouts?" Jacques asks. "It seems presumptuous to assume you will find them by wandering randomly through the forest."

"Nothing I do is random, Morozov." Darla unfolds a

map of the state park and aims her flashlight at it, illuminating a complicated code of red-marker outlines, dots, dashes, and stars. "This is where the scouts started, 'kay? This is where they were last seen by their troop; these are the areas the search parties have already covered; and *these* are the areas they're most likely to have explored based on a number of variables *including but not limited to:* their heights, weights, physical capabilities, *and* interests as declared on Facebook. Trust me, we *will* find them."

"The genius is a little sensitive about being questioned," Sophie whispers. "Don't take it personally."

We double-check our gear and set off, flashlights low to the ground: shuffling across an unending blanket of dead leaves, tripping over fat spidery tree roots and soft, rotting logs. The ground sends us hiking up and then stumbling down; we cross valleys and troop past rock ledges, cursing at near ankle-twists when holes appear out of nowhere or rocks slip loose of their moorings.

It's hard to see where you're going, and watching the ground pretty much ensures that you'll be hit in the face by skinny branches. Low, curving shrubs turn out to be full of thorns. Sophie does her best to skip over them, but her bare legs are being massacred. Nicholas's trench coat keeps getting snagged and yanking him back.

Catherine's the only one not having trouble; she doesn't even bother with a flashlight. Immune to missteps, she prowls through the woods like she owns them, frequently turning around only to see that we're at least twenty feet behind her, then asking impatiently, "Are we doing this or not? What are you waiting for?"

An hour passes, two. The muddy ground keeps sucking Sophie's shoes off, until Nicholas volunteers me as the team pack animal and I let her hop up and ride piggyback. When we hear dogs barking, or inadvertently get too close to one of the trails, we veer off in the opposite direction, cutting deeper into the woods.

"I hope we're not walking in circles," Sophie says.

"We're not," Nicholas assures her. "We've backtracked a few times but we're making progress."

Following the sound of rushing water, we come to a wide gorge with a stream at the bottom—maybe thirty feet down, and the gap itself is ten feet across. Catherine paces until she comes to a point where a fallen tree trunk is lodged across the gorge and forms a makeshift bridge.

"Score," she says. "This was getting boring."

She springs onto the trunk and pads across it before we can stop her, quick and sure-footed like the gymnast girls who show off on the balance beam during gym class. Only if she falls, she'll break every bone in her body. Thank God she doesn't do any cartwheels.

Catherine's safe on the other side before my heart has a chance to stop, smirking like, *what? You doubted me?* Maybe it was a bad idea to bring badass risk-taker girl on this mission. She's totally getting back at me for flying.

"Way to take the initiative, Catherine!" Darla says brightly. "But, um, we're not going that way."

"Why not?" Catherine says. "The missing kids had access to the trails, right? That means they could be any-where. My random decision is just as likely to result in success as your random decision."

Okay, clearly Catherine missed the tirade earlier.

"My decisions are *not* random!" Darla exclaims. "I base them on a careful series of calculations and re—"

I clamp my hand over Darla's mouth. Rude, but it has to be done. "Good call, Catherine. I'll get the others over." She's squinting to ward off my flashlight beam, but I think she's happy.

"First come, first served," I say.

"I hate to turn that down, but this is, like, the first time these crappy shoes have been useful," Sophie says, pluck-ing off her trashed ballet flats and sticky-stepping across the log bridge. "But feel free to rescue me if I fall!"

No heart attacks this time. I hover close by to make sure she gets across, then fly Darla and Nicholas to the other side, using an underarm carry. Darla tries to convince me she needs to be flown back, because she forgot something on the other side—but the whole time her eyes are darting around obvious-liar style, so I just promise to fly her again some other time.

That leaves Jacques on the other side. "You trust me, right?" I call across.

Tick, tick, tick.

Seconds pass. My flashlight beam catches glimpses of frustration, uncertainty. But when he finally answers, he's the picture of cool composure: "Why would that matter?"

Jacques extends his arms like a conductor and focuses until water from the stream below begins to rise into the air, slush turning to a bridge of rough, glistening ice. He steps to the edge of the gorge and treads calmly across the ice bridge, barely quickening his pace when the ice behind him begins to crack. Once he reaches the other side, large chunks of ice break free like puzzle pieces and fall, until there's no trace of the frozen walkway.

When I look more closely, there's a thin film of sweat on his forehead. He doesn't look chill *at all*. And I wonder: Did Jacques shatter that walkway on purpose, just to prove how badass he is? Or did he overextend his powers?

We're mostly quiet as we continue our search, ears tuned to cries for help. Leaves *shush* under our feet, stones rattle down hillsides, twigs crunch. Nicholas's bag of water bottles *glugs* with every hard step. As we near the third hour of our march, Jacques's breathing turns ragged and we stop to rest, even though he insists he's fine. After a few minutes he's still hunched over, pale as powder. Sophie sits down next to him with a worried expression on her face, tries to get him to drink some water.

Pride's kept Jacques on his feet this long, but something's definitely wrong with him. He's sick, or . . . I don't know. With our powers, it's hard to tell. Could be the flu, could be a serious side effect he hasn't told us about. I decide to play it safe, let them rest a little longer.

"Why don't you guys stay here for a while?" I say. "I want to try something else. Catherine and I can cover more ground—"

She's nodding, and then I finish:

"—from up here."

I sweep her into the air before she can protest. Soon we're treetop level, moving slowly but faster than we were before, no longer delayed by the obstacles on the ground. She's hanging from my arms: alternately limp as a doll, tense as steel wire. Not kicking, not screaming. Plotting my demise? Yeah, there's probably a good chance of that.

"Night-vision time," I tell her. "I need you to be my eyes 'cause I'm effectively blind up here." The new leaves are doing their utmost to block out the available moonlight, and it's cloudy tonight on top of it. Plus I never claimed to have eagle eyes.

"I hate this," she grumbles.

"You're doing great. Much better than last time."

Catherine and I fly north for a while and then double back before we've gone too far, to ensure we don't lose track of the team; then I pick a different direction and we try that. Rinse, repeat. Eventually Catherine complains that I'm pulling her arms out of their sockets, her armpits hurt, etc., so we switch to a different carry. I cradle her in my arms instead of swinging her around, glad that I don't have to carry a guy like this. It's a position that would embarrass your average Avenger.

In between catlike yawns and hissed reassurances that yes, she's fine, and no, she's not tired, Catherine motions for me to dive lower each time she sees something. Movement, an odd shape: animal or person? "Back up back up back up!" she finally orders. I pull higher and out of sight.

....

"You think you found them?"

"I see them—they're sleeping under leaves. And one kid's buried to the waist, sitting up keeping watch or something."

"Freaking sweet! Catherine, I knew you could do this!" Carrying her turns into a full-fledged hug, and she stiffens up again, her legs kicking out like rusty scissors.

"Down please," she says.

Back at ground level, I switch my flashlight on and charge after Catherine, stomping through leaves and trickly streams, calling out for the scouts, telling them help is on the way.

YOU'RE SAFE," I SAY. "We're going to get you home."

The kids look disoriented; most of them are still clearing dreams from their heads. Their camp is composed of piles of leaves and empty snack wrappers, a soda bottle filled with water from the stream. We're not much older than they are—I doubt we look like rescuers. More like teens who've just happened to cross paths with them.

"Pair up," Catherine tells the scouts. "Everybody keep track of each other while we're walking. Hold hands or hold on to your friend's coat or something. Odd man out sticks with him," she says, pointing to me.

"You think you can get us back to the group?" I say quietly, before kid number five has a chance to stick to me like glue. "I think I could find them from the air but it's a different story down here."

"Are you kidding? I can still smell Jacques's cologne. I could walk you there with my eyes closed."

"Excellent. Lead the way, Captain."

I bring up the rear to make sure no one wanders off, and Catherine takes the lead. None of the kids questions her lack of flashlight; they're too hungry and thirsty to be really talkative, although one insists about three times that he has to pee, which leads to the group's stopping and my becoming pee-chaperone, a role I don't exactly relish.

We're standing around trying to settle an argument over how the peeing kid and his partner should keep track of each other, since the other kid refuses to hold hands and doesn't want the peeing kid holding his jacket either—"His hands have pee on them!"—when my flashlight beam catches a mountain lion in a low crouch. Stalking us, less than ten feet away.

Crap.

I clear my throat, nudge Catherine. "Ahem. Um. Predator. Over there."

I try to say it quietly but these kids are no one's fools; they switch from overtired bicker mode to pure panic, talking all at once and then yelling at each other to shut up, it's gonna kill us, no we have to scare it, we have to seem bigger and threatening! I don't know WTF to do; I'm not a wilderness-survival person!

One of the kids throws a rock and I wince. The mountain lion closes its eyes when the rock hits it, then refocuses, as if we're the only thing that matters. Its lack of reaction seems to jar something within the kids. The collective chaos stops; we all just breathe, *breathe,* hearts drumming in time with the twitch of the mountain lion's black-tipped tail.

It watches us intently, never relaxing from that ready crouch.

Catherine moves toward it, her own face serious, holding her hand out like you do for a dog or a cat, so it can sniff you, get to know you. The mountain lion snarls when she gets too close, black-edged lips curling back—but Catherine stands her ground.

"Stop it," she orders. "No one's going off alone, so you won't get any chances. You're not even hungry; you're being greedy."

The mountain lion butts its head up against Catherine's hand, knocks her back a step. She gets this look on her face like she's gonna slap it, and I clench my fists and think, *please, please don't make me wrestle this cat*—but before either one of us makes a move, the mountain lion starts rubbing its head against her, gently but insistently. That's when I realize it wants a scratch. Catherine complies and the mountain lion starts purring: deep, rumbly sounds that are scary, but also nice. It rolls its head back and forth so she hits all the best spots.

After enjoying a few scratches, the mountain lion yawns and pads soundlessly back into the forest. We stand there in shock for a moment before the kids crowd around Catherine, awestruck like she's a rock star. *How did she do it? Ohmygod she's amazing! I'm in loooove!* And so on.

"You're lucky these kids aren't old enough to ask you on a date," I say.

She treats me to an exasperated eye-roll but I think secretly she's flattered. "Oh, shut up before I rip your guts out. And don't touch me," she snaps at the peeing kid. "Hello, you have pee on your hands!" Which I think just makes them worship her even more.

We make it back to the group in one piece, arguments kept to a minimum now that Catherine's the boss. We're greeted with cheers from Sophie and Darla when we arrive; Nicholas unzips his backpack and goes on water duty, hydrating the scouts while Sophie plies them with granola bars and I go around whacking the kids who are too obvious about staring at her butt.

"Is anyone injured?" Jacques asks. "I can provide an ice pack."

"Um. No, I don't think so." I turn back to the scouts, take a sec to look them over. Oops. I never thought to ask them that. But I'm pretty sure they're okay. "Not unless you have a balm for broken hearts," I say.

"Do you have any disinfectant?" Catherine asks. "This kid's covered in pee."

"I am not!" he cries, squatting down to rub his hands on the fallen leaves. Vigorously, like he's willing to sandpaper his skin off in exchange for her approval.

Jacques looks mildly ill and backs away.

"Uh, they're fine," I say. "But thanks for asking."

Once the kids have had a chance to rest and refuel, we get started on the long hike back. If we could get to the trail and find the official rescue team, that would probably be best—but we're all stubborn enough to want this to be *our* victory. No adults—*we* did this.

....

"Time to do your thing, Nicholas," I say, smacking his shoulders. "Think you can get us out of here?"

"It's easy," he says. "All you have to do is remember where you went before. Darla's crazy if she thinks that's a power."

"Um, okay—then how come no one else in the world can do that?"

"I'm sure someone can." He shrugs. "Most people just don't pay attention."

"You think a *genius* doesn't pay attention?" Darla huffs, butting into our conversation.

"A genius who managed to break both her compass and her GPS system right before this mission?" Nicholas says. "Hmm, I'd say she pays too much attention, except when it comes to herself and how easy it is to see through her machinations."

"I'm leaving until he stops using words like that," I say.

The return trip goes much more quickly. Sure, we're still tripping over stuff and getting gouged by thorns, but Nicholas has the uncanny ability to determine the shortest distance between two points—and then lead us right to our destination. Superpowers are back under wraps, so we cross the gorge via an actual, man-made bridge before plunging back into the forest.

Sometime between three and four in the morning, we push through the thick wall of trees and emerge next to Jacques's tarp-covered Jaguar. Nicholas dusts his hands off. "My work is done."

"Whoa. Talk about exact," I say. Even Jacques seems impressed.

The scouts sit down on the slope to rest ("My feet hurt!" one kid whines; Catherine tells him not to be a wuss) and Darla digs out her supersatellite cell phone to start making calls, before we lead the kids to another location. Within half an hour, Darla, Catherine, and I are greeting ten parents, a scattering of siblings, and the scout troop leader outside the gates of a local farm. Reunions begin, and when the adults start looking around for the rescuers, they're stunned to discover *we* found their missing kids.

"She scared away a mountain lion!" one of the scouts exclaims, pointing at Catherine. The others start jabbering excitedly, and Catherine just gives this I-don't-know-what-they're-talking-about shrug.

"They've had a long night," she says.

"And so have we," I interrupt. "It's past our bedtime. So we have to get going."

The glory is great, it's nice, I like being appreciated— but I'm exhausted and all this fresh excitement is wearing me out.

Before Catherine and Darla and I can beat a hasty retreat, one of the moms says, "I recognize you! You were on the *Today* show last summer!"

"Um." I glance around, fear crawling like spiders under my skin. "No, that was probably someone—"

"Avery something!" the mom says. "You saved a little boy who'd been trapped under his mother's car." She's getting more and more sure of herself, nodding as it comes back to her. "And here you are, doing it again. That's amazing."

I must have a save-me look on my face, because Darla jumps in to run interference.

"It's hard to get into a good college these days. You have to start early. Pick up some extracurricular activities no one else has. You know how it is."

"Oh, I know," another mom agrees. "My oldest is applying next year and it's a nightmare. There's so much competition, you have to really stand out."

"Avery wants to go Yale," Darla continues—um, pushing it a bit *far,* in my opinion. "So he has to work even harder."

"Well, good luck, honey!"

I thank the moms for their well-wishes and we get the hell out of there, disappearing into the trees across the street and running until we get to the Jaguar, now revved and ready to go. Sophie and Nicholas are belted in and bobbing along to the dreamy electronica on the radio. Jacques is sucking on a piece of peppermint candy to keep himself awake. We all trade smiles and sleepy high fives.

"We did it," Sophie says.

Darla grins big, taking some robot-shaped lollipops from her bag to celebrate and tossing one to each of us. "Was there ever any doubt?"

"Superstars!" I throw my arms around Nicholas and Catherine. "These two have futures so bright I need sunglasses. Even in the dark."

Catherine pokes me in the ribs. "Shut up, sidekick. Before you get demoted to lackey."

At this moment, I feel ridiculous, obnoxious, accomplished, and popular. (In a non-annoying way.) I can't imagine this getting any better. And yet we're just getting started.

"We need to rethink this sidekick business," I say to Catherine.

Back at my sanctuary (uh, that would be my messy room), I kick some dirty clothes out of the way and sit down at my computer. My body's ready to lose consciousness, but my brain's too wired to conk out right away. I check to see if anyone else is killing time online.

A message from Nicholas pops up.

PendulousNB: *i hate him*

Me: *??*

PendulousNB: *my dad*
he's pissd i snuck out
threatnd to snd me to military schl
he lookd in my eyes to chk if i was smokng pot

Me: *calm down ok? i'll call u*

PendulousNB: *brb he's banging on my door*

Damn it. I spin back and forth in my creaky desk chair, anxious to talk to him again and make sure that everything's okay. Minutes tick by like hours and I'm still staring at a blinking cursor. I dial Darla and hope she left her phone on.

"Hmm, hello?"

"Nicholas got in a big fight with his dad, and they're still fighting and I'm freaking out because I'm worried this might be it—"

I stop to breathe and Darla takes it from there. Her voice fades in and out as the phone gets jostled around. "I'm already getting dressed. I'll sneak over and see what's going on. I can be there in like two minutes."

"Okay," I say, swallowing hard at the sight of the blinking cursor. No news. "Please hurry." No news is bad news. I hang up with Darla and wait.

Five minutes pass. She's probably there by now.

Ten minutes later I'm shredding a magazine, nervously rolling it up and ripping it to bits. I start typing just to keep my hands busy. *U ther? U ok?* But he doesn't answer.

I'm about ready to fly over there myself when a new message appears.

PendulousNB: *sorry . . . everything's fine*

Me: *u & ur dad talked it out?*

PendulousNB: *not exactly. it's fine tho, no worries*

Me: *u saw darla?*

PendulousNB: *yep*

Me: *so what happnd?*

PendulousNB: *i'm good . . . g2g, sorry . . . erly morning 2mrrw . . . nite*

He signs off before I have a chance to ask him anything else. I lie down on my bed, woozy and sick to my stomach. Call Darla again.

"Is he really okay?"

"I think so," she says. "He's acting weird, but his eyes weren't glowing or anything. He just didn't want to talk about what happened. And his dad's fine; I heard him clearing his throat really loud, so it's not like he got sucked into the vortex."

"His dad wants to send him to military school."

Darla sighs. "I know. I think it's just a scare tactic, but I'll check in with Nicholas after I wake up. Make sure he doesn't freak out too much. He's been really on edge lately."

"Sounds good. I'm just glad he's . . . and his dad's not . . ."

"Tell me about it." Darla yawns. "Okay. Too sleepy now. Talk to you tomorrow."

"Yeah. 'Night."

I close my eyes. Tell myself that I'm overtired, worried about nothing. Tomorrow everything will be fine. Nick's dad will chill—it's not like he never snuck out when he was young. And Darla will talk to Nicholas, and my mom will make pancakes or something because now that I'm an A student I'm pancake worthy, and I'm not going to think about anything else because not everything is my problem to solve and and and . . .

Sleep.

20

MY DAD AND I are eating coffee cake for breakfast (totally acceptable behavior so long as my mom's still in the bathroom) and watching the local news on TV. I'm recording it, ostensibly for a "media" project at school, but really because I want to preserve some footage of the rescued scouts for posterity. One day when I'm old I'm going to look back on this stuff, along with my yearbooks and prom pictures or whatever, and relive my glorious youth. It's important.

Finally! After sitting through a bunch of boring local-interest segments, the newscasters start introducing the rescue story and I sit up a little straighter. They cut to footage of the rescued scouts, wrapped in blankets and surrounded by their parents. My dad's slurping his coffee, nodding approvingly. "Glad those kids are safe."

I have to hide the smile on my face when the newscasters start talking about the "mysterious circumstances" of the rescue: how the scouts were missing for almost forty-eight hours before a group of anonymous teenagers found them and led them to safety. Meanwhile, a massive search party, rescue dogs, helicopters, and even sophisticated heat-detection equipment failed in the attempt.

"That's very mysterious, Tina."

"Indeed, Jim. However, the rescue may not be so mysterious after all. Rumor has it that local teen hero Avery Pirzwick is back in action. According to an eyewitness . . ."

My dad spews his coffee as my most recent school picture appears on the screen. My giddy smile changes to a horrified *O*.

"Pirzwick made national headlines last summer when he . . ."

I don't even have a chance to get out of the kitchen before the hammer comes down.

My dad slams his fist against the kitchen table—rattling his coffee cup and shocking the crap out of me. He doesn't usually get angry like that. He's supposed to be the understanding one.

"Do you know what could have happened to you out there? You need to leave this kind of work to professionals—people who are trained to do this! You can't just . . ."

My mom comes running into the kitchen like the house is on fire. She's only half made up; one set of eyelashes is significantly thicker and blacker than the other. She stopped mid-mascara to get the details and punish me—that's how bad this is.

I am so dead.

My dad stops yelling at me long enough to fill her in, and the two of them rewind the footage so my mom can get all the sordid details. She clutches the remote, watching and rewatching the segment, her forehead knotted with instant rage.

"Yale?" she snorts. "That's your excuse?!"

"Uh . . ."

Crap.

"It's going to take a hell of a lot more than stupidly risking your life to get into an Ivy League college, let me tell you that. You need to show good judgment if you ever even want to leave this house again, Avery—do you understand me?"

"I was trying to . . ." I'm having trouble articulating what I want to say. But I feel like I have to make them understand, at least partially. "I wanted to do something good. And I did, okay?"

"If you want to do something good, you need to concentrate on your schoolwork and on not getting in trouble," my dad says. "Leave being a hero to the professionals. That's not your responsibility."

"What if the rescue crews didn't find them in time, and they died? We ran into a mountain lion and—"

"A *what*?" my mom shouts.

"And if we hadn't been there, it would have attacked one of the kids. You can't tell me I don't have the training *to do something I just did*! You have no idea what I'm capable of!"

Damn it. I've crossed the line from articulating *why* I did it to pissing my parents off royally—especially my mom. But even my dad's looking explosive. My mom starts shouting about no more going out at night, they'll nail my window shut, send me to military school! Hell, maybe I can go with Nicholas. And I'm yelling back: "Just *try* to lock me up! See what I do then! See what I do!"

My heart's racing. I don't want to fight with them; I want them to understand, to be proud of me. But it's too late. We're at the point where backing down means giving in and admitting you were totally wrong. No compromise, no apologies—just groveling. And I won't do it. We saved those kids; we were capable and we knew it, even if no one else did. It was the right thing to do.

"Go to your room," my mom says, flushed and breathless, eyes radiating warning, "while we figure out what to do about this. And don't you dare sneak out."

I storm upstairs, slam my bedroom door so hard that the frame cracks. And for the first time, I don't care about the damage, don't care how they think it happened. I'm through explaining.

So now it's irresponsible to save lives? What the hell do they even know about it? I'm not doing drugs; I'm not joining a gang or dropping out of my crappy school or stealing cars or chugging a six-pack and then puking all over the front lawn.

Their lives could be so much worse.

Like, what if they didn't have me anymore? Couldn't tell me what to do anymore?

They'll never understand who I am. I'll never be free here. Even if they knew my secret, they'd overreact, smother me. Get overprotective, freak out. Or maybe they'd be afraid of me, and try to fix me: their bone-shattering, gravity-defying, superstrong son. We're barely the same species.

I shove open my window and climb out before they think to check on me, leaving everything behind except my wallet (flush with cash from my last blowout action-figure sale to the eBay kids down the street), and a worn, silver-and-white business card.

I buy a prepaid cell phone and dial the number my fingers have been tracing for the past few weeks: *escape.* I'm sick of hiding. I need to belong somewhere; I need to be myself. I'm not going to waste my talent, pretending to be less than I am when there are bigger things out there waiting for me.

"Hello?" Leilani's voice.

"It's Avery," I say. "Can I talk to—"

"Of course! One moment, please."

I'm hiding behind a Dumpster in the loading area behind one of the big box stores, nervous that I'll be found before I can do this—that my parents are already out looking for me, that they've called the police. Or that some reporter will stumble across me and take my picture.

I'm also scared to go through with it—to really join Cherchette, to leave everything behind. The prepaid-cell-phone packaging is fresh in the garbage out front. I ripped it in half and threw it away no more than five minutes ago.

Oh God. I hear the scrape of the phone as someone

picks up on the other line. I squat down and prop my head between my knees, nauseated as hell.

"Avery!" Cherchette says. "I am stunned, absolutely stunned by your recklessness—you and your little group. What were you thinking? Do you really want to get caught over something so stupid?"

W-what? What is she talking about? "It isn't stupid," I manage.

"It is, and you have truly outdone yourself this time. The press is sure to pay more attention now. How long do you think you have before someone uncovers your secret? Enough playing. It is time for you to come home."

I'm silent. My head's throbbing. More of the same.

Stupid . . .

"Where are you? I will pick you up. Avery? Hello?"

"No, you won't," I say. "Not until you . . ." I suck in a deep, raw breath; I don't even know what I want anymore. "It wasn't stupid. I know what I'm doing."

I throw the phone down, crush it under my heel because I know I'm lying, and because I know she'll call back. I've never felt more lost, more uncertain about what to do or where to go. I want to hurl this Dumpster across the parking lot. I want my heart to slow down.

I want . . .

~~~

Catherine's doorbell is broken so I bang on the door instead, rattling the screen, not afraid of her dad today because the black pickup truck is gone. I hope she's home, I hope she called off work after being out all night . . .

The back of my T-shirt is soaked with sweat. I scrambled through fields and backyards and the back lots of strip malls to get here, scared I'd run smack into Cherchette or my parents if I dared to show my face on the street.

The TV's on and I hear it click off; I hear voices and then little feet running before a door slams somewhere inside. Catherine opens the door a few seconds later, still in her pajamas, surprised to see me.

She hesitates. "Avery . . . you can't come to my house."

I shake my head, like *I don't know why and I don't care why.* "Are your parents home?"

"No, but . . ."

I walk past her and she doesn't stop me; take a seat on the sunken brown couch, eyeing a box of Lucky Charms and two half-empty cereal bowls on the coffee table. The milk is gray from all the melted-marshmallow colors mixing together in it.

I sigh, knead my temples like something physical is going to make this feeling go away. "So how are you?" I say, as if I'm not the one who barged in here, desperate for company.

"Um, I'm okay. Look, if you need to talk, we can go somewhere . . ."

"I'm hiding," I say. "My picture was on the news, when they did the segment on the rescued scouts. I dunno if you saw it . . ."

"I saw it."

"My parents are really mad about it. I don't know what's going to happen. I think I ran away." I push my fingers through my sweat-drenched hair, one step away from ripping it out. Catherine's watching me with her head tilted awkwardly, one bare foot resting on top of the other. Her ankles are showing below her too-short, candy-cane-striped pajama bottoms. "But I'm glad you came with us last night. And that mountain-lion trick . . . I don't know what the hell you did but that was unreal. Amazing."

"Good thing it worked," she says, sinking down next to me. "Otherwise you would've had to be like Batman and punch it in the face."

"Um." I screw up my face at her. "Batman does not punch animals."

"The hell he doesn't. Look it up sometime."

Hmm. I consider this: why would Batman beat up animals? It makes no sense. Wouldn't he have, like, knockout gas he could use on them instead? I'm not sure whether Catherine's lying, but it's a welcome distraction while it lasts.

"Probably you don't know because you don't actually read anything," Catherine says. "You probably get all your info from cartoons."

"Not true. I read stuff online."

Catherine groans. "Wait." She disappears down the hall and returns a moment later with a stack of books and graphic novels. "Do you see this? This is a book. *Book*—four-letter word, you should love it."

"I don't really like where this is going . . ."

She spreads them out on the coffee table. "I did something I didn't want to do—now it's your turn. If we're going to be friends you can't be an illiterate moron. Pick one. We've got future dystopia, *Uncanny X-Men: The Dark Phoenix Saga,* golden-age Batman, homeless drug-addict kids with miserable lives—"

"That one sounds tempting."

"Don't knock it; it has pictures. And, um, this one is full of depressingly awesome poetry." She slides it toward me, her hair hanging in her face, almost like she's embarrassed.

The poetry book is the most worn-out. The corners are split apart and fraying, like she's read it a hundred times. I pick it up and flip through it. Hmm. Poems are short at least.

"So if I read some of these, we can talk about powers?"

She nods happily and we shake on it. Okay. Deal. Not that I agree with that illiterate-moron part—that was way too harsh. I stack the beat-up poetry book and the comics next to me on the couch.

"So how'd you get that mountain lion to leave us alone?" I ask. "Can you talk to cats? I mean, you were speaking English to it."

"I don't think it understood my words. I don't usually *talk* to them. That was more for your benefit, so you knew what I was doing and didn't freak out and try to come to my rescue or something. It's more of a mental nudging, like . . . trading messages and impressions." She frowns. "Sorry if that sounds weird. I've never tried to explain it before."

"No, I think I get it," I say. "It's good to know I'm not the only one who's scared of you. Lions and tigers run away, too."

Catherine flops a pillow around on her lap, biting her lip like she's guarding against too big a smile. "I've never tried to bond with a big cat before. I was scared, but when it worked, it was like . . . wow. I've never felt anything like that."

Outside, the twittering of birds is interrupted by the impatient rumble of car tires over gravel, rolling to a stop. Catherine curses and grabs the cereal bowls, dashes to the kitchen and throws them into the sink, swirls the milk and mushy cereal down the drain. "My parents aren't supposed to be back for another three hours!" Her voice is shaky, almost shrill, as she goes through the motions of putting the dishes away.

"Maybe it's just someone turning around." I go to the window and peer out—then drop to the floor bank-robbery style.

There's an ice-blue Aston Martin in the driveway.

I force myself to the window for a second look. Cherchette's alone, striding across Catherine's uneven driveway, a shiny wrapped package in her arms: metallic silver paper, glittering in the sun, topped with a flouncy red bow.

Catherine comes back, wiping her wet hands on a

towel—and stops. She sees me crouched and instinctively lowers herself to the floor. "What is it?" she whispers.

"Something bad. I didn't want to involve you. But somehow she—"

We feel the house shudder then, hear the grating metal creak of a manual garage door being raised.

Catherine curses. The walls are thin so we can hear Cherchette's voice, although not what she's saying. The fact that she's speaking at all—in that soothing, sweet, sugarcoated tone—puzzles me. Who's she talking to?

"Not again. Why won't she ever . . . ?" Catherine grits her teeth, turns to me. "You have to go. It isn't about you; she's been here before. This is something I need to deal with."

Before I can argue, Catherine yanks me up by the elbow and marches me out the door. "I mean it," she says firmly. "If I find you here afterward, I'll kick your ass. Not everything is your problem."

"Fine, I'm going," I say, looking all offended. I storm down the street, not glancing back until I hear her run across the driveway, bare feet scattering the stones. Then I haul ass right back there and hide outside the garage.

I don't feel right about this; Cherchette's pissed—at me, at all of us. And now she shows up with a present, like it's somebody's birthday? Something's going on here, and there's no way in hell I'm leaving Catherine alone.

THERE—HOW DO you like it? A present for you and your sister." Cherchette's squatting neatly beside a small boy—maybe eight or nine?—who's curled up on a dirty mattress in the Drakes' garage. She's in pearls and high-heeled boots and a designer suit; the boy's so scrawny his elbows bulge like knobs on a tree; he's wearing dirt-streaked jeans and a several-sizes-too-big Incredible Hulk shirt: the one I bought for Henry. My throat closes up.

It's a heartwarming, messed-up picture, full of possibility: a socialite lavishing attention on a stray. Like when celebrities visit suffering children and they just *glow* next to them, and you think for a sec that, yeah, something is going to change, these kids' lives are going to improve, just by virtue of having been touched by someone so special.

"I like the paper," the boy says. His voice is rough and raspy, like it doesn't get used much.

"Go on, see what's inside," Cherchette urges, a lipstick-pink smile on her face.

The garage is filthy: the cement floor is run through with cracks and stained with oil, bags of garbage are piled everywhere, and broken furniture, boxes, and a cobwebbed

Christmas tree take up the rest of the space, turning the place into a claustrophobic cavern.

But that's not what sticks with me.

As the kid in the Incredible Hulk shirt leans over the package, unwrapping it with the utmost care, his straggly, dirty hair falls forward to reveal pointed ears. A long feline tail, sparsely coated with fine golden hair, twitches limply against the mattress.

There's a plastic water bowl next to him—like the kind you would use for a dog.

What the hell's going on here?

Catherine's staying back, hands on her hips, working herself up to something—I can see it in her face. But . . . what?

I wish she'd told me about this; I wish I knew what this was about. For now all I can do is watch and wait. Try to get a feel for the situation.

The boy folds the wrapping paper carefully, sets it beside him like it's a present in itself. He grins big as he lifts a huge LEGO castle out of the box. "Cool," he says.

"I have so many more gifts for you at home. I would bring them here but I don't think your parents would like that," Cherchette says with a pout.

"No . . ."

"There's a girl who lives with me who is just like you. She also had to hide away from the world. Her teeth are like a piranha's. And her skin is like a shark's. But where I live, she is free to show herself and make friends. She is not a monster, she is special. How does that sound?"

Cherchette's voice is warm with reassurance. The boy is nodding along.

"It sounds nice."

Catherine breaks the silence then; she grips her hips with two tight fists. "We're not interested. And stop talking to him like he's five."

"I'm sorry—did I offend you?"

"He's small; he's not retarded," Catherine says. "You can't just buy him presents and expect him to fall for your lies."

"Always so hostile." Cherchette tsks. "I am only concerned for your welfare, and Charlie's. You should want your twin brother to be happy, not to remain here when a better life awaits."

Wait—*what??*

This little kid is Catherine's twin?

"He'll have a better life," Catherine says, stalking forward. "I'll make sure of it."

"Oh—your pitiful coffee-shop job?" Cherchette purses her lips. "You think you can support two people with that pittance? Where will you live—outdoors? How will you ensure that he is not discovered?"

"As long as he's away from you, he'll be fine."

"I am offering you both a lifeline," Cherchette says, "and you are foolish not to take it. You insist on having things your own way, and in the meantime your brother leads an animal's life. I have been patient with you, I have tried to make you understand—but the time is up, Catherine. We both know where you belong."

"Get out!" Catherine shouts.

Cherchette smoothes her narrow skirt as she stands up. "Charlie, darling, how would you like to sleep in a warm, clean bed tonight, in a beautiful house, with good things to eat, and friends and games to play with, and a swimming pool to swim in and a trampoline? Doesn't that sound heavenly? Wouldn't you like your sister to be there with you?"

Charlie nods, his eyes glittering, entranced by Cherchette and her promises.

Catherine's face is flushed with anger. Tears spring to her eyes. "It's too good to be true and we both know it. Charlie isn't going to fall for that any more than I would."

"Charlie and I are leaving," Cherchette says. "With or without you, Catherine. But I suggest you join us. Or else he will miss you very much." Cherchette takes the boy's tiny hand and something in Catherine snaps.

Claws splayed, she leaps at Cherchette.

Ten claws slam into an unyielding ice wall—a shield that built itself in fast-forward: from fog to rock-hard in a split second. Catherine crumples, gasping like she got the wind knocked out of her, cradling her left hand. One of her claws is broken off. Blood trickles from her injured finger.

"You little minx," Cherchette says. "That was very stupid."

Cherchette is icy cool and the air around her is getting colder. I'm frozen in place except for the uncontrollable shaking, holding tight to the wall, trying to keep my knees from banging into the garage.

"Must you fear me in order to respect me? Is that why you've never raised a hand against your parents?" Cherchette tugs Charlie's shirt up, revealing a skinny torso studded with bruises. "Explain to me—you are a coward then, so you have to be a hero now?"

"Shut up!" Catherine struggles to one knee. "Get the hell away from him!"

"You're in no position to give orders, dear. It's time you learned that."

Spikes of ice rain down from the ceiling. Catherine raises her hands to protect herself and an icy wind hits her like a massive slap, knocking her into a pile of broken furniture. Nail-ridden chairs and table legs topple with the impact, pinning her to the ground.

"It appears you were a bit too sure of yourself," Cherchette says as Catherine makes a feeble attempt to claw her way out of the wreckage. "Are you ready to behave? You're upsetting your brother, you know."

Catherine strikes back with probably the most offensive string of curse words I've ever heard. She spits them and they turn to ice on her lips. Charlie huddles against one wall, hugging himself.

"I won't tolerate such disrespect," Cherchette says. A miniature blizzard swirls above her palm, ice crystals snapping in the frigid air. Her eyes are as blank and white as frosted glass. "I've come to help you, to save you from this wretched life, but you will *not* speak to me that way. You stupid little fool—this is going to hurt terribly and it's all your fault."

Something's changing in Cherchette; Catherine's prone and helpless, but Cherchette is not backing off. The cold above her palm is gathering into a spiny, shimmering orb, spiked with icicles like the head of a frozen mace. She curls her lips back and raises her arm as if to hurl the orb at Catherine.

The sight jolts me into action, reminds me that I can move. My feet barely touch the ground as I launch myself from my hiding spot, tackling Cherchette and slamming us both into a pile of cardboard boxes. The orb explodes on contact, spiny icicles biting into my skin like blades. Frost blasts my face, blinding me. The boxes tumble around us and Cherchette cries out in pain.

I pry my frozen eyelids apart with trembling fingers.

Cherchette is guarding her ribs, fingers pressed delicately to her side. Her eyes are iced over to the point where it's like she doesn't recognize me. Nostrils flaring rhythmically. *Revenge.*

"I'm sorry," I say. "I didn't mean to—I didn't know what else to—"

My words are wasted on her. Cherchette grasps my throat and squeezes, cold shooting through her fingertips and into my jaw, my brain. I'm shuddering with pain, some kind of massive internal shutdown: throat closing up, my lungs close to frozen. And I can't think. Can't— everything is—so—slow.

Just. Blue. In front of my eyes. Blacking out. And.

Cherchette gasps. She cries out in a language I don't understand, tears herself away from me. My vision floods back, just in time to see the horrified look on her face. She stumbles out of the garage, steps as unsteady as my heartbeat. Slams herself into her car, frantic. The Aston Martin reverses quickly, kicking up stones as the heat rushes back to my brain, and I can move again.

She lost control. I could see it. I thought she was superior to us, perfectly in control of her powers and emotions at all times. Witnessing Cherchette lose it is almost as much of a shock as seeing her true self. Her anger. The violence she's ready to unleash when she doesn't get what she wants.

Catherine kicks the last piece of furniture away from her and grabs my face, turns it this way and that—scared, I think. "That bad?" I manage.

"It's like she burned you. Damn it! Damn her! She's like, she's freaking worse than—" Catherine's eyes flick around until they land on Charlie. He's busy hiding inside his Incredible Hulk shirt, tugging the front over his bent knees. "I'll get something to clean it. Alcohol or—"

"Don't worry about me," I say, struggling not to bite through my tongue the first time I stretch my neck. Agggh. It kills. "Are you all right?"

"Fine." She sucks on her injured fingertip, sourly. "But—" She turns on her brother then. "What the hell, Charlie?" she shouts. "What did I tell you about her? We're going away on our own! You can't trust her! Why don't you listen to me?"

"Leave him alone," I say. "She just scared the crap out

of him; she almost killed his sister. I know you're pissed but you're picking the wrong target."

"What are we supposed to do?" Catherine says. "How are we going to get out of this?"

She curls up and jams her head against her knees, and then she's crying, so I wrap my arms around her and squeeze—the kind of hug that could crack someone's ribs, if I wasn't careful. But I can control it. I can control it enough not to hurt my friend.

"Is this my fault?" she asks. "What they're doing to him? Because I won't—because I can't stop it yet?"

"No," I say. "Your parents are supposed to be there for you. They're supposed to help when you have a problem, not punish you for it. It's not your fault. You shouldn't have to choose between the lesser of two evils."

"Three evils," she sniffs. "I'm the third one. I can't offer him a good life either, can I? I'm trying, but . . . it's totally unrealistic, like she said."

"She can't tell you how it'll turn out. No one knows that yet."

Catherine wipes her eyes on her pajama top. Skin still red and raw, a bruise forming on her cheek. "I guess. Look, if you tell anyone about this . . ."

Not that again. I bump her with my head, squeeze a little harder. "Catherine, shut up. Seriously. Just trust me for five seconds."

I sit with her until she calms down, my mind racing—that argument with my parents seems so far away. I watch

Charlie, wonder how his mom and dad could do this to him—even though I know stuff like this happens all the time, to kids who don't even have anything supposedly "wrong" with them. He's in the corner, playing quietly, folding and unfolding the silver wrapping paper. Occasionally he looks at us—territorial or lonely or confused, I'm not sure.

Charlie's a secret. The police can't be called, social workers can't come to his rescue. If he were discovered, who knows what would happen to him? So what good is all that *professional* hero training? What good is patrolling my neighborhood every day if I can't save the one kid who has no one else to help him?

I promise Catherine I'll call her later. Right now I have to concentrate on what I *can* do: which is warn the team.

I need to tell Darla she was right about Cherchette.

22

I RUN THE WHOLE WAY to Darla's house: chest heaving, lungs and throat raw. It's too bright to fly. It's a beautiful, horrible day.

I check the shed—home of the family lawn mower and the site of Darla's workshop—first, hoping I can bypass meeting her family, doing the whole hello-how-are-you-by-the-way-I'm-Avery thing, but it's padlocked. I'm about to turn around and head for the house when I notice a folded piece of paper wedged under the door. It's most of the way inside, but with a little careful maneuvering I manage to pry it out.

It's a letter.

From Nicholas.

I don't want you to worry about me, D. And don't try to fix this, because you can't.

I've made the decision to leave with C.M.

I really think it's best for me and everyone else; it's nothing you did or didn't do. I just can't take any more risks. I came so close to doing the unthinkable

last night . . . and the scary part is, I almost wanted
to. To get it over with. I can't let that happen again.
Please tell everyone good-bye, and I'm sorry.
　—N

———————————————————

"H uh, whass—" Darla flips over in bed, blinking feebly like a mole who's suddenly been exposed to sunlight. Her Hello Kitty sheets are tangled around her legs, her camouflage fleece blanket is in a lump on the floor. She fumbles for her glasses and sits up, straightening her too-tight Transformers pajamas. They look like they were sized for a ten-year-old boy.

"Frigging hell, how late do you sleep?" I don't mean to yell at her but I can't help it. "It's three in the afternoon! You were supposed to talk to Nicholas, remember?"

"I was up till like six. Jeez. Why, did something happen?" She lifts up her glasses and rubs the sleep out of her eyes. Squints at my neck. "Um, did you burn yourself with a curling iron? Like twenty times?"

"No," I say. "Cherchette tried to choke the life out of me. But then she changed her mind, which is the only reason I'm still alive to tell you that Nicholas left with her. Presumably before she tried to kill me."

Darla's mouth opens. I can see her trying to figure out the appropriate response, like: is he joking? I pull Nick's note out of my pocket and toss it on her bed. It takes her about ten seconds to read it.

"He what?!" Darla explodes. I try to quiet her with a

fierce shushing motion. I already went through one round of interrogation with Darla's nana when I got here; I'm not really eager for round two.

"He lives right down the street and I didn't even— damn it! Why didn't I know he was really considering this?" Darla punches one of the doe-eyed Japanese stuffed animals off her bed. Punching it must not be satisfying enough, because she gets up and punts it across the room. "I was supposed to protect him! That was the whole point!"

Two more stuffed animals bear the brunt of her anger before she grabs her cell phone and punches Sophie's speed-dial number. "Code red, Soph. Nicholas blew the proverbial Popsicle stand and went over to the dark side. I hate to ask for his help, but I need to know what the ice boy knows about this." She pauses and I hear Sophie's voice chirping through the speaker. Darla grimaces. "Fine, what *Jacques* knows about this. And tell him *thank you*."

Darla starts pulling street clothes on over her pajamas. "I need information, Avery. Anything you think would be helpful."

"Cherchette's messed up. Dangerous. I think she's running out of patience. She wants some of us, and . . ." I tell Darla everything I can remember. The things Cherchette said to Catherine, the way she attacked. My mind's a jumble of sensations: the way the heat left my body as soon as we collided; the pain of my veins being shot through with ice.

By the time I finish my story, Darla's on her way to

a massive un-genius-like freak-out. "I *knew* she was corrupt—and dangerous insofar as, like, killing his belief in himself, which I was *fighting* to keep alive. But if she hurts him . . ."

Darla grabs her backpack and starts stuffing supplies into it: her Taser inhaler; a box of chamomile tea; a purple Magic 8 Ball that has a strip of masking tape across the back, labeling it CONCUSSION GRENADE PROTOTYPE. DO NOT TOUCH!! "We have to hurry! Who knows what she's done to him since she picked him up?"

"Just . . . try to calm down. We can't do anything until Jacques gets here. We don't even know where Nicholas is." I do my best to take my own advice. Sit down at the edge of Darla's messy bed and will Sophie and Jacques to hurry. I try not to torment myself with questions, but it's impossible. Nicholas doesn't know what he's gotten himself into—and the scary thing is, neither do we. What does Cherchette really intend? Why does she want us so badly? She swings back and forth between loving and vicious—where's that needle going to stop when it comes to Nicholas? And will we get there in time to save Nicholas from whatever she has in store for him?

When Sophie and Jacques finally arrive, I'm no calmer than I was thirty minutes ago. I've worked myself into a nervous frenzy, and Darla's even worse.

"Bedroom door stays open," Nana C. reminds us, eyeing Jacques and me suspiciously.

Darla looks like her brain's about to pop. "Oh yeah, right!" she grumbles. "Like I'm going to have a top-secret superhero conversation with my nana eavesdropping in the hall. Let's go to my workshop."

I fill Sophie in on the way, whispering what happened at Catherine's house. It seems rude to relate this stuff directly to Jacques, so I don't—but I'm pretty sure he hears every word. He looks nervous, especially unsettled when I tell Sophie how Cherchette attacked us, and how it seemed like she'd snapped, like she'd decided that our time was finally up.

Darla unchains the shed doors and ushers us inside, stopping to attach a tiny surveillance robot before she slams them shut. She punches a code into an electronic keypad on the wall, and a stilted, soothing voice announces: *"Defense mechanisms activated: nonlethal."* "I just know Nana will show up with cookies eventually. I need to be prepared."

The interior of the shed is ruled by the most bizarre organizational system known to man—er, Darla. Like, you know how you insist you shouldn't have to clean your messy room because *you* know where everything is? Picture that, only with a high-tech bejeweled supercomputer instead of a bed, tools and weapons and welding equipment all over the floor instead of dirty clothes, and a giant purple robot sitting where the closet would be, his tree-trunk-size legs bent in front of him, like an enormous sulky kid stuck in the corner.

"Uh, is that a giant robot?" I ask.

"Of course it's a giant robot," Darla snaps, clearly unimpressed with my observational skills. She plunks her overstuffed backpack down on her gadget-strewn inventing table—and considering she's got an untested concussion grenade in that bag, she's either gone totally mad or is insanely stressed.

I can relate. At least Darla never talked about Cherchette like she was a potential mentor, a role model just waiting for the right opportunity. I didn't know how far Cherchette was willing to go, but I *wanted* to believe in her—and I feel like it's partly my fault that Nicholas believed in her. Every time Darla brought up the warning signs, I had to play devil's advocate. So if anything bad happens to him . . . that will be partly my fault, too.

Sophie browses the new weapons stash, ever the optimist, like everything will be fine as long as we have enough firepower. She aims a futuristic-looking, pink assault rifle at the giant robot's head and mimes shooting it. "Bam! Okay, I want this one."

"It's a prototype. It's not ready yet." Darla sighs. "It's a dynamic pain cannon, also with a stun setting. It overloads the nerves with pain without causing physical damage. I haven't really been able to test it . . ."

Jacques looks uncomfortable in the midst of all this pain-producing technology—not that I blame him. I'm feeling a little queasy myself. "You wanted to know about Nicholas," he says. "What is it you think I can do for you?"

"Well, first off, you can tell us where he is," Darla says. "And what your crazy mom plans to do with him."

Jacques's jaw tightens, and Sophie shoots Darla a dirty

look. Obviously the genius is too stressed to be diplomatic, so I jump in.

"What Darla's trying to say is that she's going to shut up now. We're worried about Nicholas. We think that, um . . ." *Your mom is dangerous? Out of her mind?* I can't exactly say that to Jacques. "We think he made a hasty decision. He's been having trouble at home, and . . ."

"Of course he has been having trouble," Jacques says. "He possesses a vortex that kills people. He has gone with my mother to learn how to control it so that he will not be a danger to himself, or his family. It's not as if he's the only one. Leilani has been with us for months." The air in the workshop chills when Jacques mentions Leilani. He seems to drift for a second, his focus leaving us, his eyes growing stormy—a darker, brooding blue.

Oh yeah—you can feel the love there.

"Right," Sophie says softly. "But Leilani was alone. She didn't have anyone else. Nicholas has us. We're still going to help him. We just . . . we need your help in order to do that." Sophie stops herself and takes Jacques's arm, turns toward him. Like maybe he'll loosen up if he's less aware of Darla and me.

"I don't want to strain your relationship with your mom," Sophie says. "But Nicholas is making a huge mistake here. And you remember, you said . . . that lately she's been . . ." She bites her lip, peers up at him like she's willing him to fill in the blanks. I wish one of them would just say it.

That lately she's been . . . ?

Wild? Reckless? Erratic? Mad?

"The way she lost control with Avery and Catherine . . . doesn't that fit in with what you were worried about? You don't have to be involved," Sophie says. "She doesn't ever have to know who told us."

"Who else would tell you?" Jacques mumbles. A long sigh escapes him and he leans against Darla's inventing table, his arm trembling like mine does after too much caffeine.

"We could have heard from Nicholas." Sophie shrugs, takes a quick breath, and dives in again. "I know it's an uncomfortable situation for you, so Darla and Avery and I will go. We'll handle it. But we need to know where to find him. We can't leave him there. He's our friend. He needs our support. We need to keep him safe. Please, Jacques." She's pleading with him with big blue eyes, as sweet and earnest as the manga girls she draws. Jacques hesitates, like he's dying to say no, but can't—he crumbles under the weight of that stare.

"Fine," Jacques says. "But you have to promise to stay here."

"Me?" Sophie rapid-fire blinks. "But—"

"I'll take Avery if he's willing, but no one else."

"I'm not breaking up the team," Darla says, bristling.

"You don't have a choice," Jacques says. "Avery is the only one who has a chance at defending himself if something goes wrong."

"If something goes *wrong*?" Darla says. "I have a whole contingency plan for that scenario. It's called 'say hello to my *Carminotoxin* truth serum and tell me exactly what I want to hear, before I incapacitate you and trap you in a sauna!' I'm not leaving Avery at the mercy of you and your manipulative mother, ice boy, and if you think—"

"Darla!" Sophie shouts. "Shut! Up!"

Darla's face flushes almost as pink as that girly assault rifle, but she flops down in her inventor's chair and shuts her mouth. Sophie grabs the back of Darla's chair and wheels her into a corner, talks to her quietly. Jacques takes his cell phone out to check the time, agitated.

"What am I going to have to defend myself against?" I finally ask, fairly certain I know the answer.

Jacques shakes his head slowly, pushes his platinum hair out of his face. "I hope nothing. My mother has an appointment tomorrow morning. A follow-up with her surgeon. She may cancel it, because of Nicholas. I don't know. But it's our best chance, to go there when she is away, and then perhaps—"

"If she isn't going to be there, we can all go," Sophie says brightly. "It shouldn't matter then whether I can defend myself. I think Nicholas would feel good if he saw the whole team, and saw how much he means to us."

"No," Jacques says firmly. "I won't discuss this anymore. My mother will have brought Nicholas to the house, which is a significant distance away from here. We need to leave now or not at all."

He won't look at me; he's busy icing up his fingers and then scraping the frost away with his nails. Repeatedly. Distracted. And I wonder, is he lying to us? Is he setting me up? Jacques and I have never really been friends. But he seems nervous, ready to bolt. I don't want to push him and make him change his mind—not when Nicholas's future is at stake. Which means there's no time for questions.

"I'm ready," I say.

"Fine. But this is a horrible idea," Darla mutters, hugging me tightly, a little too long. "We're not leaving you on your own. I'm going to come up with a plan, and I'll—"

"Please don't," Jacques says. "You have no idea what you are dealing with. You'll only make things worse."

Darla does something weird then—I mean weird even for her. She throws her arms around Jacques in this intense embrace, hands roaming across his back before she pulls away. I have to blink a few times to make sure I'm not delirious. That was like watching my dad French-kiss a raccoon—I feel violated on so many levels.

"Good luck," she says, totally avoiding eye contact.

"Would you *please* reconsider?" Sophie says. "It might be good to have more support. I mean, if something bad *does* happen . . ."

"Absolutely not. I don't want you there, Sophie. Your power doesn't interest her. If you make her angry, you're completely expendable—she doesn't respond well to defiance. Promise me you won't get involved."

"But—"

"I am so serious about this," Jacques says. "I have never been more serious about anything. Please: stay here." His expression is totally bare, almost pleading with her. I feel like I'm looking at a different person, because there's no awareness of *me* in his eyes, no anger, irritation, pride. He cares about her.

And I do, too. "He's probably right. It'll be an easy in-and-out, faster with just the two of us," I say, even though I'm growing less sure of this by the moment.

I swallow. Jacques is talking about his mom here—what's he so afraid of? I mean, if her own son is taking these kinds of precautions . . . either he's determined to see me crash and burn alone, or Cherchette's even more disturbed than I thought.

"Well, okay then." Sophie hesitates; fidgets, then turns on her thousand-watt smile again. "I *do* have faith in you guys. Make us proud, team! Woot!" She steps forward and smacks me on the ass, like a too-cute football coach getting friendly before a game. I seriously cannot speak after she does that. "But be careful," Sophie says. "Bring Nicholas back safe. And if you need me . . ." She holds up her cell phone, looking worried-hopeful, and wishes us luck.

***

A nd that's how I end up in Jacques' car that evening, speeding along the highway, towns whipping by us, some kind of moody trip hop on the radio.

I rub my hands together to warm them up, but it's more a symbolic gesture than anything. Jacques's focus is barely on me and the temps seem to stay pretty regular. I try to think of something to say, some normal way to interrupt the silence.

"How long of a ride is it?"

"Not long," he says. "We're going a bit out of our way to dispose of this." He leans forward in his seat and reaches around behind him, fingers plucking awkwardly at his jacket until he comes away with a sliver of lavender plastic, about the size of a girl's fingernail, with spiky metal teeth on the back.

"Tracking device," he explains. "Unless your friend plans to kill me and has made a miniature bomb. But I doubt it."

"How did you . . . ?"

Jacques gives me a look like he knows the difference between a girl who likes him and a girl who's tagging him. "Something very strange about that good-bye."

Wow. Darla has no shame. Pretty ingenious scheme, though. I wonder what she'd think if she knew Jacques saw right through it.

Silence again. The incessant mellow beat of the music wraps around me, helps me lose myself in my thoughts. We're traveling via local roads now, not the highway, but it still all looks the same. A "Welcome to Wherever" sign, and then miles of homes, or nothingness, the endless road lulling me into a passive, thoughtful state.

"So why do you hate me?" I ask. The question bubbles up before I think to clamp down on it.

Jacques raises his eyebrows, surprised. It takes him a second to collect himself. But he looks like he's considering it, so . . . I guess that means there's something to consider. "I don't know that it's accurate to say I hate you. Maybe I did. Or I thought I did."

"Because of Sophie?"

"Why would it involve Sophie?"

I clear my throat. "No reason."

Jacques turns the wheel, hand over hand, as we take a curve. "You were an idea to me before you were a person. I knew you on paper first. And if you had remained paper, I would have shredded you. That's how I felt. I know this doesn't make sense to you. I don't expect it to. I can explain, but I'm not sure how healthy it is for you to know this."

"My life hasn't exactly been easy lately," I say. "I can take—"

"Your life is very easy," Jacques interrupts. "You have no idea how lucky you are. Your powers are a burden to you sometimes—is that what you base this 'difficulty' on? You don't wish to be discovered. You lose control on occasion and things go badly for you. But you are a diamond in the rough. You have amazing potential. Surely you know that about yourself."

"I don't know." Fields and houses speed past us in the dark. People's lives. Families. I wonder what my parents are thinking. If they're angry. Or worried. And whether this is fair. Whether I was a total A-hole to them this morning. They don't deserve me—that's for sure. And I don't mean that like I'm a prize. Like I have amazing *potential*. I mean they shouldn't have to put up with me. My dad shouldn't be working a sixth day a week because of me. My mom shouldn't be freaking that she can't leave the job she hates, the boss she hates, because they don't know when I'm going to put them in debt next.

"I don't feel very amazing," I say finally.

"Well, my mother thinks you are amazing. You're the pinnacle of what we could be. A human being who defies gravity, who has the strength of a hundred men. A human miracle. And I . . . I am a poor copy, a second-generation imitation. Of very little value, compared to you."

"She doesn't think that," I say.

"You represent something more to her," he goes on. "You are the future. We are all born with the same raw materials—but look what you've become." He smiles bitterly. "And if I don't surpass you, it's my own fault. It's because something in me is lacking. She's so simplistic it's infuriating."

The chill in the car is growing, reaching out, like ghostly tendrils slowly strangling the warmth out of me. I curl up in the seat to get smaller—I don't care how stupid it looks.

"Maybe it wouldn't be so bad if I hadn't spent my entire life trying to be what she wanted, only to be told that was impossible, because I wasn't you. I will *never* be you. And so the next best thing, I suppose, was proving to myself that you weren't what she wanted either. But you are," he says. "What am I supposed to do about that?"

My body's juddering, breath leaking out like steam. Jacques is pushing forward, lost in whatever he's feeling, and I don't know what to say to bring him back. "That can't be true," I say. "No matter what my powers are, I'm just some random kid; you're her *son*."

"Anyone can be a parent," he says quietly. "My mother needs more than that."

Jacques slows to a stop at a red light and finally notices me convulsing. The tendrils of cold retract. Blood rushes back to my fingertips. My nerves tingle as they thaw out.

"I'm sorry," he says. "That was unintentional."

I nod, wanting to believe him.

Jacques takes a few moments to compose himself, and I cup my hands together over my mouth, blow warm air into my palms. I might be stronger, but Jacques manages to nail my weak point every time. He can incapacitate me without even trying. I need him to look at this differently, or we're both in trouble.

"Your mom's opinion isn't the only one that matters," I say, forcing the words out because I know the next few are going to be even harder. "Sophie thinks you're awesome. When we caught that mugger at the park, she said you were hands down our MVP. Not a loser." The reject list conversation Darla and I had with Sophie flashes through my mind. "Or does it not matter to you what she thinks? Since according to your mom, Sophie's a loser, too?"

"I don't agree with my mother's evaluation of Sophie."

I figured that—but I'm trying to get the wheels turning. Jacques is alternating between hot and cold, flushing one moment, chilling the air the next—like he's struggling with something, but isn't sure how to say it. "My mother . . . doesn't see what she has in front of her some-times. There are very specific things that she wants to achieve, and life is too short to waste time on people she doesn't value. I . . . admit that I have spent too much of my life being frustrated with her opinions, rather than ques-tioning her judgment. But when I found Sophie on my mother's exclusion list, I was curious. My mother was oc-cupied, doting on her 'chosen ones'; I had very little to do, and here was a girl my mother deemed worthless . . . like me. I wondered if I would view her that way, too, if I met her. But I decided that my mother was wrong."

"If she was wrong about Sophie, maybe she was wrong about you, too," I say.

Jacques sighs. His tense smile seems sad, a little angry. "Maybe."

Knowing that we're starting to understand each other should probably make me feel better—but it doesn't. Everything is still so uncertain between us. And I don't just have Jacques to worry about—there's Nicholas, too. What if I tell him the truth about Cherchette, and he still wants to stay? I'm hoping that he's already having second thoughts, and that if a way out presents itself, he'll take it. But if he's firm about staying . . .

"Do we have a plan?" I ask Jacques.

"In, out," he says. "As quickly as possible. We do not use hired security; no one will be on the lookout for you, so long as my mother is absent. It's up to you to convince Nicholas. You should have about an hour to do so, but the faster we get out of there the better."

"Agreed," I say. I don't want to face Cherchette again. Once she finds out I'm unraveling the web she spun to snare Nicholas—on top of what I already did to her at Catherine's—there's no telling how she'll react. She stopped herself from killing me once, but I might not be so lucky a second time. And considering how easily Jacques's power can bring me to my knees, I don't think I'll stand much of a chance if Cherchette unleashes her full fury.

When Jacques finally stops the car, it's at a fast-food restaurant hours away. The sun's starting to set. Jacques pulls me out of the Jaguar and instructs me to lift my arms up, then proceeds to brush off my shirt like he's trying to dislodge a stubborn insect. Or, uh, maybe a tracking device.

"Your hands are really cold," I say.

"Deal with it. We can't have the girls following us." I wince and make faces and wait for it to be over. I mean, I agree with him—but it wouldn't kill the guy to wear gloves.

When beating my shirt, and even checking the inside of my collar, doesn't produce a second lavender sliver, Jacques steps back. Satisfied that I haven't been tagged, he drops his own tracking device down a sewer grate.

"Don't you think it'll be a little suspicious when Darla's GPS leads her here?"

Jacques smirks. "It will fit perfectly with what she already assumes about my family. A subterranean fortress below Burger King."

We stop inside for dinner, kill time slurping shakes. We

still have to drive back—cover all the ground we covered to get here, but in reverse. After that, Jacques claims it won't take us long to get to Cherchette's. But we'll have to wait until morning to enter the house so that we can grab Nicholas while she's gone. That means hours and hours before we'll see him.

Hours and hours for something to go wrong.

I try not to think about that on the way back. Instead I try to visualize success, walk myself through a house I've never been in, imagine the moment we find Nicholas, imagine myself making this perfect argument and Nick agreeing to come home. I try to psych myself up like I would before a match. But this isn't a game. It's *too* real. Jacques's moody music holds on to me and pushes me deeper into my thoughts.

Sometime later that night, Jacques murmurs that we're nearing his home. He drives the Jaguar down a dead-end road, empty except for trees and the "Private Property: No Trespassing" signs that are staked into the ground every few hundred feet. He parks beneath a tree with heavy, drooping branches, a threatening sentinel in the dark. "We'll wait here until morning." My heart's thudding, just knowing Cherchette's so close—almost afraid she'll sense us, come crashing through the trees that border the abandoned road.

Jacques shifts in his seat, stares into the darkness, a chill wafting from his skin with every creak of the leather. I need to get some sleep, but my mind's racing, impatient for the seconds to tick away and bring us closer to

Nicholas so this can all be over—so we can be okay. Back home. Safe. I try to hold on to these thoughts, to keep the icy fears at bay, but memories of my last encounter with Cherchette swirl through my mind. Like waking nightmares. Only worse, because they've already come true.

I must drift off at some point, because when I open my eyes, the Jaguar is gliding toward an immense, Victorian-style mansion: a cross between a fairy-tale palace and a haunted house. The grounds extend as far as I can see, wild with a sea of unkempt grass. Barren rosebushes tangle together into a wall of thorns—and there are no neighbors for miles, no one to get too curious or ask questions. Flaking paint and crooked shingles reveal themselves as we drive closer. I yawn, stretch, too bleary to be really nervous. My muscles are stiff and the warmth of the early morning sun lingers on my clothes.

"This is good," Jacques says as we pull into the empty four-car garage. "I worried she might cancel her appointment because of Nicholas. But her car is gone. We have until . . . at least ten. Leilani sleeps in; I don't think we'll see her. But keep your voice down."

With that last bit of advice, Jacques unlocks the house door with a resounding *thunk.*

The house is quiet except for the hum of appliances, the ticking of various clocks. Our footsteps are muted by plush, dark carpets patterned with flowers. Jacques motions *this way,* and I follow him through a series of rooms, all furnished elaborately like we're in Versailles or something.

The air is stuffy with strong perfume, the cloying scent of candles and furniture polish. The whole place is sealed up like a crypt. Most of the curtains are pulled. In the rare place where the sun filters in, it bounces off clear glass display cases filled with warped, plastic fashion dolls. Their cheekbones are sharp, like Barbie went under the knife. Every last one of them has platinum-blond hair, and full lips the color of blood.

Jacques only does a cursory walk-through of the main floor; he says Nicholas is probably asleep, so we head upstairs to where the bedrooms are. Jacques points out his own, Leilani's, Cherchette's, the bathrooms; we avoid those. He runs his hand across the rest of the doorknobs in the long, narrow corridor: twin rows of rooms like in an old hotel.

"He's not here. Not enough body heat. The rooms are empty."

"Check again." The hinges creak as I open one of the doors. Inside I find a perfectly made bed, open curtains, sunshine streaming in. Fresh flowers on a bedside table.

Nothing.

But there are other rooms. I abandon the first one, check the adjacent room. And then the room across the hall. And—

Jacques stops me with an icy hand. "He's not here."

"Where then?"

We descend the stairs to the first floor again—creaky

wood steps covered by thin, rose-colored carpet—and Jacques heads to a sort of den or TV room and flops down on a leather couch. Searches under it for the remote. "Where is it?" he murmurs, practically upside down now, shoving books and papers aside in his search.

There's a huge flat-panel TV mounted on the wall—the one nod to the current century. "Uh, are you missing your favorite show or something?"

"Hardly," Jacques says, emerging with the remote. He punches a series of buttons and the wall that holds the TV slides away, revealing a heavy steel door.

Jacques steps forward to be identified by the door's retinal scanner. "This is where the real work is done," he says as the door beeps in recognition and swings open. "If my mother is serious about him, Nicholas will be here."

We step through into a stark-white, auditorium-size room, shiny and sterile like a hospital: a supersecret headquarters tacked onto the back of Cherchette's mansion. The floor is covered with white tiles, and there are no windows—only glass panels that allow you to look into other rooms, like when you're at the gym and you want to check out what's going on in the racquetball court or the swimming pool.

And there *is* a swimming pool. Through the observation window, I see a gray-skinned girl doing laps, what look like webbed hands and feet gliding through the water. Jacques motions for me to follow (actually it's more of a "stop staring, idiot; we have work to do") and we hurry across the room to a sort of hub: a main desk equipped with monitor screens and a control panel. Jacques keys in a password, rotates the surveillance screens until we see Nicholas.

He's alone. A grainy figure in a barren room. Leaning closer, I realize he's not wearing his trench coat. He's bare-chested, clenching his fists.

"What's he doing? His coat is, like, his one safeguard. I don't understand why he'd—"

"Shall we find out?" Jacques says.

The steel door beeps again and we freeze. Jacques has the sense to close down the surveillance screens, but other than that, he doesn't move. Doesn't turn around. His grip tightens on the mouse.

Please let it be Leilani, I think. *Please.*

The hospital-style flooring turns Cherchette's strut into a tap dance. *Click. Click. Clickclickclick.* Mixed with a defeated sound. Something heavy being dragged along the floor. We're mostly hidden behind the monitors. I don't think she's noticed me yet.

"Jacques," Cherchette says—her voice harsh but shrill, wavering along its upper register. "Here you are. Well, look at me. I require your assistance."

We both step out to greet her. I need to look composed. To show her I'm not afraid of her. To . . .

But I can't.

Damn it. Damnitdamnitdamnit.

She went back. After I left Catherine's, she went back.

Cherchette's standing a few feet away from the steel door: hair mussed, a fresh red scratch on her face. One gloved hand clutches Catherine's shirt, which she's using as a sort of handle to drag her around. Catherine's head is slumped forward; her whole body's limp.

"Very interesting," Cherchette says curtly. "To what do I owe this surprise?"

Jacques grabs my shoulders and urges me forward. "I brought him to you. Avery knows he made a mistake."

What? This had better be part of the plan to save our asses, and not the ultimate goal of the treacherous plot Darla's been so freaked about.

Leilani's posed with one hand on her hip, ponytailed and dressed for a workout. "Well, I'm glad we have some muscle here. I thought I was going to have to shift into a big hulking thing to get the cat-girl into observation."

"That won't be necessary," Jacques says, lifting Catherine's limp body off the floor. Cherchette's watching us curiously. And I'm . . . shaking. What happened to Cherchette's appointment? Did Jacques just screw up or . . . ?

"Avery," Cherchette coos. She wraps her arms around me, pulls me into her floral-scented embrace. My face sinks into the fur of her collar and she won't let me go. It's like the time my mom hugged me after I got on the wrong bus in kindergarten and ended up getting home an hour late. Back before I was a screwup. When I could still grow up to be anything.

"Jacques convinced me that I was wrong." The words come out like they're part of a script, but she doesn't seem to notice. She wants to hear it, so she hugs me tighter. "I don't belong anywhere else."

. . . .

259

I don't have an explanation for what happened at Catherine's because it's something I can't lie about. I can't think of a way to excuse Cherchette's behavior and apologize for my own. But she doesn't ask for it. I'm here. That's what matters.

When she releases me, Cherchette gazes at me for a long time. Proudly, her eyes misting up. "You've come home."

I force myself to smile. I don't have a clue what I'm supposed to do anymore. "Can I . . . can I see Catherine? I think she'd feel more comfortable if I had a chance to explain to her . . . why this is best." It sounds like an outright lie to me, but Cherchette nods her approval.

"Yes, of course, of course. And Nicholas is here, too—it will be like a reunion. Would you like to see him as well?" She links arms with me and leads me to an observation room. Leilani follows, squeaking along in her sneakers—a sound that quickly shifts to the sharp click of stiletto heels, knocking in sync with Cherchette's. I glance back to see that Leilani's all glam now, wearing sunglasses and tight jeans; her legs seem impossibly longer.

"You made the right choice, Avery," Cherchette says.

But my mind rearranges the words—and in my head I hear what she really means: I made the *only* choice.

23

I'M WAITING WITH JACQUES in the observation room, sitting on a gurney next to Catherine, two fingers on her wrist, obsessively checking her pulse, pushing her hair out of her face and trying to wake her up.

Cherchette and Leilani finally left a few minutes ago. We haven't seen Nicholas.

"She's sedated," Jacques says. "It has to run its course."

"She's tough, though," I say. "We might be able to speed it along." It's crap reasoning and I know it, but I don't like seeing Catherine out of it like this; that's so not her style. She should be bristling, raging, scowling. I want to go back to that.

"So what now?" I say.

"I'm not sure. The situation has become more complicated."

Jacques takes out his cell phone, breathes deeply, and dials. It's set to speakerphone, so I hear Sophie's hopeful voice when she says, "Jacques! How's it going? Did you guys find him? Are you coming home yet?"

"Things have gone awry," Jacques says.

Darla's voice: "Awry? What do you mean, 'awry'? What the hell are you up to, Morozov?"

"It isn't your concern because your getting involved is not an option," he snaps. Whoa. Jacques is losing his cool.

"It's okay, Jacques." Sophie again, after a muffled argument with the genius. "Just tell us what happened."

"Cherchette showed up," I say. "At a very inopportune time. She has Catherine now, and she brought her here by force."

Double gasps.

"Do not try to come after us," Jacques adds. "I dislodged the tracking device you planted on me, Darla Carmine, so the beacon will lead you to the wrong location."

"Jacques, come on." Sophie again. "You have to tell us where you are. We can't just leave you—"

"Have it your way, Morozov!" Darla shouts into the phone. "You two are on your own! Good freaking luck getting out of this without my help!"

Um, what?? What happened to "I'll never let you down"? Or: "We're a team"? Or any of those other sentiments?

Jacques raises his eyebrows. "Well. I'm surprised at your sudden change of heart. But I appreciate it. You are finally showing some of that intellect you are famous for."

And then the girls hang up on us. I stare at Jacques, openmouthed. I can't believe that just happened, that it's over just like that.

"So much for the team," Jacques says.

When Catherine comes to, she's wobbly like a cat on too much catnip, but her attitude is intact. Before she notices Jacques, she promises to flay Cherchette into tiny pieces. Cherchette must be watching us on the surveillance monitors, because no sooner is Catherine upright and spouting threats than Cherchette instructs us, via loudspeaker, to strap her down.

"I'm surprised you didn't think of that already, Jacques," she says. "I'm disappointed in you."

"Anyone comes close to me and I'll—" Catherine sways backward, slams her shaky hands against the gurney to catch herself, nails piercing the vinyl. She's sweating like someone in the throes of a fever, but she's fighting hard to keep up a good front.

"I've got this one," I say, slipping the straps around Catherine's wrists and securing them before she can take my eye out. I lower my voice and say, "It'll take me two seconds to rip these off. Just trust me. Nicholas is still here somewhere, and you're in no state to make a break for it. We need to play along if we want to get out of here."

"If you're lying to me, I'll rip your heart out," Catherine mutters. She's breathing hard. I swear, if that stuff Cherchette gave her messed her up, if any of this is permanent . . .

I shake my head to clear it—can't think about that now. Thumbs up at the camera. "She's good."

"Thank you, Avery," Cherchette coos. "Nicholas and I will be there shortly."

Irritably, Jacques flicks his hand toward the camera and freezes it. He leans against one of the hospital-style cabinets, checks his phone, but doesn't say anything.

Catherine's staring at me. "Why are you here, Avery? Is this your choice?"

"Long story. I'm going to get you out of here, though. Don't pay attention to anything I say to Cherchette."

Five minutes more and Cherchette and a very war-torn-looking Nicholas are with us. His trench coat is back in place, but his face glistens with sweat. His normally sharp eyes are dim.

"Well," Cherchette says. "How is our patient?"

I edge in front of Catherine. "Fine. Calming down pretty well." I put my hand on Catherine's, squeeze it in a physical *shhhh* gesture, because I know she's not going to like my next question. "So where's Charlie?"

Cherchette waves her hand dismissively. "Charlie—the poor dear simply doesn't belong here. I have to concentrate my resources on those who can truly benefit from my help."

Translation: Charlie's on the reject list. Like Sophie. Like anyone whose powers aren't impressive enough.

My hand is practically swallowing Catherine's at this point, trying to calm her down. "Really?" I screw up my forehead, feigning confusion. "'Cause, I mean, if you're offering sanctuary, Charlie needs it more than anyone."

"He'll be all right," Cherchette says with a smile. "Now please, sit down. Today is about the three of you."

Cherchette indicates the hard plastic chairs in the room. I drag mine over to Catherine's gurney and take a seat. Nicholas settles in, too. He hasn't quite met my gaze yet, almost like he's ashamed. Like maybe he wanted to do this alone.

"I want to offer you something very exciting: a chance to live up to your full potential—surpass it, even." Cherchette's eyes glimmer and a smile twists her lips. "Imagine eliminating your weaknesses and, in the process, gaining power beyond measure. What would you say?"

"You know what I would say," Jacques mutters.

Cherchette blinks at him, the flutter of her eyelashes masking . . . irritation? "Jacques, darling—if you're going to remain here, you could at least make yourself useful. Right now you're failing to do that."

"Sounds all right." I shrug. What's she getting at?

"Oh, it's better than all right," Cherchette says. Her cold white fingers curl around my chin, tilt it upward until my throat is stretched and exposed. She runs her nails lightly along my frost-burned wound. "I didn't mean to hurt you. You startled me, and I reacted, and it's unfortunate—but it brings us to an important point, Avery."

The straps creak behind me. "That you're a psycho b—"

"Like what?" I say quickly, shooting Catherine a look, like: *no, that does* not *count as playing along!*

"You are strong, but you can still be hurt. You are invulnerable to blunt trauma, but I can prick you with a simple needle. A knife or a bullet could pierce your skin and kill you. You are worried about being captured, held as a test subject, dissected perhaps? We could render that an impossibility with Stage Two."

"Stage Two?"

"It is a formula," Cherchette explains, "designed to be used on extraordinary individuals once their powers have manifested. It will push you to the next stage of development, enhancing your strengths, eliminating your weaknesses, and quite possibly adding new abilities to your arsenal. It's almost a crime to be as advanced as you are, and yet be held back by an Achilles' heel. Checks and balances are for the weak, you know." She winks conspiratorially.

"This formula . . ." Nicholas begins, his voice rusty. "Would it help me control my power? Or is it just an option for Avery?"

"Stage Two is for all of you. You would truly be the master of your power, Nicholas—it is yours, after all; there's no reason you should be at its mercy. And Catherine, you are a remarkable girl: so powerful, yet so frail. Why be a kitty cat when you could be a tigress?"

"I'll show you a tigress," Catherine mutters, straining against her wrist straps. I whack the gurney to settle her down.

"I want it," Nicholas says. "Can you do it now?"

"Administer the formula?" Cherchette asks. "Of course. The results won't be immediate—the incubation process takes time. But we can begin almost at once. I only need to prepare a few things."

"As soon as you can do it," Nicholas says, "I'm ready." He's shaking a little, his hands clenched around a thermos.

He has no idea what he's doing.

First of all, we don't even *know* if this formula is legit. I mean, our origins are a mystery; maybe we were born this way. Pumping us full of chemicals isn't going to bring about some miraculous change that supes us up to the nth power.

"Have a drink," Cherchette says, stroking his hair on her way out. "Be sure you don't get too excited."

Nicholas nods bashfully, twists the cap off the thermos, and sips from it slowly. Almost instantaneously, his shaking stops and his breathing slows. Huh? Did she give him some kind of sedative?

Once the door shuts, I count to twenty, figuring that gives Cherchette ample time to come back if she forgot something. Through the windows in the observation room I see her pass the surveillance desk. Leilani's sitting there with her feet on the desk, blowing pink bubble-gum bubbles; she bolts up when Cherchette gets there, nods obediently for a while, then darts off toward one of the research labs.

"You're not doing it," I tell Nicholas.

He sips from his thermos—I know that's not chamomile tea. Already his eyes are getting this glazed look.

"People can overdose on *prescription* drugs, okay? And those are regulated. You have no idea what kind of toxin she'll put in your body. You could *die*, Nicholas."

"I don't care. Better me than someone else."

I almost want to smack some sense into him. Maybe I would, if I didn't think I'd take his head off.

"You really want to die?" Jacques says. "Maybe you'll get your wish."

"Shut up, Jacques," I snap.

Words are failing me. I want to break something, but I don't want to alert Cherchette to the mutiny raging in my heart. How do you save someone who doesn't want to be saved?

Cherchette's busy preparing the Stage Two formula, measuring doses of the thick, phosphorescent liquid while Nicholas watches from a paper-lined exam table, the sleeve of his trench coat rolled up to his elbow.

He's sucking in deep breaths. "I don't like needles."

"It will be over in an instant," Cherchette says. "You'll barely feel it." She swabs his hand with something and Nicholas averts his eyes, grimaces as she slides the thick IV needle into his vein. A shiver runs through his body. "If you want to lie down," she begins—but then Jacques interrupts her.

"Stage Two isn't foolproof, you know. Not even close."

My body tenses as the air grows colder. What is he doing?

"That's enough," Cherchette says, securing the plastic tube to Nicholas's hand with tape.

Jacques flips a quarter into the air, slaps one hand on

top of the other to catch it. "Call it—heads or tails? Success or failure? So far there is a fifty percent chance it will fulfill all your dreams. The other fifty percent says it ruins you." His eyes are blazing blue fury—I've never seen him like this: angry, almost righteous. It's not the simmering contempt I first saw at Sophie's. It's wild, reckless.

"If your mouth doesn't close on its own, I can do it for you," Cherchette says. She snaps her fingers and a crust of ice freezes Jacques's lips shut. Snow dust falls to the ground as he claws it away.

"What's he talking about?" I ask. Jacques doesn't give her a chance to answer.

"You're full of enthusiasm until something goes wrong," he says. "And then it's *my* fault. My fault that I didn't live up to your hopes, and you can just explain it away with 'survival of the fittest,' as if—" He stops to catch his breath, watching his mother warily, uncertain. Like maybe he's already said too much. "As if it was meant to be this way."

"It is your fault," Cherchette says coolly. "No one forced you to undergo the procedure—you believed you were ready. And I've learned from your mistake. I've become more selective; I see now who is ready to develop and who is not. Blaming me isn't going to change anything."

"I was a child. You promised me greatness! What was I supposed to think?"

The empty IV tube still hangs limply from Nicholas's hand. Cherchette sighs. "This is growing tiresome, Jacques. Please get your emotions under control so we can move on."

....

Nicholas lies down on the exam table, his chest heaving with short, shallow breaths. "What does he mean, it could 'ruin me'?"

"Jacques's experience was anomalous, dear. He doesn't know what he's talking about."

"Stage Two has only been given to two people," Jacques says. "My mother and myself. I was a child when she first attempted it. She was ill for weeks; she was barely mobile and I feared she would die. But when she pulled through, she was ten times stronger. And so when I reached adolescence, when I felt I had begun to peak—"

"This isn't about you, Jacques," Cherchette says. "Stop interfering."

"She convinced me I could go much, much further. I was more powerful than she had been at my age—that's what she told me. But when my new powers failed to manifest—when, in fact, I escaped death only to emerge from the experience weaker, with a whole host of defects, a heart that beats as though it's been ravaged by disease—"

Jacques breaks down. The temperature in the room is spiking and falling dramatically. My body's acting as a thermometer, bordering on paralyzed every time the temperature plunges.

"You think she wants to help you?" Jacques shouts. "She's the one who did this to you! Who gave you these powers in the first place!"

Nicholas stiffens like he's been slapped. I wonder if we all look like that—not sure what to believe. A hush descends on the room, leaving only the steady hum of electronics.

"Are you finished?" Cherchette says. "If you're not through behaving hysterically, perhaps you should leave."

Jacques meets my eyes, his stare ghostly. "I don't care anymore, what telling you the truth is going to mean for me. You have to know that it's a mistake."

"Please," Nicholas says. He lifts his hand carefully, two fingers pressed to the tape. "Can we stop delaying this? I'm ready; I don't care if I end up weaker. Or anything worse. It would make things a lot easier." He's swallowing again and again, and I don't believe him for a second—he's terrified. He has to be.

"Nick, you're not strong enough," I say.

"Of course he is," Cherchette says tartly, catching me with a warning glare. "No more outbursts please. Have some respect for the transformation Nicholas is about to undergo. All your problems will soon be over," she assures him.

"Wait!" I grab Cherchette's arm before she can inject the first dose of the formula into Nicholas's waiting bloodstream. "It isn't fair that Nicholas gets to be first. I'm your favorite, right? It should be me."

I puff out my chest, try to look stronger, more formidable. To make myself believe it. Because this is it. No turning back. It's me or Nicholas—and I know which one of us has a better chance of surviving.

Cherchette's watching me curiously, her eyes sparkling. She caresses my wounded throat with one gloved hand.

"Of course you're my favorite." She says it like I'm the only one in the room.

"Okay then." I take a deep breath. "Don't you want to see what I'll become?"

ISWEAR TO GOD I'm going to cry," Catherine says. "And then I'm going to kill someone."

I'm sitting on a gurney with IVs in both my hands. Waves of heat spread throughout my body as the formula pumps slowly into my veins. My heart burns like an ember in my chest.

In my mind, a coin keeps flipping back and forth. Heads, I come out of this a force to be reckoned with. Amazing, spectacular, more powerful than ever. Tails, and I'm ruined. I lose everything that makes me unique. Or maybe there's a third option. Jacques isn't exactly a weakling. Maybe he isn't as strong as he once was—but what if he used to be stronger than I am now? What if there's something special in the Morozov bloodline that allowed Jacques to even *survive* Stage Two?

Option three means that the coin crumbles in midair. Total body shutdown.

Nicholas hasn't said a word to me since I demanded his spot and Cherchette bumped him to the waiting list. But now that she's gone—off to check on some things, or deal with Leilani or maybe hunt down someone else—he finds his voice.

"You shouldn't have done that. It's not going to stop me. As soon as she's finished with you, I'm going next. And I shouldn't have to feel guilty about what happens to you." His Adam's apple bobs painfully. "I feel guilty about enough already."

"I'm buying us time, Nicholas," I say. "And you're not going next because I'm getting you out of here before—"

A surge of heat floods my head and I swoon forward. My vision goes gray and sweat pours down my face: the floodgates have opened. Cold hands seize my shoulders and prop me back up. "This is the worst thing you could have done," Jacques says.

"Can't we just rip the IV out?" Catherine asks.

A blurry Jacques shakes his head. "I don't know what would happen if we interfered with it. It might make things worse."

God. My head is spinning so violently I literally don't know which way is up, down, sideways . . .

"He looks awful," Catherine says. "There has to be something we can do!"

I'm lying flat but I feel like I'm falling, falling . . . I don't stay conscious long enough to hear Jacques's answer.

Drifting in and out. Fever dreams drip with reality. I roll over, hyperaware of the damp shirt clinging to my neck and chest, the sensation of vinyl slick against my cheek.

"Perhaps he'll make it through—there's no real prec-edent. He's the first of the second generation, if you don't count . . . but my origin is different."

"Did your mother really create us?" a male voice asks. "What does that even mean?"

An exhalation like a whistle. "There was an earlier for-mula. And the specifics—"

Someone touches my face. My eyelids spasm and light filters in, dims again.

"I think he's awake. Maybe . . ."

"—various children in cities all over the country. Ad-ministered in place of the polio vaccine."

"Nice," a girl says sarcastically. "So we're not even im-mune to polio."

"I think that's the least of our problems . . ."

A gray hand descends like a shroud and smothers me, blocks out the sound. I jerk away from it, panting—but I can't move. Flickers appear. Snaps and pops of light. Vein-colored flares against a night sky.

"So there are others? How many?"

"Many did not survive. We have recorded deaths throughout infancy and beyond . . . Although typically af-ter age seven, the survival rate is very high. Some of her subjects gained no powers, but suffered disfigurements."

"Like . . ." Deep breath. Mine or someone else's. Swol-len in my ears. "My brother."

A golden glow attacks my retinas, when all they want is darkness. Something soothing to get lost in. The orb expands, pounces on my brain, relentlessly . . .

....

"It's almost midnight. That means . . ."

"How long until he's, you know, lucid?"

"I really can't say. My mother was weak but coherent, for the most part. Of course, she was an adult by then. For me, Stage Two was mainly a time of nightmares."

Nightmares. I roll the taste of the word around on my tongue. The flavor is bitter, too hot. I get up and leave the room, flee through the steel door, and escape . . . and then I find myself back on the gurney, going through the motions all over again. Mechanically. Effortlessly. But I'm always in the same place.

"So if Cherchette created us, who created her? Where does this—"

Begin?

"My grandfather. He . . . it's a long story . . ."

A very, dear." Cherchette's cool hand touches my face, relieving some of the heat, the delirium. "You are doing very well. Do you want to try to sit up?"

We're alone. I'm on a real bed now, still in a sterile white room, surrounded by office furniture and medical equipment, and it's mostly dark. Easy on my eyes. The walls and the door are plated with glass so that I can see the rest of the complex. Blue light from the pool room slithers across the ceiling.

With Cherchette's help, I manage to pull myself into a sitting position. The room sways at first but eventually the vertigo passes and I can hold a cup of water without dropping it.

"The pain is only temporary. It will be much better soon." She strokes my hair, like a mother tending to a sick child, and I wonder if she did this for Jacques. If she reassured him the same way. How can she be sure?

"I'm not afraid of pain," I say.

Pain, at least, I can withstand, battle through it to emerge on the other side. But weakness . . . I'm so used to being strong; I'm terrified that this formula flipped a switch in me and I'll never be the same. All my power-related problems will be gone, but the person I've become will cease to exist.

Normal—I've never been more afraid of that word.

Cherchette tells me to take a deep breath, presses her stethoscope to my back as I slowly exhale. She checks all my vital signs, records the results on her clipboard. She even measures my arms, my chest, my waist, as if my body's going to spontaneously change shape or something.

Hell, I don't know; maybe it will.

"Can you stand, Avery? Stage Two may affect your mass, so I would like to get a starting weight for you." She gestures to the medical scale next to the bed, takes my arm, and lets me lean on her as I step onto the scale—a strangely familiar feeling, since I've been weighed probably hundreds of times for wrestling. She steps behind me, picks up her clipboard, and stops. "What is—"

I turn, and see her squint before she quickly plucks

something off the back of my pants. I'm about to tell her—politely—*not* to touch my butt when I see it: pinched between her nails is a small lavender sliver of plastic, the size of a girl's fingernail. With spiky metal teeth on the back.

Holy—

Darla didn't tag me. Sophie did.

"What's this?" Cherchette turns it over, pokes the metal teeth that have held on to my pants all this time.

"Um." Before I can think of a good answer, Cherchette lifts the sliver to her lips and blows, coating it with frost until it looks like it's been dipped in liquid nitrogen. Then she flicks it with her fingertip and it disintegrates. "Clever. Does this mean I should be expecting company?"

"N-no, I don't think so."

"You know, I was perfectly content to leave your little friends alone." Cherchette slams her tools into a drawer and locks it. "I can't help them; they'll never be more than they are. But I don't take this sort of interference lightly. It's bad enough that Jacques's ambition has suffered and his defiance has virtually exploded since he began spending time with that girl. I could let that go; the children don't know what they're getting themselves into. But this is too much."

"They're not—" I'm fumbling; damn it, why can't I get out a coherent thought? "It's an earring or something. Probably my mom's; she leaves her crap all over the house."

"Avery. Look around you at the resources I possess. Do you think that I was born yesterday?"

"Listen: no one's coming here! Jacques told Sophie to stay out of it and she listens to him! And Darla's totally distanced herself; she doesn't care what happens to us! I swear to you. And if I'm lying you can . . ." And I *am* lying; it's never been more clear how *obvious* it is that Darla and Sophie would never leave their friends hanging out to dry. Darla's loyal to a fault, and Sophie sticks to her friends like glue—even Jacques, when no one else trusted him. We're in this together. All or nothing. "If I'm lying you can . . ."

My words fade away. I'm staring at the frosty dust that used to be solid plastic and metal. I'm remembering— even as my own body is failing me—that Cherchette came through Stage Two more powerful than ever. She could snuff me out in a second. She could end any one of us with a simple flick of her fingers.

"Avery—do not make deals with me. I am building a family here. And when I allow newcomers into my family, when I trust them and show them I care for them, I expect their loyalty."

I bow my head, wondering where the others are, whether Catherine and Nicholas are okay. Heads or tails. My mind flips, the coin landing on *you're screwed*. If we end up in trouble, I won't be able to save them. I'm not the alpha-perfect-golden-boy anymore.

I'm a liability. Weaker than I've ever been.

"I have dedicated my life to this," Cherchette says quietly. "I have been mistreated so many times by people who could not understand me—who would *never* accept me.

And it has taken me years, to . . . to find others who would understand. I won't be betrayed by my own kind. It's unacceptable. I have worked too hard to bring us together."

"What happened to you?" I say. "Why are you doing this?" My voice breaks. I don't understand. Why does she throw around words like *family* with kids like Leilani and me, but then discard Charlie and Sophie like trash?

"Ah, Avery." Cherchette sighs. "You are opening Pandora's box, asking me that. I don't wish to burden you with the darkness and despair that has come before. We can move on from this."

"Obviously you can't," I say, almost wincing as the words leave my lips, expecting her to lash out in retaliation. Cherchette blinks at me, dumbfounded, her eyes suddenly wide, like a child's. Stage Two is breaking down my self-censor—either that or my will to live. Because I can't stop myself. I let everything out. "You can't move on or you wouldn't be doing this, playing with us. How am I supposed to feel safe here—how are any of us?—if you're so willing to lay down the law as soon as one of us fails to play by your rules? We didn't come looking for you. We haven't agreed to anything."

The innocence in Cherchette's face closes up. She seems angry again, and fully aware of the power discrepancy between us. "You said you *wanted* to be here. That you knew that you belonged here. You came to be better than you are, more special. Stage Two is not something to toy with. And if you can't appreciate that, or the other things I've done for you . . ."

"I know, I know," I say. "I wouldn't be what I am without you. You made us like this—that's what Jacques said. And it's true, isn't it? You gave us these powers, you threw us into a world that didn't know what to do with us, and now you pick and choose who you want to help. Why would you play with our lives like that if you don't even—if some of us don't even warrant your time?" *Like Charlie. Like Sophie. Like your own son, Jacques.* I manage to bite back that much.

Arguing is wearing me down, sending me spiraling into the draining depths of Stage Two–based exhaustion. There's no adrenaline here to save me. No super energy. Just my own body fighting not to kill itself.

Cherchette touches my hand gently. "You don't understand, Avery. Let's not be enemies," she murmurs. "I didn't know what would happen, when I . . . when Stage One began. I had to take chances, because I couldn't be alone. I couldn't. I've opened up your world, Avery—I've given you a gift other boys your age would die to have. And some of them did die. Some of the children didn't make it—I admit that, and it's very unfortunate. But it's a natural test, you see—like natural selection. It makes what *you've* become all the more special."

She smiles and strokes my hand, almost happy. I shiver each time her fingers make contact with my skin.

"Nature doesn't make mistakes. Nature weeds out the weak, the unfit. We have to accept that we are different. I . . . have been different. Since I was a young girl. My father . . ."

She pauses, her face contorting with bitterness, maybe sadness, like she's struggling to contain something. "My father was far more ambitious than I could ever be. He was driven by the thrill of discovery, the power that comes with shaping the future, adapting humanity. A forced evolution of sorts. What might mankind require to survive in the future? What skills or specialties might be buried within us, waiting for the right mutation to act as a catalyst and change our race forever?

"He used me as his test subject. I was an only child and he wasn't fond of children, but he found a use for me—his perfect little experiment. A subject who would always keep her mouth shut, who would dutifully suffer the injections and the analysis.

"The pain that I endured as the experiments wrought changes upon my body was so intense that I cannot describe it. And yet my father, the scientist, continued to administer his revised formulas as if I were a tower he was building, and all he cared about was how tall it could become, with no thought as to what might make it collapse. I think he imagined that he would one day create a race of supermen, once he had perfected his formula. But he failed to account for what I might do once I was truly strong, truly my own person, unwilling to endure any more. And that . . . that is all I wish to say about my father. You want to know why I created you, why I would inflict that transformation on others, when I had suffered so terribly?"

I do want to know. "Please."

"I inherited my father's formula—I inherited every-thing. I told myself I would live a simple, normal life—dull, even."

She smiles at me, like this is our private joke.

"But as I made my way in the world, I realized that a normal life was out of my grasp. I would forever be hiding my true self. I wished for siblings and peers who did not exist. I had been the first, but now I possessed my father's formula. Perhaps I could create others, and we could be our own family, our own society. The strongest, the fittest and most special, as chosen by nature. You understand me now, don't you?"

She flashes a bright, fervent smile, and I give a tight, upturned grimace in return, too sick and conflicted to really know how to feel about this.

On the one hand, I love my powers. I claim them, I own them (or at least what's left of them); they make me who I am. But kids died because of Stage One. And others have had their lives ruined—like Charlie. That's not nature; it's not "meant to be." That's what Cherchette doesn't under-stand. With her it's black or white; we're either fit or unfit for survival. Like she said about Jacques, when Stage Two brought him down: it was his own fault. No apologies.

I open my mouth to say something neutral, searching for a way to soothe her, to make her forget about Darla and Sophie. But something within me is still shocked, speechless. Too sick, too weak, too scared to know how to tell her that it doesn't have to be this way. Precious seconds go by in silence, and Cherchette's introspective air slips away, replaced by something stiff and wounded. Slowly, her eyes drift back to the pulverized remains of Darla's tracking device, and as her features grow hard and begin to freeze over, I know that any chance I may have had to stop this is gone.

"Enough. I have a mess to clean up." Cherchette's voice is cold, sharp. "It is hard on you now, but one day you will understand that I act only out of necessity—to protect our family from those who wish to hurt us."

"Cherchette, wait," I say.

"It is time for you to rest." She shuts the door solidly behind her and locks it. I thump my fists against the observation window, try to get her attention as she's walking away—"Wait! Let's talk about this!"—but she ignores me. I *know* what she's doing—and I can't just sit here while she masterminds my friends' deaths.

Using the walls for balance, I shove my way over to the desk where she keeps her medical equipment, searching for a misplaced key or a phone that makes outgoing calls. If I can at least *contact* Darla and Sophie, I can tell them Cherchette's expecting them: ABORT! ABORT!

I'm busy trying to break into the desk—an act that would've taken me two seconds back before Cherchette pumped my veins full of phosphorescent poison—when an explosion rocks the whole headquarters. I whip around, the sudden spin making me dizzy, and see a cloud of brick dust and debris fill the pool room as the outer wall crumbles. A huge, boxy, shadowed figure appears in the opening—like in those old Kool-Aid commercials where

Kool-Aid man busts through a wall to save kids from their own thirstiness, yelling: *Ohhhh yeah!*

Only it's not Kool-Aid man. It's a giant purple robot with Sophie stuck to its shoulder. She's in skimpy, bright blue neoprene, armed with the massive pink gun from Darla's workshop.

Darla's voice explodes from the robot's loudspeaker, all garbled and metallic but still Darla enough to be recognizable: "It's ON like Donkey Kong, Ice Queen! You're going DOWN!"

The robot crashes through the rubble next to the Olympic-size swimming pool—then jerks forward a few steps too many and plunges into the shallow end, sinking in up to its knees. I rattle the doorknob of my prison, a fresh wave of sweat pouring down—

But I can't budge the lock.

I ram the door with my shoulder—but it's like I've got nothing to give. I collapse against it, slide down in slow motion before I realize what's happening and pull myself up. I give it another shot: I visualize my leg thrusting forward, boot slamming the door at its center, cracking it in half. But when I throw my first kick, it's with zero force. Just lifting my leg off the ground seems like too much effort; I have to grip the bed to keep from falling down.

The robot reverses and sloshes backward, awkwardly trying to mount the pool stairs before it short-circuits. Sophie leaps off its shoulder and lands poolside, rolling across the cement to break her fall. "Shut it down!" she cries.

"No one told me there was a pool here! Who puts a pool in their evil lair?!" Robotic limbs punch and thrash in all directions as Darla tries to navigate her creation out of the water.

Water that is quickly turning to ice.

Silver frost races across the water like the pool's been touched by a magic wand, freezing the surface first and then sinking deeper, transforming the entire pool into a massive ice cube, trapping Darla's robot in place. Spidery cracks split the cement around the pool, glittering frost filling them as soon as they form.

I press my face to the observation window, determined to focus whatever strength I have left—so that when I go to use it, it'll count. I have to get out of here.

Cherchette makes her grand entrance like an actress taking the stage, dressed for the part of villainess in a white fur cape, boots, and sleek white bodysuit—only her face and hands are bare. Blue light bounces off the ice, lending her skin a ghostly pallor, like all the humanity drained out of her a long time ago.

"Intruders," she says. "Allow me to welcome you properly!"

Cold air rushes through the corridors, blowing under my door and clutching my heart like an icy fist. Poolside, Sophie's breath heaves out of her like smoke. She's crouched, mostly bare skin flushing pink from the assault. She flips a switch on her oversize pink gun and fires, sending an almost colorless beam shooting forth.

Darla's dynamic pain cannon.

Cherchette screams when it hits her, convulses like every one of her nerves is on fire; but when it's over, instead of collapsing in defeat, she straightens to her full height, angrier than ever.

"Why is she still conscious?" Darla shouts via loudspeaker.

"I don't know! I set it on stun!"

"Impossible! If you'd set it on *stun* she'd be—"

Before she can finish, Cherchette cracks Darla's robot open like a crab, wedging a huge ice spike into its back. Darla hits her emergency eject button and goes flying, an inflatable sled opening beneath her just in time to cushion the impact as she shoots across the pool-turned-ice-rink—spandex-clad and wearing aviator goggles, shrieking the whole way.

"Plan B!" Darla shouts. "Plan Beeeeeeee!"

Sophie takes cover behind the gutted robot and charges up the pain cannon for a second shot.

I hear the *crash* of glass shattering and see a chair go flying through the window next door, followed by the batwing flap of a trench coat as Nicholas climbs out. Catherine kicks through next, one chewed-up strap still dangling from her wrist. I pound on my own window—then duck as Nicholas picks up the chair and hurls it through.

Glass rains down all around me, piercing my skin. Tiny cuts fill with blood. But I don't have much time to think about that. Catherine and Nicholas reach through the broken window and haul me out.

Nicholas's eyes are glowing like two eerie spotlights—

so blue it blocks out the whites of his eyes. He's shaking, not even close to the calm, sedated Nicholas we saw earlier. Catherine seems to be ordering him around, keeping him somewhat stable, but once we enter the war zone, there's no way that's going to last.

"You're shivering like a Chihuahua," Catherine says, throwing my arm around her shoulders for support.

I nod, teeth chattering—can't argue with that. "Where's Jacques? Do you think he could displace some of the cold, so I can f-function?"

"No idea. He left with Cherchette when she moved you to another room. We haven't seen him since."

Inside the pool room, Darla and Sophie are getting their asses handed to them. Darla must have been counting on the invincibility of her robot, because she doesn't have a weapon—and Cherchette is taking full advantage of that fact. Right now a spider made of animated ice is chasing her around the room, brittle legs tinkling across the pool, leaving traces of frost wherever they touch down. Sophie's smacking her gun against the floor and cursing it, grappling with the frozen dial. The barrel and the controls are clogged with ice, and her right hand is frozen to the grip like a deformed claw.

"We need to get in there!" I say.

"The doors are iced shut," Catherine says. "I can claw through but it'll take a while." She bites her lip, dissatisfied. "It has to be sooner than that. Those two don't have a chance by themselves."

"I think I can be of assistance."

I turn around, shocked to see Jacques standing behind me. Not just because he's here, but because he's so messed up: the skin around one eye is swollen black and purple; the corner of his mouth is torn and his shirt collar is stained with blood.

Jacques ignores my stare and lifts his hand, focusing his energy on the ice seal, whittling it down until the floor is littered with ice crystals and the door opens easily.

"Before we go in there," Catherine says. "Jacques, are you any match for your mom?"

A bitter smile forms on his face. "Not even close. And I'm guessing you are not either."

Catherine bristles but doesn't deny it—probably remembering the fight that brought her here. She rakes her claws down the wall, agitated. "Okay then. Last resort: Avery, tell me you're all better now and you're ready to save the day. This whole weak-delirious thing is part of your act. Please?"

"I'll pull my weight," I say. I lean over, cheeks bulging with sudden pressure, and—

I spew a stream of blue, blood-spattered liquid onto the floor. Like some kind of alien vomit. Holy hell, Batman. My throat burns like I choked up a razor blade. My eyes are dying to roll back in my skull. Jacques and Catherine collide, swooping toward me to boost me up.

"You're staying here," Catherine orders.

"No, no, I'm good. I always puke before a match." Blatant lie. "I'm ready now. Bring it."

Catherine glares at me and shoves through the door to

the pool room, Jacques at her heels. I grab Nicholas and drag him in after them. He's verging on catatonic: eyes glazed with light, limbs statue-rigid—and I'm about as robust as a zombie. But our friends are in trouble. Either we make it through this—all of us—or we go down together.

Entering the pool room is like stepping into an industrial-size freezer that wants to kill you. Hailstones rain down amid the blinding snow like an arctic air strike. Frost clings to Darla and Sophie like fur; a monstrous ice spider lunges at Darla with its pincered mouth. And in the center of the storm: Cherchette. The mad conductor of her own icy symphony, cloaked in mink and mania and completely beyond reason. The potential of Stage Two, live and in the flesh. More power than we ever dreamed of.

And not one of us can get near her.

Instead we're dodging every deadly creation she throws at us.

Catherine launches herself at the ice spider, amputates a leg with twin claw-slashes before her momentum sends her skidding across the surface of the pool. Seven more legs to go. Darla batters the spider's face with her sled, doing her damnedest to keep it at bay.

Sophie's busy chipping away at the ice clogging her gun, using a jagged metal lever that she snapped off Darla's robot, fighting to bring the pain cannon back into commission. Cherchette's been bombarding her with hail for a while now: her flushed legs and arms are showing golf-ball-size welts; her knees are knocking together and the tool she's using keeps missing its target. But when Jacques rushes to help her, Cherchette switches gears.

The hailstorm abruptly ceases. Sophie looks up, dazed—just in time to see a cage of ice imprison Jacques, ice spikes slicing the air mere inches from his face.

"You've betrayed me for the last time!" Cherchette's chest heaves, her fists clenching and unclenching rhythmically, bloodless white nails digging into her flesh.

Jacques works at thawing the cage, but Cherchette builds the walls back up before he can break them down. As the bars grow thicker, the cage gets narrower, until it's pressing Jacques from all sides like a torture device, crushing the air out of his lungs.

Sophie rips the black boomerang off her utility belt and wings it at Jacques's cage; then dives out of the way as it explodes, blowing a gorilla-size hole in the ice. My heart's thumping in time with my tremors, fast and frantic; I feel like a plague victim but this deep-rooted desire's kicking in. This is still who I am. I grab Jacques by the shirt and wrench him out.

Watching my friends, I see everyone's giving it their all. Working their adrenaline for whatever it's worth.

And it's not enough. We're going down, fast.

A gale-force icy wind slams Sophie against the wall; she sticks like a fly that's been swatted, head lolling forward.

Nicholas is the last remaining source of heat in the room. His eyes are swirling milky-blue neon; his body's vibrating like it's been electrified.

Catherine's managed to saw three more legs off the ice

spider, felling it like a chopped-down tree. It lies on its bulbous side, spindly legs twitching uselessly. But Cherchette has moved on to the next line of attack: hypothermia. Catherine's a fighter—but the cold is wearing her down. Darla's huddling in the shadow of the giant robot, shivering so hard she can barely move, let alone strategize. And Sophie's glued to the wall; Jacques is struggling to catch his breath; the wind around Nicholas is whipping wildly, tornado-style—

Nicholas . . .

Cold steamrollers us, battering us down, forcing us to our knees. First numbness, then unconsciousness—and once we're unconscious, we'll be at her mercy. Cherchette's desperate to protect her twisted dream, and there's no room for forgiveness. She'll crush anyone who tries to take it away from her.

I can't say that what I'm about to do is right. That I expect it to ever be okay. But I know who I care about. I know how far I'm willing to go to protect them.

"Catherine!" I shout. I stow Jacques behind the giant robot and hurry toward her. "Fastball special at twelve o'clock!"

She gapes at me in disbelief, but I know she knows what I'm talking about. It's a classic superhero move—any girl who drops obscure Batman references *has* to know what it is. I stumble toward her, eyes narrowed against the icy wind. We meet on the slick surface of the pool, twenty feet behind Nicholas. Draw a line straight from us to Cherchette and he'd be the center point.

The wintry wind howls all around us. I cup my hands around my mouth and speak directly into Catherine's ear, setting up my plan in as few words as possible.

"Hold on tight," I finish. "Dig your claws in! Whatever you have to do! Ready?"

Catherine climbs into my waiting arms, body poised in a tight crouch. Her eyes are narrowed to slits, frost ringing her lids. "Let's do this!"

I channel it all: the strength I do have, the strength I used to have; the desire that makes it possible, that makes me more than what everyone thinks I am, more than a reckless daredevil, a destroyer of property and trust and friendships and . . .

And I throw Catherine with everything I've got, her feline-girl body soaring through the storm like a tightly wound spring, ready to uncurl, pounce, and stir it up. She lands perfectly on Nicholas's back, shreds his trench coat open in a single fierce motion, claws ripping through it, exposing his vortex to the air.

Catherine plunges her claws into his shoulders and the vortex roars, expands until it's almost encompassing Nicholas's entire torso, and parts of his face are vanishing in the blackness. Snow and ice crystals and wind and hail are drawn into the vortex. The suction snags me and pulls me forward, my feet can't get a grip on the slippery floor; Jacques and Darla are sliding toward it, scrabbling wildly on the ice . . .

But the black void is aimed directly at Cherchette. Her eyes stretch in horror and she fumbles to create a handhold, to root herself to the ground with ice—but every weapon at her disposal is being devoured by the vortex. Her fur cape begins to pleat; her model-severe features distort, lose dimension. She flattens, shrinks—

And then she's gone.

ICICLES WASTE AWAY to needle-thin slivers, and the air fills with the musical *drip, drip, drip* of ice melting, tinkling, teardropping to the ground. As the room thaws, the reality of what I've done dawns on me:

I killed Cherchette.

Nicholas is on his knees, blood trickling down the shoulders of his trench coat, when Leilani bursts in and starts pummeling him, anywhere and everywhere she can. "What the hell have you done? Bring her back!" Her face contorts, becoming more like Cherchette's until Catherine grabs her and shoves her. But Leilani grips back and they both go down, splashing into a puddle of water on the chipped poolside cement. Leilani kicks at Catherine with her sharp heels, scrambles away, and lunges at me next.

"You've frigging betrayed her like everyone else!" Leilani shouts. "She believed in you, she would have helped you to become anything you wanted! You would have been part of our family! We trusted you, and you destroyed everything!"

"Leilani, I'm sorry," I say as the rest of the group

joins us. "No one wanted this. But she didn't leave me a choice."

Leilani's smacking fat tears off her cheeks as soon as they fall. "You forced her hand. You treated her like a criminal, like some creature to be gunned down, and *she* didn't have a choice. Can't you see that?"

She turns on Jacques. "And you—you should be ashamed. Your own mother! Do you know how lucky you are? And you just go and throw it away like that, like she's nothing to you!"

"I won't discuss this with you," Jacques says. "You don't know anything about her." He's still staring at the place where Cherchette was last standing, like he expects her to appear again.

"This is hard on all of us," Sophie says. "Yelling at each other isn't going to make it easier."

"Oh, shut up! You pathetic parasite! As if you're not thrilled to be a part of something so big. You never should have survived Stage One, let alone—"

A plate of ice clamps her lips together before she can finish. "That's enough," Jacques says. He's trembling. Sophie buries her head in his chest and hugs him. Stage One? It's all Greek to her. She and Darla still don't know the truth. Right now is about comforting Jacques, because . . . maybe Cherchette was messed up, but she was his *mom*. His only family, as far as we know.

And it's my fault that he lost her.

This is the one thing I've done that can't be fixed. That won't heal or improve with the passage of time. I cost

Jacques his mother; Leilani lost her mentor, the person she loved more than anyone; and I forced Nicholas to do the one thing he didn't ever want to do—destroy a human life.

Can that ever be justified? Could I have done anything else?

Catherine digs a claw into my sleeve and drags me away from the others.

"Stop it," she says.

"What?"

"Stop tearing yourself up over this. We did what we had to do; you're not the only one who thought it was a good idea, okay? This woman killed people. *Babies*—kids who could've lived normal, healthy lives if she hadn't decided to play mad scientist. She could have easily killed all six of us tonight.

"If you think someone needs to be blamed for what happened to her, you're gonna have to put that on both of us. I'm the one who opened Nicholas's coat, not you. Do you think I'm a horrible person?"

"No, but—"

"Then stop it—or I'll claw your face off. I still haven't forgiven you for strapping me to that hospital bed, you know."

"No fair killing me now—I'm still recovering."

"About that . . . how do you feel? Are you any better?"

I sigh. "I'm not sure. I'm tired. And when I . . ." My throat clenches up. My eyes burn and Catherine's face blurs as two tears roll down, too quick for me to catch. "When I tried to fly, I couldn't get off the ground. Not even a few inches. I did everything I normally do, but my body . . . my body won't listen anymore."

"It's temporary," Catherine says. "It's . . ." She swallows, avoiding my eyes, and then I know she's as worried as I am. "You'll be stronger. After."

"What if I lose everything?" Damn it. My throat feels like there's a sharp stone wedged inside, like I'll choke if I don't let it out. I'm trying to hide it and Catherine's pretending it's working. "Here." She tugs the waist of her T-shirt away from her body and slices a section off with her claws. Hands it to me. "You're leaking antifreeze again."

"Yeah, thanks," I mumble, wiping my face before anyone else comes to check on me.

"Seriously, I'm not doing this again—so I hope this is a good time for it." Catherine takes a quick breath, then pounces forward and throws her arms around me and hugs me hard, the way you hug someone when you're afraid they'll disappear. "It'll be okay. Whatever happens, Avery. I'll be here, and . . . your friends will be here—"

"They're your friends, too," I murmur.

"And no matter how this Stage Two crap changes things, you'll still be Avery. Even if we have to buy you a jetpack, you'll fly again. You're not going back to the way you were before."

"I can't."

"I know. I know, and we won't let that happen to you. You're so past normal it's sick. And if you end up with a heart defect, or whatever Jacques has, Darla can build you a robotic bodysuit with a built-in pacemaker, Iron Man–style. She'd probably love that."

"Oh God, no," I groan.

"Buck up," she whispers. "I only get this supportive once or twice a year. So . . . I hope you enjoyed it. After tonight you're on your own."

"Storing it away in my memory," I say.

She pulls away and I don't feel as heavy anymore. Still tired, but . . . I'm still here. And I've got more than just myself to lean on.

Leilani's gone—who knows where to. Nicholas is sitting with his feet propped on the wobbly ice rink, sipping Gatorade with Darla while Sophie sticky-scrambles up the side of the robot and into the cockpit, on a mission to salvage the most essential of Darla's gadgets. Jacques stands below, playing spotter in case she slips.

I approach kind of hesitantly, not sure who's gonna be pissed at me. "Is everyone okay?"

Darla points at Nicholas. "Rehydrating. And totally exhausted. But other than that, good."

Sophie models the welts on her legs. "I feel like I got cornered by a very angry pitching machine. I want some hot chocolate. And I think I have five more adrenaline-fueled minutes before I pass out."

"Enough," Jacques says, motioning for her to climb down.

I take a few deep breaths then, working myself up to this. "Nicholas?"

The last time we spoke to each other, we were arguing about how I shouldn't have taken his place in Cherchette's Stage Two experiment. All he wanted was for his power to *stop*. To not be out of his control, violent, unpredictable, and dangerous.

And now, after what I did . . .

He downs the rest of his Gatorade, leans his head back, and closes his eyes. "I'm not going to say what you think I'm going to say, Avery. I'm not mad. You know what my brother says about battle? He says it's not about the enemy—it's about the person next to you. Your friend, your teammate. You're fighting to protect them, and they're doing the same thing for you. I never wanted it to end like that. I feel like it's my fault that it happened, in a way, because I came here in the first place. None of this would have happened if not for that. But I didn't know what to expect. I never thought you guys would be in danger. And I guess, when it comes down to it . . . I'm grateful I was here to help when you needed me."

Darla flashes me a thumbs-up and a not-so-discreet wink through her cracked aviator goggles. She looks like she just ran a four-day marathon through the Sahara with only a juice box and some scorpion sweat for hydration—she should be passed out on the ground right now. But nothing gets this girl down. No matter what happens, she bounces right back. That's got to be a superpower in itself.

Sophie covers her mouth with both hands as she yawns. "Ready to go home, team?"

We all nod with zero energy, giving in to the crash after so much fury: the calm *after* the storm.

Jacques catches Darla with a stern glance as she gets to her feet. "Is Benedict Arnold part of the team?"

Darla looks taken aback; she blinks so hard the cracked lens in her goggles wobbles. Then Jacques manages a small smile and she realizes he's joking. Darla grins back big, a mix between embarrassment and giddy glee.

"No, but Jacques Morozov is on the team."

"Told yooooou!" Sophie sings. She waves the two-fingered victory *V* in the air and yawns again, falls against Darla's shoulder, green mascara'd eyelashes fluttering with exhaustion. "Good call, Mr. Wayne."

"I guess you had *one* good idea," Darla says. "But I was the one who first thought Jacques had potential. If you recall the time I . . ."

Nicholas rolls his not-glowing, back-to-normal eyes at me. Catherine groans and bumps my shoulder. "Why doesn't she just write a *poem* about him? How did I end up with you people?" She growls when I throw my arm around her—half hug, half headlock, all awesome.

I look around at them—all my friends, people I didn't even know a few months ago—and I'm just blown away. I can't imagine being who I am without them in my life. They've become as much a part of me as my powers. Flight, superstrength, invulnerability. Darla, Nicholas, Sophie, Jacques. Catherine.

They're freaking extraordinary.

EPILOGUE

RUNNING AWAY DIDN'T WIN ME ANY POINTS with my parents. My chores have increased, like, tenfold, and I have to do the really crappy jobs, like laundry—which is full of untold secrets I did *not* need to know. My dad's underwear is so much bigger than his actual butt it's frightening.

Night flights and the daily neighborhood patrol?—they've kind of come to an end. I can't stay on my feet for hours, and flying . . . isn't a reality right now. Fingers crossed that it's only temporary. I'm trying not to think about it. I borrowed a few books from Catherine to distract myself. But it's hard to ignore all the weird stuff going on with my body.

Occasionally I'm overwhelmed by extreme nausea and delirium. For a split second I even imagined I could see through my bedroom wall.

Crazy, right?

I wake with night sweats. Bad dreams that I never remember—only the unsettled feeling remains. And sometimes this intense pain racks my body, like my muscles are being torn apart. I wake up and have to bite down on my pillow to keep from crying out. The other night I bit *through* it.

I haven't told anyone about that.

———————————————

Do you like it?" Jacques asks Charlie, showing off his shiny silver Jaguar. Charlie nods shyly from under his oversize baseball cap, tail tucked into a pair of baggy sweatpants, XL Incredible Hulk shirt making him look like any other kid.

Charlie's prepped for an extended sleepover. Catherine has reluctantly agreed to let her brother move in with Jacques, now that Cherchette's gone from the mansion. No more garage living. No more abuse. Just country life and open air—Charlie will be free to be himself. But that doesn't mean this change is easy for her.

"You ready?" I ask Catherine.

Catherine shifts Charlie's overnight bag to her other shoulder. "I don't know . . ."

"Give it a chance," I say. "Charlie wants to go, doesn't he?"

"Yeah, but . . . he's never been away from me before."

"He'll be fine. If anything, he'll just end up spoiled and refuse to leave the house without his diamond cuff links." I block before Catherine can gouge me with her claws. "Hey! Still recovering here! No cheap shots."

Charlie says something to Jacques, his voice so raspy-whispery we can barely hear him. "What's that?" Jacques leans closer.

"Is there really a trampoline?"

"Ah . . ." Jacques smiles. "I think it may be in the shop. But we can buy one."

"Cool." Charlie ducks his head again, tugging the hat tighter over his ears.

"Be good," Catherine says, smothering him in a feral-sister hug. "I have a phone now. Call me anytime you miss me. And eat all of your cereal, not just the marshmallows."

"I will take good care of him," Jacques assures her. "I promise. Whenever you want to see him, just call and I will come get you."

"We can jump on the trampoline," Charlie says. "And do backflips."

Catherine manages a reluctant smile and helps Charlie load his stuff into the car, still full of instructions. "Don't fight with the fish girl. And if Leilani plays any tricks on you, tell her I'll rip her face off."

"So we'll see you next weekend?" I ask Jacques.

"Team meeting," he says. "Of course I'll be there."

"Good." I slap him on the shoulder. "We're training Nicholas next week, so come ready to play football."

After some last-minute adjustments they're finally ready to go. Charlie waves good-bye as the Jaguar pulls away, and we wave back wildly, with big, enthusiastic grins to match his smile. But Catherine deflates a little once he's out of sight.

She takes out her new phone, starts to dial Jacques's number, but stops. "He'll be fine, right? I'm doing the right thing?"

"Definitely." I know this is hard for her—she wants her brother to be safe, and happy, and she doesn't trust anyone else to protect him. She's taking a huge chance. But I think this will actually work out.

She exhales, long and loud, and her shoulders loosen as the tension leaves her. "Okay. I'm going to try to believe that."

⚡⚡⚡

The smell of pizza and fresh-baked cookies hits us as soon as we enter Sophie's basement.

"Woo!" Sophie hops up and does her own version of a touchdown dance. "Score!"

"This is ridiculous." Nicholas sighs and tosses his controller on the floor. He and Sophie are playing a newly purchased game of Madden on her Xbox, trying to get a feel for the mechanics of football. Nicholas is losing 42–0.

"You'll be better at the real game," I promise. "This is just a crash course in the rules. And learning what the various positions are."

"I don't *want* to go out for the football team," Nicholas groans.

"It's getting your dad off your back, isn't it?" Darla says. "It's like when I signed up for cheerleading camp one summer so my dad would stop harassing me about my inventions. It'll work, trust me."

"But my dad's on the phone with the coach practically every night," Nicholas says. "He's so excited it's sick.

What's going to happen when I *don't* make the team? This might be the worst idea you've ever had, Darla."

I cram the controller back in his hand. "You'll make the team," I say. "We'll make sure of it."

"Besides, I've never had a truly *bad* idea," Darla says.

"That's true," Sophie says. "That heartfelt poem you read at Roast? Great idea."

"It was excellent!" Darla protests.

"Yeah, and the 'R.I.P. Marie Curie' shirt," I throw in.

"Ooh, good one!"

Darla sinks lower into her beanbag chair, face hidden behind her blingtastic Hello Kitty laptop. She's doing her typical genius grumbling, insulting us with words we don't understand.

"Hmm, she must be really mad," Sophie says with a grin. "That last one was in Latin."

Catherine's watching us like an anthropologist observing aliens for the first time. She's working her way through the plate of football-shaped, pink-frosted sugar cookies, scrunching her nose each time I point sternly at the pizza, trying to get her to eat something that doesn't have frosting on it.

"Ohmygod!" Darla spins her laptop around on her knees, so forcefully it nearly goes crashing to the ground.

It's a news report from a few days ago.

We gather around to read it. Nicholas mouths the words, his eyes opening wide—amazed or in disbelief or both.

AMNESIA VICTIM FOUND IN VIRGINIA

A picture of the victim accompanies the article—and it's definitely Cherchette. Platinum-blond hair, blue eyes, supermodel-tall, etc. The report says she's been taken to an area hospital, and that police are seeking to establish her identity.

"Virginia?" Catherine says.

Nicholas rubs his hands over his face. "I used to live there. That means she's . . ."

"Alive," I say. My heart wrenches. I'm relieved and I'm not. What does this mean for us?

"Your vortex," Darla says. She slams her fist down on the carpet. "I can't believe I never thought of that! It doesn't destroy things! It teleports them! Ohmygod barbeque eureka what-what!" She hops up and starts dancing; links hands with Sophie and they whoop it up and scream and twirl around.

"Nicholas! Aren't you excited?"

He nods, still in shock. "My dog, Boots. He could still be alive. I have to find him."

Catherine's rocking back and forth restlessly, like a dark cloud just drifted over her. "Amnesia. How long does *that* last? Do you know how freaking bad this is for us? How long before she uses her ice powers in front of someone? What if her powers are completely out of control? Does she even know she *has* them?"

Darla stops dancing. "Um . . . crap."

"Yeah, exactly. And unlike some people who end up in the news"—Catherine nods in my direction—"there's no good way to cover up her powers. Adrenaline doesn't go far toward explaining an indoor ice storm."

"I have to call Jacques," Sophie says. She picks up her phone and starts dialing. "We could find her. Maybe even rehabilitate her! So that like . . . when she *does* regain her memory, she'll be a better person."

Catherine snorts. "That's realistic."

We all wait as Sophie excitedly informs Jacques that his mother's alive—a victim of teleportation, not destruction. But as they talk, her voice goes from cheery to troubled. Her eyebrows turn upward, perplexed. "So, what does that mean?" she asks him.

Finally she hangs up. "Um, you guys? Jacques says Leilani left yesterday morning. At first he thought it was random. But she took Cherchette's passport. He thinks she went to find her."

Leilani: the girl who thinks we destroyed her life and considers us her enemies. Who can slip in and out of crowds anonymously and become anyone she wants at will. If she finds Cherchette before we do, and fills in the blanks with her one-sided view of how things went down, Cherchette will be poisoned against us forever; there's no chance we'll be able to help her. She'll be coming for us, and not to bring us "home"—this time it's going to be all about revenge.

We can't just wait to see how this turns out. We have to do something.

It looks like our superteam is coming out of retirement.

SUPER THANKS TO...

My agent, Laura Rennert: ninja, goddess, and all-around purveyor of awesome. You believed in *Dull Boy* from the very beginning, and found the perfect home for it—that means the world to me and I am so glad you're on my team.

My editor, Sarah Shumway: visionary, champion, and a true marvel with a red pencil. You saw *Dull Boy's* potential and helped me to make the book a thousand times better. Working with you has been nothing but fun every step of the way.

Thanks also to Stephanie Owens Lurie, Mark McVeigh, Andrew Harwell, and everyone at Dutton who has had a hand in bringing *Dull Boy* to readers.

Miscellaneous thanks to sassy librarians—you make the world go 'round; to my butler, Alfred, for cookies and pep talks—but especially cookies; to Brian K. Vaughan, whose *Runaways* inspired me to finally put my superhero dreams into book form.

Extra-special thanks to Peter, my husband and BFF, who read this book more times than any sane person should have to, and wasn't afraid to tell me exactly what was wrong with it—even when I threatened him with my laser eyes and scowl of doom. You're cute and your critiquing skills are awesome! I promise you only have to read this book one more time.